The corpse handler moved back, step by slow step. His own crew was in front of him now, stumbling toward him with weapons raised. It was a chilling sight. Their arms moved, and they walked. But their eyes were blank and their faces were dead — *DEAD!* For the first time, Kabaraijian understood the horror some people felt near dead men.

He looked over his shoulder. Both of Cochran's corpses were heading his way, armed. Cochran still had not risen. He lay with his face in the sand and the waters lapping at his boots.

His mind began to work again, in the short breather he was granted. His hand went to his belt. The controller was still on, still warm and humming. He tested it. He reached out to his corpses, into them. He told them to stand still, to drop their tools, to freeze.

They continued to advance.

Kabaraijian shivered. The controller was still working; he could still feel the echoes in his head. But somehow, the corpses weren't responding. He felt very cold.

And colder when it finally hit him, like ice water. Cochran's corpses hadn't responded either. Both crews had turned on their handlers.

Override!

A Song for Lya

and Other Stories

Also by George R.R. Martin

NOVELS:
Dying of the Light
Windhaven (with Lisa Tuttle)
Fevre Dream
The Armageddon Rag
Dead Man's Hand (with John J. Miller)

<u>A Song of Ice and Fire</u>
A Game of Thrones
A Clash of Kings
A Storm of Swords
A Dance with Dragons

SHORT STORY COLLECTIONS:
A Song for Lya and Other Stories
Songs of Stars and Shadows
Sandkings
Songs the Dead Men Sing
Nightflyers
Tuf Voyaging
Portraits of His Children

EDITED BY GEORGE R.R. MARTIN:
New Voices in Science Fiction, Volumes 1-4
The Science Fiction Weight-Loss Book (with Isaac Asimov and Martin
Harry Greenberg)
The John W. Campbell Awards, Volume 5
Night Visions 3
Wildcards I-XV

A Song for Lya

and Other Stories

George R.R. Martin

BABBAGE PRESS • NORTHRIDGE, CA

A SONG FOR LYA AND OTHER STORIES

Copyright © 1976, 2001 by George R. R. Martin

Cover art and design ©2001 by Lydia C. Marano

ISBN: 1-930235-11-9
Babbage Press edition: April, 2001

Babbage Press
8740 Penfield Avenue
Northridge, California 91324

www.babbagepress.com

Printed in the United States of America

to Parris
second time's the charm

ACKNOWLEDGMENTS

"With Morning Comes Mistfall" copyright © 1973 by Condé Nast Publications, Inc. From *Analog Science Fiction/Fact*, May 1973.

"The Second Kind of Loneliness" copyright © 1972 by Condé Nast Publications, Inc. From *Analog Science Fiction/Fact*, December 1972.

"Override" copyright © 1973 by Condé Nast Publications, Inc. From *Analog Science Fiction/Fact*, September 1973.

"Dark, Dark Were The Tunnels" copyright © 1973 by Mankind Publishing Company. From *Vertex Magazine*, December 1973.

"The Hero" copyright © 1971 by UPD Publishing Corporation. From *Galaxy Magazine* February 1971.

"FTA" copyright © 1974 by Condé Nast Publications, Inc. From *Analog Science Fiction/Fact*, May 1974.

"Run To Starlight" copyright © 1974 by Ultimate Publishing Company, Inc. From *Amazing Science Fiction*, December 1974.

"The Exit to San Breta" copyright © 1971 by Ultimate Publishing Co., Inc. From *Fantastic Stories*, February 1972.

"Slide Show" copyright © 1973 by Roger Elwood. From *Omega* (Walker and Company, 1973).

"A Song for Lya" copyright © 1974 by Condé Nast Publications, Inc. From *Analog Science Fiction/Fact*, June 1974.

CONTENTS

With Morning Comes Mistfall   1

The Second Kind of Loneliness   19

Override   35

Dark, Dark Were the Tunnels   63

The Hero   81

fta   95

Run to Starlight   99

The Exit to San Breta   129

Slide Show   143

A Song for Lya   157

With Morning Comes Mistfall

I was early to breakfast that morning, the first day after landing. But Sanders was already out on the dining balcony when I got there. He was standing alone by the edge, looking out over the mountains and the mists.

I walked up behind him and muttered hello. He didn't bother to reply. "It's beautiful, isn't it?" he said, without turning.

And it was.

Only a few feet below balcony level the mists rolled, sending ghostly breakers to crash against the stones of Sanders' castle. A thick white blanket extended from horizon to horizon, cloaking everything. We could see the summit of the Red Ghost, off to the north; a barbed dagger of scarlet rock jabbing into the sky. But that was all. The other mountains were still below mist level.

But we were above the mists. Sanders had built his hotel atop the tallest mountain in the chain. We were floating alone in a swirling white ocean, on a flying castle amid a sea of clouds.

Castle Cloud, in fact. That was what Sanders had named the place. It was easy to see why.

"Is it always like this?" I asked Sanders, after drinking it all in for a while.

"Every mistfall," he replied, turning toward me with a wistful smile. He was a fat man, with a jovial red face. Not the sort who should smile wistfully. But he did.

He gestured toward the east, where Wraithworld's sun rising above the mists made a crimson and orange spectacle of the dawn sky.

"The sun," he said. "As it rises, the heat drives the mists back into the valleys, forces them to surrender the mountains they've conquered during the night. The mists sink, and one by one the peaks come into view. By noon the whole range is visible for miles and miles. There's nothing like it on Earth, or anywhere else."

He smiled again, and led me over to one of the tables scattered around the balcony. "And then, at sunset, it's all reversed. You must watch mistrise tonight," he said.

We sat down, and a sleek robowaiter came rolling out to serve us as the chairs registered our presence. Sanders ignored it. "It's war, you know," he continued. "Eternal war between the sun and the mists. And the mists have the better of it. They have the valleys, and the plains, and the seacoasts. The sun has only a few mountaintops. And them only by day."

He turned to the robowaiter and ordered coffee for both of us, to keep us occupied until the others arrived. It would be fresh-brewed, of course. Sanders didn't tolerate instants or synthetics on his planet.

"You like it here," I said, while we waited for the coffee.

Sanders laughed. "What's not to like? Castle Cloud has everything. Good food, entertainment, gambling, and all the other comforts of home. Plus this planet. I've got the best of both worlds, don't I?"

"I suppose so. But most people don't think in those terms. Nobody comes to Wraithworld for the gambling, or the food."

Sanders nodded. "But we do get some hunters. Out after rockcats and plains devils. And once in a while someone will come to look at the ruins."

"Maybe," I said. "But those are your exceptions. Not your rule. Most of your guests are here for one reason."

"Sure," he admitted, grinning. "The wraiths."

"The wraiths," I echoed. "You've got beauty here, and hunting and fishing and mountaineering. But none of that brings the tourists here. It's the wraiths they come for."

The coffee arrived then, two big steaming mugs accompanied by a pitcher of thick cream. It was very strong, and very hot, and very good. After weeks of spaceship synthetic, it was an awakening.

Sanders sipped at his coffee with care, his eyes studying me over the mug. He set it down thoughtfully. "And it's the wraiths you've come for, too," he said.

I shrugged. "Of course. My readers aren't interested in scenery, no matter how spectacular. Dubowski and his men are here to find wraiths, and I'm here to cover the search."

Sanders was about to answer, but he never got the chance. A sharp, precise voice cut in suddenly. "If there are any wraiths to find," the voice said.

We turned to face the balcony entrance. Dr. Charles Dubowski, head of the Wraithworld Research Team, was standing in the doorway, squinting at the light. He had managed to shake the gaggle of research assistants who usually trailed him everywhere.

Dubowski paused for a second, then walked over to our table, pulled out a chair, and sat down. The robowaiter came rolling out again.

Sanders eyed the thin scientist with unconcealed distaste. "What makes you think the wraiths aren't there, Doctor?" he asked.

Dubowski shrugged, and smiled lightly. "I just don't feel there's enough evidence," he said. "But don't worry. I never let my feelings interfere with my work. I want the truth as much as anyone. So I'll run an impartial expedition. If your wraiths *are* out there, I'll find them."

"Or they'll find you," Sanders said. He looked grave. "And that might not be too pleasant."

Dubowski laughed. "Oh, come now, Sanders. Just because you live in a castle doesn't mean you have to be so melodramatic."

"Don't laugh, Doctor. The wraiths have killed people before, you know."

"No proof of that," said Dubowski. "No proof at all. Just as there's no proof of the wraiths themselves. But that's why we're here. To find proof. Or disproof. But come, I'm famished." He turned to our robo-waiter, who had been standing by and humming impatiently.

Dubowski and I ordered rockcat steaks, with a basket of hot, freshly-baked biscuits. Sanders took advantage of the Earth supplies our ship had brought in last night, and got a massive slab of ham with a half-dozen eggs.

Rockcat has a flavor that Earth meat hasn't had in centuries. I loved it, although Dubowski left much of his steak uneaten. He was too busy talking to eat.

"You shouldn't dismiss the wraiths so lightly," Sanders said after the robowaiter had stalked off with our orders. "There is evidence. Plenty of it. Twenty-two deaths since this planet was discovered. And eyewitness accounts of wraiths by the dozens."

"True," Dubowski said. "But I wouldn't call that real evidence. Deaths? Yes. Most are simple disappearances, however. Probably people who fell off a mountain, or got eaten by a rockcat, or something. It's impossible to find the bodies in the mists. More people vanish every day on Earth, and nothing is thought of it. But here, every time someone disappears, people claim the wraiths got him. No, I'm sorry. It's not enough."

"Bodies have been found, Doctor," Sanders said quietly. "Slain horribly. And not by falls or rockcats, either."

It was my turn to cut in. "Only four bodies have been recovered that I know of," I said. "And I've backgrounded myself pretty thoroughly on the wraiths."

Sanders frowned. "All right," he admitted. "But what about those four cases? Pretty convincing evidence, if you ask me."

The food showed up about then, but Sanders continued as we ate. "The first sighting, for example. That's never been explained satisfactorily. The Gregor Expedition."

I nodded. Dave Gregor had captained the ship that had discovered Wraithworld, nearly seventy-five years earlier. He had probed through the mists with his sensors, and set his ship down on the seacoast plains. Then he sent teams out to explore.

There were two men in each team, both well armed. But in one case, only a single man came back, and he was in hysteria. He and his partner had gotten separated in the mists, and suddenly he heard a blood-curdling scream. When he found his friend, he was quite dead. And something was standing over the body.

The survivor described the killer as man-like, eight feet tall, and somehow insubstantial. He claimed that when he fired at it, the blaster bolt went right through it. Then the creature had wavered, and vanished in the mists.

Gregor sent other teams out to search for the thing. They recovered the body, but that was all. Without special instruments, it was difficult to find the same place twice in the mists. Let alone something like the creature that had been described.

So the story was never confirmed. But nonetheless, it caused a sensation when Gregor returned to Earth. Another ship was sent to conduct a more thorough search. It found nothing. But one of its search teams disappeared without a trace.

And the legend of the mist wraiths was born, and began to grow. Other ships came to Wraithworld, and a trickle of colonists came and went, and Paul Sanders landed one day and erected the Castle Cloud so the public might safely visit the mysterious planet of the wraiths.

And there were other deaths, and other disappearances, and many people claimed to catch brief glimpses of wraiths prowling through the mists. And then someone found the ruins. Just tumbled stone blocks, now. But once, structures of some sort. The homes of the wraiths, people said.

There was evidence, I thought. And some of it was hard to deny. But Dubowski was shaking his head vigorously.

"The Gregor affair proves nothing," he said. "You know as well as I this planet has never been explored thoroughly. Especially the plains area, where Gregor's ship put down. It was probably some sort of animal that killed that man. A rare animal of some sort native to that area."

"What about the testimony of his partner?" Sanders asked.

"Hysteria, pure and simple."

"The other sightings? There have been an awful lot of them. And the witnesses weren't always hysterical."

"Proves nothing," Dubowski said, shaking his head. "Back on Earth, plenty of people still claim to have seen ghosts and flying saucers. And here, with those damned mists, mistakes and hallucinations are naturally even easier."

He jabbed at Sanders with the knife he was using to butter a biscuit. "It's these mists that foul up everything. The wraith myth would have died long ago without the mists. Up to now, no one has had the equipment or the money to conduct a really thorough investigation. But we do. And we will. We'll get the truth once and for all."

Sanders grimaced. "If you don't get yourself killed first. The wraiths may not like being investigated."

"I don't understand you, Sanders," Dubowski said. "If you're so afraid of the wraiths and so convinced that they're down there prowling about, why have you lived here so long?"

"Castle Cloud was built with safeguards," Sanders said. "The brochure we send prospective guests describes them. No one is in danger here. For one thing, the wraiths won't come out of the mists. And we're in sunlight most of the day. But it's a different story down in the valleys."

"That's superstitious nonsense. If I had to guess, I'd say these mist wraiths of yours were nothing but transplanted Earth ghosts. Phantoms of someone's imagination. But I won't guess — I'll wait until the results are in. Then we'll see. If they are real, they won't be able to hide from us."

Sanders looked over at me. "What about you? Do you agree with him?"

"I'm a journalist," I said carefully. "I'm just here to cover what happens. The wraiths are famous, and my readers are interested. So I've got no opinions. Or none that I'd care to broadcast, anyway."

Sanders lapsed into a disgruntled silence, and attacked his ham and eggs with a renewed vigor. Dubowski took over for him, and steered the conversation over to the details of the investigation he was planning. The rest of the meal was a montage of eager talk about wraith traps, and search plans, and roboprobes, and sensors. I listened carefully and took mental notes for a column on the subject.

Sanders listened carefully, too. But you could tell from his face that he was far from pleased by what he heard.

Nothing much else happened that day. Dubowski spent his time at the spacefield, built on a small plateau below the castle, and supervised the unloading of his equipment. I wrote a column on his plans for the expedition, and beamed it back to Earth. Sanders tended to his other guests, and did whatever else a hotel manager does, I guess.

I went out to the balcony again at sunset, to watch the mists rise.

It was war, as Sanders had said. At mistfall, I had seen the sun victorious in the first of the daily battles. But now the conflict was renewed. The mists began to creep back to the heights as the temperature fell. Wispy gray-white tendrils stole up silently from the valleys, and curled around the jagged mountain peaks like ghostly fingers. Then the fingers began to grow thicker and stronger, and after a while they pulled the mists up after them.

One by one the stark, wind-carved summits were swallowed up for another night. The Red Ghost, the giant to the north, was the last mountain to vanish in the lapping white ocean. And then the mists began to pour in over the balcony ledge, and close around Castle Cloud itself.

I went back inside. Sanders was standing there, just inside the doors. He had been watching me.

"You were right," I said. "It was beautiful."

He nodded. "You know, I don't think Dubowski has bothered to look yet," he said.

"Busy, I guess."

Sanders sighed. "Too damn busy. C'mon. I'll buy you a drink."

The hotel bar was quiet and dark, with the kind of mood that promotes good talk and serious drinking. The more I saw of Sanders' castle, the more I liked the man. Our tastes were in remarkable accord.

We found a table in the darkest and most secluded part of the room, and ordered drinks from a stock that included liquors from a dozen worlds. And we talked.

"You don't seem very happy to have Dubowski here," I said after the drinks came. "Why not? He's filling up your hotel."

Sanders looked up from his drink, and smiled. "True. It is the slow season. But I don't like what he's trying to do."

"So you try to scare him away?"

Sanders' smile vanished. "Was I that transparent?"

I nodded.

He sighed. "Didn't think it would work," he said. He sipped thoughtfully at his drink. "But I had to try something."

"Why?"

"Because. Because he's going to destroy this world, if I let him. By the time he and his kind get through, there won't be a mystery left in the universe."

"He's just trying to find some answers. Do the wraiths exist? What about the ruins? Who built them? Didn't you ever want to know those things, Sanders?"

He drained his drink, looked around, and caught the waiter's eye to order another. No robowaiters in here. Only human help. Sanders was particular about atmosphere.

"Of course," he said when he had his drink. "Everyone's wondered about those questions. That's why people come here to Wraithworld, to the Castle Cloud. Each guy who touches down here is secretly hoping he'll have an adventure with the wraiths, and find out all the answers personally.

"So he doesn't. So he slaps on a blaster and wander around the mist forests for a few days, or a few weeks, and finds nothing. So what? He can come back and search again. The dream is still there, and the romance, and the mystery.

"And who knows? Maybe one trip he glimpses a wraith drifting through the mists. Or something he thinks is a wraith. And then he'll go home happy, because he's been part of a legend. He's touched a little bit of creation that hasn't had all the awe and the wonder ripped from it yet by Dubowski's sort."

He fell silent, and stared morosely into his drink. Finally, after a long pause, be continued. "Dubowski! Bah! He makes me boil. He comes here with his ship full of lackeys and his million-credit grant and all his gadgets, to hunt for wraiths. Oh, he'll get them all right. That's what frightens me. Either he'll prove they don't exist, or he'll find them, and they'll turn out to be some kind of submen or animals or something."

He emptied his glass again, savagely. "And that will ruin it. Ruin it, you hear! He'll answer all the questions with his gadgets, and there'll be nothing left for anyone else. It isn't fair."

I sat there and sipped quietly at my drink and said nothing. Sanders ordered another. A foul thought was running around in my head. Finally I had to say it aloud.

"If Dubowski answers all the questions," I said, "then there will be no reason to come here anymore. And you'll be put out of business. Are you sure that's not why you're so worried?"

Sanders glared at me, and I thought he was going to hit me for a second. But he didn't. "I thought you were different. You looked at mistfall, and understood. I thought you did, anyway. But I guess I was wrong." He jerked his head toward the door. "Get out of here," he said.

I rose. "All right," I said. "I'm sorry, Sanders. But it's my job to ask nasty questions like that."

He ignored me, and I left the table. When I reached the door, I turned and looked back across the room. Sanders was staring into his drink again, and talking loudly to himself.

"Answers," he said. He made it sound obscene. "Answers. Always they have to have answers. But the questions are so much finer. Why can't they leave them alone?"

I left him alone then. Alone with his drinks.

The next few weeks were hectic ones, for the expedition and for me. Dubowski went about things thoroughly, you had to give him that. He had planned his assault on Wraithworld with meticulous precision.

Mapping came first. Thanks to the mists, what maps there were of Wraithworld were very crude by modern standards. So Dubowski sent out a whole fleet of roboprobes, to skim above the mists and steal their secrets with sophisticated sensory devices. From the information that came pouring in, a detailed topography of the region was pieced together.

That done, Dubowski and his assistants then used the maps to carefully plot every recorded wraith sighting since the Gregor Expedition. Considerable data on the sightings had been compiled and analyzed long before we left Earth, of course. Heavy use of the matchless collection on wraiths in the Castle Cloud library filled in the gaps that remained. As expected, sightings were most common in the valleys around the hotel, the only permanent human habitation on the planet.

When the plotting was completed, Dubowski set out his wraith traps, scattering most of them in the areas where wraiths had been reported most frequently. He also put a few in distant, outlying regions, however, including the seacoast plain where Gregor's ship had made the initial contact.

The traps weren't really traps, of course. They were squat duralloy pillars, packed with most every type of sensing and recording equipment known to Earth science. To the traps, the mists were all but nonexistent. If some unfortunate wraith wandered into survey range, there would be no way it could avoid detection.

Meanwhile, the mapping roboprobes were pulled in to be overhauled and reprogrammed, and then sent out again. With the topography known in detail, the probes could be sent through the mists on low-level patrols without fear of banging into a concealed mountain. The sensing equipment carried by the probes was not the equal of that in the wraith traps, of course. But the probes had a much greater range, and could cover thousands of square miles each day.

Finally, when the wraith traps were deployed and the roboprobes were in the air, Dubowski and his men took to the mist forests themselves. Each carried a heavy backpack of sensors and detection devices. The human search teams had more mobility than the wraith traps, and more sophisticated equipment than the probes. They covered a different area each day, in painstaking detail.

I went along on a few of those trips, with a backpack of my own. It made for some interesting copy, even though we never found anything. And while on search, I fell in love with the mist forests.

The tourist literature likes to call them "the ghastly mist forests of haunted Wraithworld." But they're not ghastly. Not really. There's a strange sort of beauty there, for those who can appreciate it.

The trees are thin and very tall, with white bark and pale gray leaves. But the forests are not without color. There's a parasite, a hanging moss of some sort, that's very common, and it drips from the overhanging branches in cascades of dark green and scarlet. And there are rocks, and vines, and low bushes choked with misshapen purplish fruits.

But there's no sun, of course. The mists hide everything. They swirl and slide around you as you walk, caressing you with unseen hands, clutching at your feet.

Once in a while, the mists play games with you. Most of the time you walk through a thick fog, unable to see more than a few feet in any direction, your own shoes lost in the mist carpet below. Sometimes, though, the fog closes in suddenly. And then you can't see at all. I blundered into more than one tree when that happened.

At other times, though, the mists — for no apparent reason — will roll back suddenly, and leave you standing alone in a clear pocket within a cloud. That's when you can see the forest in all its grotesque beauty. It's a brief, breathtaking glimpse of never-never land. Moments like that are few and short-lived. But they stay with you.

They stay with you.

In those early weeks, I didn't have much time for walking in the forests, except when I joined a search team to get the feel of it. Mostly I was busy writing. I did a series on the history of the planet, highlighted by the stories of the most famous sightings. I did feature profiles on some of the more colorful members of the expedition. I did a piece on Sanders, and the problems he encountered and overcame in building Castle Cloud. I did science pieces on the little known about the planet's ecology. I did mood pieces about the forests and the mountains. I did speculative thought pieces about the ruins. I wrote about rockcat hunting, and mountain climbing, and the huge and dangerous swamp lizards native to some offshore islands.

And, of course, I wrote about Dubowski and his search. On that I wrote reams.

Finally, however, the search began to settle down into dull routine, and I began to exhaust the myriad other topics Wraithworld offered. My output began to decline. I started to have time on my hands.

That's when I really began to enjoy Wraithworld. I began to take daily walks through the forests, ranging wider each day. I visited the ruins, and flew half a continent away to see the swamp lizards firsthand instead of by holo. I befriended a group of hunters passing through, and shot myself a rockcat. I accompanied some other hunters to the western seacoast, and nearly got myself killed by a plains devil.

And I began to talk to Sanders again.

Through all of this, Sanders had pretty well ignored me and Dubowski and everyone else connected with the wraith research. He spoke to us grudgingly if at all, greeted us curtly, and spent all his free time with the other guests.

At first, after the way he had talked in the bar that night, I worried about what he might do. I had visions of him murdering someone out in the mists, and trying to make it look like a wraith killing. Or maybe just sabotaging the wraith traps. But I was sure he would try something to scare off Dubowski or otherwise undermine the expedition.

Comes of watching too much holovision, I guess. Sanders did nothing of the sort. He merely sulked, glared at us in the castle corridors, and gave us less than full cooperation at all times.

After a while, though, he began to warm up again. Not, toward Dubowski and his men. Just toward me.

I guess that was because of my walks in the forests. Dubowski never went out into the mists unless he had to. And then he went out reluctantly, and came back quickly. His men followed their chiefs example. I was the only joker in the deck. But then, I wasn't really part of the same deck.

Sanders noticed, of course. He didn't miss much of what went on in his castle. And he began to speak to me again. Civilly. One day, finally, he even invited me for drinks again.

It was about two months into the expedition. Winter was coming to Wraithworld and Castle Cloud, and the air was getting cold and crisp. Dubowski and I were out on the dining balcony, lingering over coffee after another superb meal Sanders sat at a nearby table, talking to some tourists.

I forget what Dubowski and I were discussing. Whatever it was, Dubowski interrupted me with a shiver at one point. "It's getting cold out here," he complained. "Why don't we move inside?" Dubowski never liked the dining balcony very much.

I sort of frowned. "It's not that bad," I said. "Besides, it's nearly sunset. One of the best parts of the day."

Dubowski shivered again, and stood up. "Suit yourself," he said. "But I'm going in. I don't feel like catching a cold just so you can watch another mistfall."

He started to walk off. But he hadn't taken three steps before Sanders was up out of his seat, howling like a wounded rockcat.

"Mistfall," he bellowed. "*Mistfall!*" He launched into a long, incoherent string of obscenities. I had never seen Sanders so angry, not even when he threw me out of the bar that first night. He stood there, literally trembling with rage, his face flushed, his fat fists clenching and unclenching at his sides.

I got up in a hurry, and got between them. Dubowski turned to me, looking baffled and scared. "Wha — " he started.

"Get inside," I interrupted. "Get up to your room. Get to the lounge. Get somewhere. Get anywhere. But get out of here before he kills you."

"But — but — what's wrong? What happened? I don't — "

"Mistfall is in the morning," I told him. "At night, at sunset, it's mistrise. Now *go*."

"That's *all*? Why should that get him so — so — "

"*GO!*"

Dubowski shook his head, as if to say he still didn't understand what was going on. But he went.

I turned to Sanders. "Calm down," I said. "Calm down."

He stopped trembling, but his eyes threw blaster bolts at Dubowski's back. "Mistfall," he muttered. "Two months that bastard has been here, and he doesn't know the difference between mistfall and mistrise."

"He's never bothered to watch either one," I said. "Things like that don't interest him. That's his loss, though. No reason for you to get upset about it."

He looked at me, frowning. Finally he nodded. "Yeah," he said. "Maybe you're right." He sighed. "But *mistfall!* Hell." There was a short silence, then, "I need a drink. Join me?"

I nodded.

We wound up in the same dark corner as the first night, at what must have been Sanders' favorite table. He put away three drinks before I had finished my first. Big drinks. Everything in Castle Cloud was big.

There were no arguments this time. We talked about mistfall, and the forests, and the ruins. We talked about the wraiths, and Sanders lovingly told me the stories of the great sightings. I knew them all already, of course. But not the way Sanders told them.

At one point, I mentioned that I'd been born in Bradbury when my parents were spending a short vacation on Mars. Sanders' eyes lit up at that, and he spent the next hour or so regaling me with Earthman jokes. I'd heard them all before, too. But I was getting more than a little drunk, and somehow they all seemed hilarious.

After that night, I spent more time with Sanders than with anyone else in the hotel. I thought I knew Wraithworld pretty well by that time. But that was an empty conceit, and Sanders proved it. He showed me hidden spots in the forests that have haunted me ever since. He took me to island swamps, where the trees are of a very different sort and sway horribly without a wind. We flew to the far north, to another mountain range where the peaks are higher and sheathed in ice, and to a southern plateau where the mists pour eternally over the edge in a ghostly imitation of a waterfall.

I continued to write about Dubowski and his wraith hunt, of course. But there was little new to write about, so most of my time was spent with Sanders. I didn't worry too much about my output. My Wraithworld series had gotten excellent play on Earth and most of the colony worlds, so I thought I had it made.

Not so.

I'd been on Wraithworld just a little over three months when my syndicate beamed me. A few systems away, a civil war had broken out on a planet called New Refuge. They wanted me to cover it. No news was coming out of Wraithworld anyway, they said, since Dubowski's expedition still had over a year to run.

Much as I liked Wraithworld, I jumped at the chance. My stories had been getting a little stale, and I was running out of ideas, and the New Refuge thing sounded like it could be very big.

So I said good-bye to Sanders and Dubowski and Castle Cloud, and took a last walk through the mist forests, and booked passage on the next ship through.

The New Refuge civil war was a firecracker. I spent less than a month on the planet, but it was a dreary month. The place had been colonized by religious fanatics, but the original cult had schismed, and both sides accused the other of heresy. It was all very dingy. The planet itself had all the charm of a Martian suburb.

I moved on as quickly as I could, hopping from planet to planet, from story to story. In six months, I had worked myself back to Earth. Elections were coming up, so I got slapped onto a political beat. That was fine by me. It was a lively campaign, and there was a ton of good stories to be mined.

But throughout it all, I kept myself up on the little news that came out of Wraithworld. And finally, as I'd expected, Dubowski announced a press conference. As the syndicate's resident wraith, I got myself assigned to cover, and headed out on the fastest starship I could find.

I got there a week before the conference, ahead of everyone else. I had beamed Sanders before taking ship, and he met me at the spaceport. We adjourned to the dining balcony, and had our drinks served out there.

"Well?" I asked him, after we had traded amenities. "You know what Dubowski's going to announce?"

Sanders looked very glum. "I can guess," he said. "He called in all his damn gadgets a month ago, and he's been cross-checking findings on a computer. We've had a couple of wraith sightings since you left. Dubowski moved in hours after each sighting, and went over the areas with a fine-tooth comb. Nothing. That's what he's going to announce, I think. Nothing."

I nodded. "Is that so bad, though? Gregor found nothing."

"Not the same," Sanders said. "Gregor didn't look the way Dubowski has. People will believe him, whatever he says."

I wasn't so sure of that, and was about to say so, when Dubowski arrived. Someone must have told him I was there. He came striding out on the balcony, smiling, spied me, and came over to sit down.

Sanders glared at him, and studied his drink. Dubowski trained all of his attention on me. He seemed very pleased with himself. He asked what I'd been doing since I left, and I told him, and he said that was nice.

Finally I got to ask him about his results. "No comment," he said. "That's what I've called the press conference for."

"C'mon," I said. "I covered you for months when everybody else was ignoring the expedition. You can give me some kind of beat. What have you got?"

He hesitated. "Well, O.K.," he said doubtfully. "But don't release it yet. You can beam it out a few hours ahead of the conference. That should be enough time for a beat."

I nodded agreement. "What do you have?"

"The wraiths," he said. "I have the wraiths, bagged neatly. They don't exist. I've got enough evidence to prove it beyond a shadow of a doubt." He smiled broadly.

"Just because you didn't find anything?" I started. "Maybe they were avoiding you. If they're sentient, they might be smart enough. Or maybe they're beyond the ability of your sensors to detect."

"Come now," Dubowski said. "You don't believe that. Our wraith traps had every kind of sensor we could come up with. If the wraiths existed, they would have registered on something. But they didn't. We had the traps planted in the areas where three of Sanders' so-called sightings took place. Nothing. Absolutely nothing. Conclusive proof that those people were seeing things. Sightings, indeed."

"What about the deaths, the vanishings?" I asked. "What about the Gregor Expedition and the other classic cases?"

His smile spread. "Couldn't disprove all the deaths, of course. But our probes and our searches turned up four skeletons." He ticked them off on his fingers. "Two were killed by a rockslide, and one had rockcat claw marks on the bones."

"The fourth?"

"Murder," he said. "The body was buried in a shallow grave, clearly by human hands. A flood of some sort had exposed it. It was down in the records as a disappearance. I'm sure all the other bodies could be found, if we searched long enough. And we'd find that all died perfectly normal deaths."

Sanders raised his eyes from his drink. They were bitter eyes. "Gregor," he said stubbornly. "Gregor and the other classics."

Dubowski's smile became a smirk. "Ah, yes. We searched that area quite thoroughly. My theory was right. We found a tribe of apes nearby. Big brutes. Like giant baboons, with dirty white fur. Not a very successful species, either. We found only one small tribe, and they were dying out. But clearly, that was what Gregor's man sighted. And exaggerated all out of proportion."

There was silence. Then Sanders spoke, but his voice was beaten. "Just one question," he said softly. "Why?"

That brought Dubowski up short, and his smile faded. "You never have understood, have you, Sanders?" he said. "It was for truth. To free this planet from ignorance and superstition."

"Free Wraithworld?" Sanders said. "Was it enslaved?"

"Yes," Dubowski answered. "Enslaved by foolish myth. By fear. Now this planet will be free, and open. We can find out the truth behind those ruins now, without murky legends about half-human wraiths to fog the facts. We can open this planet for colonization. People won't be afraid to come here, and live, and farm. We've conquered the fear."

"A colony world? Here?" Sanders looked amused. "Are you going to bring big fans to blow away the mists, or what? Colonists have come before. And left. The soil's all wrong. You can't farm here, with all these mountains. At least not on a commercial scale. There's no way you can make a profit growing things on Wraithworld.

"Besides, there are hundreds of colony worlds crying for people. Did you need another so badly? Must Wraithworld become yet another Earth?"

Sanders shook his head sadly, drained his drink, and continued. "You're the one who doesn't understand, Doctor. Don't kid yourself.

You haven't freed Wraithworld. You've destroyed it. You've stolen its wraiths, and left an empty planet."

Dubowski shook his head. "I think you're wrong. They'll find plenty of good, profitable ways to exploit this planet. But even if you were correct, well, it's just too bad. Knowledge is what man is all about. People like you have tried to hold back progress since the beginning of time. But they failed, and you failed. Man needs to know."

"Maybe," Sanders said. "But is that the only thing man needs? I don't think so. I think he also needs mystery, and poetry, and romance. I think he needs a few unanswered questions, to make him brood and wonder."

Dubowski stood up abruptly, and frowned. "This conversation is as pointless as your philosophy, Sanders. There's no room in my universe for unanswered questions."

"Then you live in a very drab universe, Doctor."

"And you, Sanders, live in the stink of your own ignorance. Find some new superstitions if you must. But don't try to foist them off on me with your tales and legends. I've got no time for wraiths." He looked at me. "I'll see you at the press conference," he said. Then he turned and walked briskly from the balcony.

Sanders watched him depart in silence, then swiveled in his chair to look out over the mountains. "The mists are rising," he said.

Sanders was wrong about the colony too, as it turned out. They did establish one, although it wasn't much to boast of. Some vineyards, some factories, and a few thousand people; all belonging to no more than a couple of big companies.

Commercial farming did turn out to be unprofitable, you see. With one exception — a native grape, a fat gray thing the size of a lemon. So Wraithworld has only one export, a smoky white wine with a mellow, lingering flavor.

They call it mistwine, of course. I've grown fond of it over the years. The taste reminds me of mistfall somehow, and makes me dream. But that's probably me, not the wine. Most people don't care for it much.

Still, in a very minor way, it's a profitable item. So Wraithworld is still a regular stop on the spacelanes. For freighters, at least.

The tourists are long gone, though. Sanders was right about that. Scenery they can get closer to home, and cheaper. The wraiths were why they came.

Sanders is long gone, too. He was too stubborn and too impractical to buy in on the mistwine operations when he had the chance. So he stayed behind his ramparts at Castle Cloud until the last. I don't know what happened to him afterwards, when the hotel finally went out of business.

The castle itself is still there. I saw it a few years ago, when I stopped for a day en route to a story on New Refuge. It's already crumbling, though. Too expensive to maintain. In a few years, you won't be able to tell it from those other, older ruins.

Otherwise the planet hasn't changed much. The mists still rise at sunset, and fall at dawn. The Red Ghost is still stark and beautiful in the early morning light. The forests are still there, and the rockcats still prowl.

Only the wraiths are missing.

Only the wraiths.

Bayonne, New Jersey
June, 1971

The Second Kind of Loneliness

My relief left Earth today.

It will be at least three months before he gets here, of course. But he's on his way.

Today he lifted off from the Cape, just as I did, four long years ago. Out at Komarov Station he'll switch to a moon boat, then switch again in orbit around Luna, at Deepspace Station. There his voyage will really begin. Up to then he's still been in his own backyard.

Not until the *Charon* casts loose from Deepspace Station and sets out into the night will he feel it, *really* feel it, as I felt it four years ago. Not until Earth and Luna vanish behind him will it hit. He's known from the first that there's no turning back, of course. But there's a difference between knowing it and feeling it. Now he'll feel it.

There will be an orbital stopover around Mars, to send supplies down to Burroughs City. And more stops in the belt. But then the *Charon* will begin to gather speed. It will be going very fast when it reaches Jupiter. And much faster after it whips by, using the gravity of the giant planet like a slingshot to boost its acceleration.

After that there are no stops for the *Charon*. No stops at all until it reaches me, out here at the Cerberus Star Ring, six million miles beyond Pluto.

My relief will have a long time to brood. As I did.

I'm still brooding now, today, four years later. But then, there's not much else to do out here. Ringships are infrequent, and you get pretty weary of films and tapes and books after a time. So you brood. You think about your past, and dream about your future. And you try to keep the loneliness and the boredom from driving you out of your skull.

It's been a long four years. But it's almost over now. And it will be nice to get back. I want to walk on grass again, and see clouds, and eat an ice cream sundae.

Still, for all that, I don't regret coming. These four years alone in the darkness have done me good, I think. It's not as if I had left much. My days on Earth seem remote to me now, but I can still remember them if I try. The memories aren't all that pleasant. I was pretty screwed up back then.

I needed time to think, and that's one thing you get out here. The man who goes back on the *Charon* won't be the same one who came out here four years ago. I'll build a whole new life back on Earth. I know I will.

June 20

Ship today.

I didn't know it was coming, of course. I never do. The ringships are irregular, and the kind of energies I'm playing with out here turn radio signals into crackling chaos. By the time the ship finally punched through the static, the station's scanners had already picked it up and notified me.

It was clearly a ringship. Much bigger than the old system rust-buckets like the *Charon*, and heavily armored to withstand the stresses of the nullspace vortex. It came straight on, with no attempt to decelerate.

While I was heading down to the control room to strap in, a thought hit me. This might be the last. Probably not, of course. There's still three months to go, and that's time enough for a dozen ships. But you can never tell. The ring-ships are irregular, like I said.

Somehow the thought disturbed me. The ships have been part of my life for four years now. An important part. And the one today might have been the last. If so, I want it all down here. I want to remember it. With good reason, I think. When the ships come, that makes everything else worthwhile.

The control room is in the heart of my quarters. It's the center of everything, where the nerves and the tendons and the muscles of the station are gathered. But it's not very impressive. The room is very small, and once the door slides shut the walls and floor and ceiling are all a featureless white.

There's only one thing in the room: a horseshoe-shaped console that surrounds a single padded chair.

I sat down in that chair today for what might be the last time. I strapped myself in, and put on the earphones, and lowered the helmet. I reached for the controls, and touched them, and turned them on.

And the control room vanished.

It's all done with holographs, of course. I *know* that. But that doesn't make a bit of difference when I'm sitting in that chair. Then, as far as I'm concerned, I'm not inside anymore. I'm out *there*, in the void. The control console is still there, and the chair. But the rest has gone. Instead, the aching darkness is everywhere, above me, below me, all around me. The distant sun is only one star among many, and all the stars are terribly far away.

That's the way it always is. That's the way it was today. When I threw that switch I was alone in the universe with the cold stars and the ring. The Cerberus Star Ring.

I saw the ring as if from outside, looking down on it. It's a vast structure, really. But from out here, it's nothing. It's swallowed by the immensity of it all, a slim silver thread lost in the blackness.

But I know better. The ring is huge. My living quarters take up but a single degree in the circle it forms, a circle whose diameter is more than a hundred miles. The rest is circuitry and scanners and power banks. And the engines, the waiting nullspace engines.

The ring turned silent beneath me, its far side stretching away into nothingness. I touched a switch on my console. Below me, the nullspace engines woke.

In the center of the ring, a new star was born.

It was a tiny dot amid the dark at first. Green today, bright green. But not always, and not for long. Nullspace has many colors.

I could see the far side of the ring then, if I'd wanted to. It was glowing with a light of its own. Alive and awake, the nullspace engines were pouring unimaginable amounts of energy inward, to rip wide a hole in space itself.

The hole had been there long before Cerberus, long before man. Men found it, quite by accident, when they reached Pluto. They built the ring around it. Later they found two other holes, and built other star rings.

The holes were small, too small. But they could be enlarged. Temporarily, at the expense of vast amounts of power, they could be ripped open. Raw energy could be pumped through that tiny, unseen hole in the universe until the placid surface of nullspace roiled and lashed back, and the nullspace vortex formed.

And now it happened.

The star in the center of the ring grew and flattened. It was a pulsing disc, not a globe. But it was still the brightest thing in the heavens. And it swelled visibly. From the spinning green disc, flame-like orange spears lanced out, and fell back, and smoky bluish tendrils uncoiled. Specks of red danced and flashed among the green, grew and blended. The colors all began to run together.

The flat, spinning, multicolored star doubled in size, doubled again, again. A few minutes before it had not been. Now it filled the ring, lapped against the silver walls, seared them with its awful energy. It began to spin faster and faster, a whirlpool in space, a maelstrom of flame and light.

The vortex. The nullspace vortex. The howling storm that is not a storm and does not howl, for there is no sound in space.

To it came the ringship. A moving star at first, it took on visible form and shape almost faster than my human eyes could follow. It became a dark silver bullet in the blackness, a bullet fired at the vortex.

The aim was good. The ship hit very close to the center of the ring. The swirling colors closed over it.

I hit my controls. Even more suddenly than it had come, the vortex was gone. The ship was gone too, of course. Once more there was only me, and the ring, and the stars.

Then I touched another switch, and I was back in the blank white control room, unstrapping. Unstrapping for what might be the last time, ever.

Somehow I hope not. I never thought I'd miss anything about this place. But I will. I'll miss the ringships. I'll miss moments like the ones today.

I hope I get a few more chances at it before I give it up forever. I want to feel the nullspace engines wake again under my hands, and watch the vortex boil and churn while I float alone between the stars. Once more, at least. Before I go.

JUNE 23

That ringship has set me to thinking. Even more than usual.

It's funny that with all the ships I've seen pass through the vortex, I've never even given a thought to riding one. There's a whole new world on the other side of nullspace; Second Chance, a rich green planet of a star so far away that astronomers are still unsure whether it shares the same galaxy with us. That's the funny thing about the holes — you can't be sure where they lead until you go through.

When I was a kid, I read a lot about star travel. Most people didn't think it was possible. But those who did always mentioned Alpha Centauri as the first system we'd explore and colonize. Closest, and all that. Funny how wrong they were. Instead, our colonies orbit suns we can't even see. And I don't think we'll *ever* get to Alpha Centauri.

Somehow I never thought of the colonies in personal terms. Still can't. Earth is where I failed before. That's got to be where I succeed now. The colonies would be just another escape.

Like Cerberus?

JUNE 26

Ship today. So the other wasn't the last, after all. But what about this one?

JUNE 29

Why does a man volunteer for a job like this? Why does a man run to a silver ring six million miles beyond Pluto, to guard a hole in space? Why throw away four years of life alone in the darkness?

Why?

I used to ask myself that, in the early days. I couldn't answer it then. Now I think I can. I bitterly regretted the impulse that drove me out here, then. Now I think I understand it.

And it wasn't really an impulse. I ran to Cerberus. Ran. Ran to escape from loneliness.

That doesn't make sense?

Yes it does. I know about loneliness. It's been the theme of my life. I've been alone for as long as I can remember.

But there are two kinds of loneliness.

Most people don't realize the difference. I do. I've sampled both kinds.

They talk and write about the loneliness of the men who man the star rings. The lighthouses of space, and all that. And they're right.

There are times, out here at Cerberus, when I think I'm the only man in the universe. Earth was just a fever dream. The people I remember were just creations of my own mind.

There are times, out here, when I want someone to talk to so badly that I scream, and start pounding on the walls. There are times when the boredom crawls under my skin and all but drives me mad.

But there are *other* times, too. When the ringships come. When I go outside to make repairs. Or when I just sit in the control chair, imaging myself out into the darkness to watch the stars.

Lonely? Yes. But a solemn, brooding, tragic loneliness. A loneliness tinged with grandeur, somehow. A loneliness that a man hates with a passion — and yet loves so much he craves for more.

And then there is the second kind of loneliness.

You don't need the Cerberus Star Ring for that kind. You can find it anywhere on Earth. I know. I did. I found it everywhere I went, in everything I did.

It's the loneliness of people trapped within themselves. The loneliness of people who have said the wrong thing so often that they don't have the courage to say anything anymore. The loneliness, not of distance, but of fear.

The loneliness of people who sit alone in furnished rooms in crowded cities, because they've got nowhere to go and no one to talk to. The loneliness of guys who go to bars to meet someone, only to discover they don't know how to strike up a conversation, and wouldn't have the courage to do so if they did.

There's no grandeur to that kind of loneliness. No purpose and no poetry. It's loneliness without meaning. It's sad and squalid and pathetic, and it stinks of self-pity.

Oh yes, it hurts at times to be alone among the stars.

But it hurts a lot more to be alone at a party. A lot more.

JUNE 30

Reading *yesterday's* entry. Talk about self-pity

JULY 1

Reading yesterday's entry. My flippant mask. After four years, I still fight back whenever I try to be honest with myself. That's not good. If things are going to be any different this time, I have to understand myself.

So why do I have to ridicule myself when I admit that I'm lonely and vulnerable? Why do I have to struggle to admit that I was scared of life? No one's ever going to read this thing. I'm talking to myself, about myself.

So why are there some things I still can't bring myself to say?

JULY 4

No ringship today. Too bad. Earth ain't never *had* no fireworks that could match the nullspace vortex, and I felt like celebrating.

But why do I keep Earth calendar out here, where the years are centuries and the seasons a dim memory? July is just like December. So what's the use?

JULY 10

I dreamed of Karen last night And now I can't get her out of my skull.

I thought I buried her long ago. It was all a fantasy anyway. Oh, she liked me well enough. Loved me, maybe. But no more than a half-dozen other guys. I wasn't really *special* to her, and she never realized just how special she was to me.

Nor how much I wanted to be special to her — how much I needed to be special to someone, somewhere.

So I elected her. But it was all a fantasy. And I knew it was, in my more rational moments. I had no right to be so hurt. I had no special claim on her.

But I thought I did, in my daydreams. And I was hurt. It was my fault, though, not hers. Karen would never hurt anyone willingly. She just never realized how fragile I was.

Even out here, in the early years, I kept dreaming. I dreamed of how she'd change her mind. How she'd be waiting for me. Et cetera.

But that was more wish fulfillment. It was before I came to terms with myself out here. I know now that she won't be waiting. She doesn't need me, and never did. I was just a friend.

So I don't much like dreaming about her. That's bad. Whatever I do, I must *not* look up Karen when I get back. I have to start all over again. I have to find someone who does need me. And I won't find her if I try to slip back into my old life.

JULY 18

A month since my relief left Earth. The *Charon* should be in the belt by now. Two months to go.

JULY 23

Nightmares now. God help me.

I'm dreaming of Earth again. And Karen. I can't stop. Every night it's the same.

It's funny, calling Karen a nightmare. Up to now she's always been a dream. A beautiful dream, with her long, soft hair, and her laugh, and that funny way she had of grinning. But those dreams were always wish fulfillments. In the dreams Karen needed me and wanted me and loved me.

The nightmares have the bite of truth to them. They're all the same. It's always a replay of me and Karen, together on that last night.

It was a good night, as nights went for me. We ate at one of my favorite restaurants, and went to a show. We talked together easily, about many things. We laughed together, too.

Only later, back at her place, I reverted to form. When I tried to tell her how much she meant to me. I remember how awkward and stupid I felt, how I struggled to get things out, how I stumbled over my own words. So much came out wrong.

I remember how she looked at me then. Strangely. How she tried to disillusion me. Gently. She was always gentle. And I looked into her eyes and listened to her voice. But I didn't find love, or need. Just — just pity, I guess.

Pity for an inarticulate jerk who'd been letting life pass him by without touching it. Not because he didn't want to. But because he was afraid to, and didn't know how. She'd found that jerk, and loved him, in her way — she loved everybody. She'd tried to help, to give him some of her self-confidence, some of the courage and bounce that she faced life with. And, to an extent, she had.

Not enough, though. The jerk liked to make fantasies about the day he wouldn't be lonely anymore. And when Karen tried to help him, he thought she was his fantasy come to life. Or deluded himself into thinking that. The jerk suspected the truth all along, of course, but he lied to himself about it.

And when the day came that he couldn't lie any longer, he was still vulnerable enough to be hurt. He wasn't the type to grow scar tissue easily. He didn't have the courage to try again with someone else. So he ran.

I hope the nightmares stop. I can't take them, night after night. I can't take reliving that hour in Karen's apartment.

I've had four years out here. I've looked at myself hard. I've changed what I didn't like, or tried to. I've tried to cultivate that scar tissue, to gather the confidence I need to face the new rejections I'm going to meet before I find acceptance. But I know myself damn well now, and I know it's only been a partial success. There will always be things that will hurt, things that I'll never be able to face the way I'd like to.

Memories of that last hour with Karen are among those things. God, I hope the nightmares end.

July 26

More nightmares. Please, Karen. I loved you. Leave me alone. Please.

July 29

There was a ringship yesterday, thank God. I needed one. It helped take my mind off Earth, off Karen. And there was no nightmare last night, for the first time in a week. Instead I dreamed of the nullspace vortex. The raging silent storm.

August 1

The nightmares have returned. Not always Karen, now. Older memories too. Infinitely less meaningful, but still painful. All the stupid things I've said, all the girls I never met, all the things I have never done.

Bad. Bad. I have to keep reminding myself. I'm not like that anymore. There's a new me, a me I built out here, six million miles beyond Pluto. Made of steel and stars and null-space, hard and confident and self-assured. And not afraid of life.

The past is behind me. But it still hurts.

AUGUST 2

Ship today. The nightmares continue. Damn.

AUGUST 3

No nightmare last night Second time for that, that I've rested easy after opening the hole for a ringship during the day. (Day? Night? Nonsense out here — but I still write as if they had some meaning. Four years haven't even touched the Earth in me.) Maybe the vortex is scaring Karen away. But I never wanted to scare Karen away before. Besides, I shouldn't need crutches.

AUGUST 13

Another ship came through a few nights ago. No dream afterwards. A pattern!

I'm fighting the memories. I'm thinking of other things about Earth. The good times. There were a lot of them, really, and there will be lots more when I get back. I'm going to make sure of that.

These nightmares are stupid. I won't permit them to continue. There was so much else I shared with Karen, so much I'd like to recall. Why can't I?

AUGUST 18

The *Charon* is about a month away. I wonder who my relief is. I wonder what drove *him* out here?

Earth dreams continue. No. Call them Karen dreams. Am I even afraid to write her name now?

AUGUST 20

Ship today. After it was through I stayed out and looked at stars. For several hours, it seems. Didn't seem as long at the time.

It's beautiful out here. Lonely, yes. But such a loneliness! You're alone with the universe, the stars spread out at your feet and scattered around your head.

Each one is a sun. Yet they still look cold to me. I find myself shivering, lost in the vastness of it all, wondering how it got there and what it means.

My relief, whoever it is, I hope he can appreciate this, as it should be appreciated. There are so many who can't, or won't. Men who walk at night, and never look up at the sky. I hope my relief isn't a man like that.

AUGUST 24

When I get back to Earth, I will look up Karen. I must. How can I pretend that things are going to be different this time if I can't even work up the courage to do that? And they are going to be different. So I *must* face Karen, and prove that I've changed. Really changed.

AUGUST 25

The nonsense of yesterday. How could I face Karen? What would I say to her? I'd only start deluding myself again, and wind up getting burned all over again. No. I must *not* see Karen. Hell, I can't even take the dreams.

AUGUST 30

I've been going down to the control room and flipping myself out regularly of late. No ringships. But I find that going outside makes the memories of Earth dim.

More and more I know I'll miss Cerberus. A year from now, I'll be back on Earth, looking up at the night sky, and remembering how the ring shone silver in the starlight. I know I will.

And the vortex. I'll remember the vortex, and the ways the colors swirled and mixed. Different every time.

Too bad I was never a holo buff. You could make a fortune back on Earth with a tape of the way the vortex looks when it spins. The ballet of the void. I'm surprised no one's ever thought of it.

Maybe I'll suggest it to my relief. Something to do to fill the hours, if he's interested. I hope he is. Earth would be richer if someone brought back a record.

I'd do it myself, but the equipment isn't right, and I don't have the time to modify it.

SEPTEMBER 4

I've gone outside every day for the last week, I find. No nightmares. Just dreams of the darkness, laced with the colors of nullspace.

SEPTEMBER 9

Continue to go outside, and drink it all in. Soon, soon now, all this will be lost to me. Forever. I feel as though I must take advantage of every second. I must memorize the way things are out here at Cerberus, so I can keep the awe and the wonder and the beauty fresh inside me when I return to Earth.

SEPTEMBER 10

There hasn't been a ship in a long time. Is it over, then? Have I seen my last?

SEPTEMBER 12

No ship today. But I went outside and woke the engines and let the vortex roar.

Why do I always write about the vortex roaring and howling? There is no sound in space. I hear nothing. But I watch it. And it does roar. It does.

The sounds of silence. But not the way the poets meant.

SEPTEMBER 13

I watched the vortex again today, though there was no ship.

I've never done that before. Now I've done it twice. It's forbidden. The costs in terms of power are enormous, and Cerberus lives on power. So why?

It's almost as though I don't want to give up the vortex. But I have to. Soon.

SEPTEMBER 14

Idiot, idiot, idiot. What have I been doing? The *Charon* is less than a week away, and I've been gawking at the stars as if I'd never seen them before. I haven't even started to pack, and I've got to clean up my records for my relief, and get the station in order.

Idiot! Why am I wasting time writing in this damn *book!*

SEPTEMBER 15

Packing almost done. I've uncovered some weird things, too. Things I tried to hide in the early years. Like my novel. I wrote it in the first six months, and thought it was great. I could hardly wait to get back to Earth, and sell it, and become an Author. Ah, yes. Read it over a year later. It stinks.

Also found a picture of Karen.

SEPTEMBER 16

Today I took a bottle of Scotch and a glass down to the control room, set them down on the console, and strapped myself in. Drank a toast to the blackness and the stars and the vortex. I'll miss them.

SEPTEMBER 17

A day, by my calculations. A day. Then I'm on my way home, to a fresh start and a new life. If I have the courage to live it.

SEPTEMBER 18

Nearly midnight. No sign of the *Charon*. What's wrong?

Nothing, probably. These schedules are never precise. Sometimes as much as a week off. So why do I worry? Hell, I was late getting here myself. I wonder what the poor guy I replaced was thinking then?

SEPTEMBER 20

The *Charon* didn't come yesterday, either. After I got tired of waiting, I took that bottle of Scotch and went back to the control room. And out. To drink another toast to the stars. And the vortex. I woke the vortex and let it flame, and toasted it.

A lot of toasts. I finished the bottle. And today I've got such a hangover I think I'll never make it back to Earth.

It was a stupid thing to do. The crew of the *Charon* might have seen the vortex colors. If they report me, I'll get docked a small fortune from the pile of money that's waiting back on Earth.

SEPTEMBER 21

Where is the *Charon*? Did something happen to it? Is it coming?

SEPTEMBER 22

I went outside again.

God, so beautiful, so lonely, so vast. Haunting, that's the word I want. The beauty out there is haunting. Sometimes I think I'm a fool to go back. I'm giving up all of eternity for a pizza and a lay and a kind word.

31

NO! What the hell am I writing! No. I'm going back, of course I am. I need Earth, I miss Earth, I want Earth. This time it will be different.

I'll find another Karen, and this time I won't blow it.

SEPTEMBER 23

I'm sick. God, but I'm sick. The things I've been thinking. I thought I had changed, but now I don't know. I find myself actually thinking about staying, about signing on for another term. I don't want to. No. But I think I'm still afraid of life, of Earth, of everything.

Hurry, *Charon*. Hurry, before I change my mind.

SEPTEMBER 24

Karen or the vortex? Earth or eternity?

Dammit, how can I *think* that! Karen! Earth! I have to have courage, I have to risk pain, I have to taste life.

I am not a rock. Or an island. Or a star.

SEPTEMBER 25

No sign of the *Charon*. A full week late. That happens sometimes. But not very often. It will arrive soon. I know it.

SEPTEMBER 30

Nothing. Each day I watch, and wait. I listen to my scanners, and go outside to look, and pace back and forth through the ring. But nothing. It's never been this late. What's wrong?

OCTOBER 3

Ship today. Not the *Charon*. I thought it was at first, when the scanners picked it up. I yelled loud enough to wake the vortex. But then I looked, and my heart sank. It was too big, and it was coming straight on without decelerating.

I went outside and let it through. And stayed out for a long time afterward.

OCTOBER 4

I want to go home. Where are they? I don't understand. I don't understand.

They can't just leave me here. They can't. They won't.

OCTOBER 5

Ship today. Ringship again. I used to look forward to them. Now I hate them, because they're not the *Charon*. But I let it through.

OCTOBER 7

I unpacked. It's silly for me to live out of suitcases when I don't know if the *Charon* is coming, or when.

I still look for it, though. I wait. It's coming, I know. Just delayed somewhere. An emergency in the belt maybe.

There are lots of explanations.

Meanwhile, I'm doing odd jobs around the ring. I never did get it in proper shape for my relief. Too busy star watching at the time, to do what I should have been doing,

JANUARY 8 *(or thereabouts)*

Darkness and despair.

I know why the *Charon* hasn't arrived. It isn't due. The calendar was all screwed up. It's January, not October. And I've been living on the wrong time for months. Even celebrated the Fourth of July on the wrong day.

I discovered it yesterday when I was doing those chores around the ring. I wanted to make sure everything was running right. For my relief.

Only there won't be any relief.

The *Charon* arrived three months ago. I — I destroyed it. Sick. It was sick. I was sick, mad. As soon as it was done, it hit me. What I'd done. Oh, God. I screamed for hours.

And then I set back the wall calendar. And forgot. Maybe deliberately. Maybe I couldn't bear to remember. I don't know. All I know is that I forgot.

But now I remember. Now I remember it all.

The scanners had warned me of the *Charon*'s approach. I was outside, waiting. Watching. Trying to get enough of the stars and the darkness to last me forever.

Through that darkness, *Charon* came. It seemed so slow compared to the ringships. And so small. It was my salvation, my relief, but it looked fragile, and silly, and somehow ugly. Squalid. It reminded me of Earth.

It moved towards docking, dropping into the ring from above, groping toward the locks in the habitable section of Cerberus. So very slow. I watched it come. Suddenly I wondered what I'd say to the crewmen, and my relief. I wondered what they'd think of me. Somewhere in my gut, a fist clenched.

And suddenly I couldn't stand it. Suddenly I was afraid of it. Suddenly I hated it.

So I woke the vortex.

A red flare, branching into yellow tongues, growing quickly, shooting off bluegreen bolts. One passed near the *Charon*. And the ship shuddered.

I tell myself, now, that I didn't realize what I was doing.

Yet I knew the *Charon* was unarmored. I knew it couldn't take vortex energies. I knew.

The *Charon* was so slow, the vortex so fast. In two heartbeats the maelstrom was brushing against the ship. In three it had swallowed it.

It was gone so fast. I don't know if the ship melted, or burst asunder, or crumpled. But I know it couldn't have survived. There's no blood on my star ring, though. The debris is somewhere on the other side of nullspace. If there is any debris.

The ring and the darkness looked the same as ever.

That made it so easy to forget. And I must have wanted to forget very much.

And now? What do I do *now*? Will Earth find out? Will there ever be relief? I want to go home.

Karen, I —

JUNE 18

My relief left Earth today.

At least I think he did. Somehow the wall calendar was broken, so I'm not precisely sure of the date. But I've got it back into working order.

Anyway, it can't have been off for more than a few hours. or I would have noticed. So my relief is on the way. It will take him three months to get here, of course.

But at least he's coming.

Bayonne, New Jersey
July, 1971

Override

Dusk was settling softly over the High Lakes as Kabaraijian and his crew made their way home from the caves. It was a calm, quiet dusk; a twilight blended of green waters, and mellow night winds, and the slow fading of Grotto's gentle sun. From the rear of his launch, Kabaraijian watched it fall, and listened to the sounds of twilight over the purring of the engine.

Grotto was a quiet world, but the sounds were there, if you knew how to listen. Kabaraijian knew. He sat erect in the back of the boat, a slight figure with swarthy skin, and long black hair, and brown eyes that drifted dreamy. One thin hand rested on his knee, the other, forgotten, on the motor. And his ears listened to the bubbling of the water in the wake of the launch, and the swish-splash of the lakeleapers breaking surface, and the wind moving the trailing green branches of the trees along the near shore. In time, he'd hear the night-flyers, too, but they were not yet up.

There were four in the boat, but only Kabaraijian listened or heard. The others, bigger men with pasty faces and vacant eyes, were long past hearing. They wore the dull gray coveralls of dead men, and there was a steel plate in the back of each man's skull. Sometimes, when his corpse controller was on, Kabaraijian could listen with their ears, and see with their eyes. But that was work, hard work, and not worth it. The sights and sounds a corpse handler felt through his crew were pale echoes of real sensation, seldom useful and never pleasurable.

And now, Grotto's cooling dusk, was an off-time. So Kabaraijian's corpse controller was off, and his mind, disengaged from the dead men, rested easy in its own body. The launch moved purposefully along the lake shore, but Kabaraijian's thoughts wandered lazily, when he thought at all. Mostly he just sat, and watched the water and the trees, and listened. He'd worked the corpse crew hard that day, and now he was drained and empty. Thought — thought especially — was more effort than he was prepared to give. Better to just linger with the evening.

It was a long, quiet voyage, across two big lakes and one small one, through a cave, and finally up a narrow and swift-running river. Kabaraijian turned up the power then, and the trip grew noisier as the launch sliced a path through the river's flow. Night had settled before he reached the station, a rambling structure of blue-black stone set by the river's edge. But the office windows still glowed with a cheery yellow light

A long dock of native silverwood fronted the river, and a dozen launches identical to Kabaraijian's were already tied up for the night. But there were still empty berths. Kabaraijian took one of them, and guided the boat into it.

When the launch was secure, he slung his collection box under one arm, and hopped out onto the dock. His free hand went to his belt, and thumbed the corpse controller. Vague sense blurs drifted into his mind, but Kabaraijian shunted them aside, and shook the dead men alive with an unheard shout. The corpses rose, one by one, and stepped out of the launch. Then they followed Kabaraijian to the station.

Munson was waiting inside the office — a fat, scruffy man with gray hair, and wrinkles around his eyes, and a fatherly manner. He had his feet up on his desk and was reading a novel. When Kabaraijian entered, he smiled and sat up and put down the book, inserting his leather placemark carefully. "'Lo, Matt," he said. "Why are you always the last one in?"

"Because I'm usually the last one out," Kabaraijian said, smiling. It was his newest line. Munson asked the same question every night, and always expected Kabaraijian to come up with a fresh answer. He seemed only moderately pleased by this one.

Kabaraijian set the collection box down on Munson's desk and opened it. "Not a bad day," he said. "Four good stones, and twelve smaller ones."

Munson scooped a handful of small, grayish rocks from inside the padded metal box and studied them. Right now they weren't much to look at. But cut and polished they'd be something else again: swirl-stones. They were gems without fire, but they had their own beauty. Good ones looked like crystals of moving fog, full of soft colors and softer mysteries and dreams.

Munson nodded, and dropped the stones back into the box. "Not bad," he said. "You always do good, Matt. You know where to look."

"The rewards of coming back slow and easy," Kabaraijian said. "I look around me."

Munson put the box under his desk, and turned to his computer console, a white plastic intruder in the wood-paneled room. He entered the swirlstones into the records, and looked back up. "You want to wash down your corpses?"

Kabaraijian shook his head. "Not tonight. I'm tired. I'll just flop them for now."

"Sure," said Munson. He rose, and opened the door behind his desk. Kabaraijian followed him, and the three dead men followed Kabaraijian. Behind the office were barracks, long and low-roofed, with row on row of simple wooden bunks. Most of them were full. Kabaraijian guided his dead men to three empty ones and maneuvered them in. Then he thumbed his controller off. The echoes in his head blinked out, and the corpses sagged heavily into the bunks.

Afterwards, he chatted with Munson for a few minutes back in the office. Finally the old man went back to his novel, and Kabaraijian back to the cool night.

A row of company scooters sat in back of the station, but Kabaraijian left them alone, preferring the ten-minute walk from the river to the settlement. He covered the forest road with an easy, measured pace, pausing here and there to brush aside vines and low branches. It was always a pleasant walk. The nights were calm, the breezes fragrant with the fruity scent of local trees and heavy with the songs of the nightflyers.

The settlement was bigger and brighter and louder than the river station; a thick clot of houses and bars and shops built alongside the spaceport. There were a few structures of wood and stone, but most of the settlers were still content with the plastic prefabs the company had given them free.

Kabaraijian drifted through the new-paved streets, to one of the outnumbered wooden buildings. There was a heavy wooden sign over the tavern door, but no lights. Inside he found candles and heavy, stuffed chairs, and a real log fire. It was a cozy place, the oldest bar on Grotto, and still the favorite watering hole for corpse handlers and hunters and other river station personnel.

A loud shout greeted him when he entered. "Hey! Matt! Over here!"

Kabaraijian found the voice, and followed it to a table in the corner, where Ed Cochran was nursing a mug of beer. Cochran, like Kabaraijian, wore the blue-and-white tunic of a corpse handler. He was tall and lean, with a thin face that grinned a lot and a mass of tangled red-blond hair.

Kabaraijian sank gratefully into the chair opposite him.

Cochran grinned. "Beer?" he asked. "We could split a pitcher."

"No thanks. I feel like wine tonight. Something rich and mellow and slow."

"How'd it go?" said Cochran.

Kabaraijian shrugged. "O.K.," he said. "Four nice stones, a dozen little ones. Munson gave me a good estimate. Tomorrow should be better. I found a nice new place." He turned toward the bar briefly, and gestured. The bartender nodded, and the wine and glasses arrived a few minutes later.

Kabaraijian poured and sipped while Cochran discussed his day. It hadn't gone well; only six stones, none of them very big.

"You've got to range farther," Kabaraijian told him. "The caves around here have been pretty well worked out. But the High Lakes go on and on. Find someplace new."

"Why bother?" Cochran said, frowning. "Don't get to keep them anyway. What's the percentage in knocking yourself out?"

Kabaraijian twirled the wine glass slowly in a thin, dark hand, and watched the dream-red depths. "Poor Ed," he said, in a voice half-sadness and half-mockery. "All you see is the work. Grotto is a pretty planet. I don't *mind* the extra miles, Ed, I enjoy them. I'd probably travel in my off-time if they didn't pay me to do it. The fact that I get bigger swirlstones and my estimates go up — well, that's extra gravy."

Cochran smiled and shook his head. "You're crazy, Matt," he said affectionately. "Only corpse handler in the universe who'd be happy if they paid him off with scenery."

Kabaraijian smiled too, a slight lifting at the corners of his mouth. "Philistine," he said accusingly.

Cochran ordered another beer. "Look, Matt, you've got to be practical. Sure, Grotto is O.K., but you're not gonna be here all your life." He set down his beer, and pulled up the sleeve of his tunic, to flash his heavy wristlet. The gold shone softly in the candlelight, and the sapphires danced with dark blue flame. "Junk like this was valuable once," Cochran said, "before they learned how to synthesize it. They'll crack swirlstones, too, Matt. You know they will. They already have people working on it. So maybe you've got two years left, or three. But what then? Then they won't need corpse handlers anymore. So you'll move on, no better off than when you first landed."

"Not really," said Kabaraijian. "The station pays pretty good, and my estimates haven't been bad. I've got some money put away. Besides, maybe I won't move on. I like Grotto. Maybe I'll stay, and join the colonists, or something."

"Doing what? Farming? Working in an office? Don't give me that crap, Matt. You're a corpse handler, always will be. And in a couple years Grotto won't need corpses."

Kabaraijian sighed. "So?" he said. "So?"

Cochran leaned forward. "So have you thought about what I told you?"

"Yes," Kabaraijian said. "But I don't like it. I don't think it would work, first of all. Spaceport security is tight to keep people from smuggling out swirlstones, and you want to do just that. And even if it would work, I don't want any part of it. I'm sorry, Ed."

"I think it *would* work," Cochran said stubbornly. "The spaceport people are human. They can be tempted. Why should the company get all the swirlstones when we do all the work?"

"They've got the concession," Kabaraijian said.

Cochran waved him silent. "Yeah, sure. So what? By what right? We *deserve* some, for ourselves, while the damn things are still valuable."

Kabaraijian sighed again, and poured himself another glass of wine. "Look," he said, lifting the glass to his lips, "I don't quarrel with that. Maybe they should pay us more, or give us an interest in the swirlstones. But it's not worth the risk. We'll lose our crews if they catch us. *And* we'll get expelled.

"I don't want that, Ed, and I won't risk it. Grotto is too good to me, and I'm not going to throw it away. You know, some people would say we're pretty lucky. Most corpse handlers never get to work a place like Grotto. They wind up on the assembly lines of Skrakky, or in the mines of New Pittsburgh. I've seen those places. No thanks. I'm not going to risk returning to *that* sort of life."

Cochran threw imploring eyes up to the ceiling, and spread his hands helplessly. "Hopeless," he said, shaking his head. "Hopeless." Then he returned to his beer. Kabaraijian was smiling.

But his amusement died short minutes later, when Cochran suddenly stiffened and grimaced across the table. "Damn," he said. "Bartling. What the hell does *he* want here?"

Kabaraijian turned toward the door, where the newcomer was standing and waiting for his eyes to adjust to the dim light. He was a big man, with an athletic frame that had gone to pot over the years and now sported a considerable paunch. He had dark hair streaked with white and a bristling black beard, and he was wearing a fashionable multicolored tunic.

Four others had entered behind him, and now stood flanking him on either side. They were younger men than he was, and bigger, with hard faces and impressive builds. The bodyguards made sense. Lowell Bartling was widely known for his dislike of corpse handlers, and the tavern was full of them.

Bartling crossed his arms, and looked around the room slowly. He was smirking. He started to speak.

Almost before he got the first word out of his mouth, he was interrupted. One of the men along the bar emitted a loud, rude noise, and laughed. "Hiya, Bartling," he said. "What are you doing down here? Thought you didn't associate with us low-lifes?"

Bartling's face tightened, but his smirk was untouched. "Normally I don't, but I wanted the pleasure of making this announcement personally."

"You're leaving Grotto!" someone shouted. There was laughter all along the bar. "I'll drink to that," another voice added.

"No," said Bartling. "No, friend, *you* are." He looked around, savoring the moment. "Bartling Associates has just acquired the swirlstone concession, I'm happy to tell you. I take over management of the river station at the end of the month. And, of course, my first act will be to terminate the employment of all the corpse handlers currently under contract."

Suddenly the room was very silent, as the implications of that sank in. In the corner in the back of the room, Cochran rose slowly to his feet. Kabaraijian remained seated, stunned.

"You can't do that," Cochran said belligerently. "We've got contracts."

Bartling turned to face him. "Those contracts can be broken," he said, "and they will be."

"You son of a bitch," someone said.

The bodyguard tensed. "Watch who you call names, meat-mind," one of them answered. All around the room, men started getting to their feet.

Cochran was livid with anger. "Damn you, Bartling," he said. "Who the hell do you think you are? You've got no right to run us off the planet."

"I have every right," Baffling said. "Grotto is a good, clean, beautiful planet. There's no place here for your kind. It was a mistake to bring you in, and I've said so all along. Those *things* you work with contaminate the air. And you're even worse. You work with those things, those corpses, *voluntarily*, for money. You disgust me. You don't belong on Grotto. And now I'm in a position to see that you leave." He paused, then smiled. "Meatmind," he added, spitting out the word.

"Bartling, I'm going to knock your head off," one of the handlers bellowed. There was a roar of agreement. Several men started forward at once.

And jerked to a sudden stop when Kabaraijian interjected a soft, "No, wait," over the general hubbub. He hardly raised his voice at all, but it still commanded attention in the room of shouting men.

He walked through the crowd and faced Bartling, looking much calmer than he felt. "You realize that without corpse labor your costs will go way up," he said in a steady, reasonable voice, "and your profits down."

Bartling nodded. "Of course I realize it. I'm willing to take the loss. We'll use *men* to mine the swirlstones. They're too beautiful for corpses, anyway."

"You'll be losing money for nothing," Kabaraijian said.

"Hardly. I'll get rid of your stinking corpses."

Kabaraijian cracked a thin smile. "Maybe some. But not all of us, Mr. Bartling. You can take away our jobs, perhaps, but you can't throw us off Grotto. I for one refuse to go."

"Then you'll starve."

"Don't be so melodramatic. I'll find something else to do. You don't own all of Grotto. And I'll keep my corpses. Dead men can be used for a lot of things. It's just that we haven't thought of them all yet."

Bartling's smirk had vanished suddenly. "If you stay," he said, fixing Kabaraijian with a hard stare, "I promise to make you very, very sorry."

Kabaraijian laughed. "Really? Well, personally, I promise to send one of my dead men by your house every night after you go to bed, to make hideous faces at the window and moan." He laughed again, louder. Cochran joined him, then others. Soon the whole tavern was laughing.

Bartling turned red and began a slow burn. He came here to taunt his enemies, to crow his triumph, and now they were laughing at him. Laughing in the face of victory, cheating him. He seethed a long minute, then turned and walked furiously out the door. His bodyguards followed.

The laughter lingered a while after his exit, and several of the other handlers slapped Kabaraijian on the back as he made his way back to his seat. Cochran was happy about it, too. "You really took the old man apart," he said when they reached the corner table.

But Kabaraijian wasn't smiling anymore. He slumped down into his seat heavily, and reached almost immediately for the wine. "I sure did," he said slowly, between sips. "I sure did."

Cochran looked at him curiously. "You don't seem too happy."

"No," said Kabaraijian. He studied his wine. "I'm having second thoughts. That insufferable bigot riled me, made me want to get to him. Only I wonder if I can pull it off. What *can* corpses do on Grotto?"

His eyes wandered around the tavern, which had suddenly become very somber. "It's sinking in," he told Cochran. "I'll bet they're all talking about leaving."

Cochran had stopped grinning. "Some of us will stay," he said uncertainly. "We can farm with the corpses, or something."

Kabaraijian looked at him. "Uh-uh. Machinery is more efficient for farming. And dead men are too clumsy for anything but the crudest kind of labor, much too slow for hunting." He poured more wine, and mused aloud. "They're O.K. for cheap factory labor, or running an auto-mole in a mine. But Grotto doesn't have any of that. They can hack out swirlstones with a vibrodrill, only Bartling is taking that away from us." He shook his head.

"I don't know, Ed," he continued. "It's not going to be easy. And maybe it'll be impossible. With the swirlstone concession under his belt, Bartling is bigger than the settlement company now."

"That was the idea. The company sets us up, and we buy it out as we grow."

"True. But Bartling grew a little too fast. He can really start throwing his weight around now. It wouldn't surprise me if he amended the charter, to keep corpses off-planet. That *would* force us out."

"Can he get away with that?" Cochran was getting angry again, and his voice rose slightly.

"Maybe," Kabaraijian said, "if we let him. I wonder ... "

He sloshed his wine thoughtfully. "You think this deal of his is final?"

Cochran looked puzzled. "He said he had it."

"Yes. I don't suppose he'd crow about it if it wasn't in his pocket. Still, I'm curious what the company would do if someone made them a better offer."

"Who?"

"Us, maybe?" Kabaraijian sipped his wine and considered that. "Get all the handlers together, everybody puts in whatever they have. That should give us a fair sum. Maybe we could buy out the river station ourselves. Or something else, if Bartling has the swirlstones all locked up. It's an idea."

"Nah, it'd never work," Cochran said. "Maybe you've got some money, Matt, but I sure as hell don't. Spent most of it here. Besides, even the guys that have money, you'd never be able to get them together."

"Maybe not," Kabaraijian said. "But it's worth trying. Organizing against Bartling is the only way we're going to be able to keep ourselves on Grotto in the long run."

Cochran drained his beer, and signaled for another. "Nah," he said. "Bartling's too big. He'll slap you down hard if you bother him too much. I got a better idea."

"Swirlstone smuggling," Kabaraijian said, smiling.

"Yeah," Cochran said with a nod. "Maybe now you'll reconsider. If Bartling's gonna throw us off-planet, at least we can take some of his swirlstones with us. That'd set us up good wherever we go."

"You're incorrigible," Kabaraijian said. "But I'll bet half the handlers on Grotto will try the same thing now. Bartling will expect that. He'll have the spaceport screwed up tight when we start leaving. He'll catch you, Ed. And you'll lose your crew, or worse. Bartling might even try to force through dead-man laws, and start exporting corpses."

Cochran looked uneasy at that. Corpse handlers saw too much of dead men to relish the idea of becoming one. They tended to cluster on planets without dead-man laws, where capital crimes still drew prison terms or "clean" executions. Grotto was a clean planet now, but laws could change.

"I might lose my crew anyway, Matt," Cochran said. "If Bartling throws us out, I'll have to sell some of my corpses for passage money."

Kabaraijian smiled. "You still have a month, even with the worst. And there are plenty of swirlstones out there for the finding." He raised his glass. "Come. To Grotto. It's a lovely planet, and we may stay here yet."

Cochran shrugged and lifted his beer. "Yeah," he said. But his grin didn't hide his worry.

Kabaraijian reported to the station early the next morning, when Grotto's sun was fighting to dispel the river mists. The row of empty launches was still tied to the dock, bobbing up and down in the rapidly thinning fog.

Munson was inside the office, as always. So, surprisingly, was Cochran. Both of them looked up when Kabaraijian entered.

"Morning, Matt," Munson said gravely. "Ed's been telling me about last night." Today, for some reason, he looked his age. "I'm sorry, Matt. I didn't know anything about it."

Kabaraijian smiled. "I never thought you did. If you *do* hear anything, though, let me know. We're not going to go without a fight." He looked at Cochran. "What are you doing here so early? Usually you're not up until the crack of noon."

Cochran grinned. "Yeah. Well, I figured I'd start early. I'm going to need good estimates this month, if I want to save my crew."

Munson had dug two collection boxes out from under his desk: He handed them to the two corpse handlers, and nodded. "Back room's open," he said. "You can pick up your dead men whenever you like."

Kabaraijian started to circle the desk, but Cochran grabbed his arm. "I think I'll try way east," he said. "Some caves there that haven't really been hit yet. Where you going?"

"West," said Kabaraijian. "I found a good new place, like I told you."

Cochran nodded. They went to the back room together, and thumbed their controllers. Five dead men stumbled from their bunks and followed them, shuffling, from the office. Kabaraijian thanked Munson before he left. The old man had washed down his corpses anyway, and fed them.

The mists were just about gone when they reached the dock. Kabaraijian marched his crew into the boat and got set to cast off. But Cochran stopped him, looking troubled.

"Uh — Matt," he said, standing on the dock and staring down into the launch. "This new place — you say it's real good?"

Kabaraijian nodded, squinting. The sun was just clearing the tree-tops, and framing Cochran's head.

"Can I talk you into splitting?" Cochran said, with difficulty. It was an unusual request. The practice was for each handler to range alone, to find and mine his own swirlstone cave. "I mean, with only a month left, you probably won't have time to get everything, not if the place is as good as you say. And I need good estimates, I really do."

Kabaraijian could see that it wasn't an easy favor to ask. He smiled. "Sure," he said. "There's plenty there. Get your launch and follow me."

Cochran nodded and forced a grin. He walked down the dock to his launch, his dead men trailing behind.

Going downriver was easier than going up, and faster. Kabaraijian hit the lake in short order, and sent his launch surging across the spar-kling green surface in a spray of foam. It was an exhilarating morning, with a bright sun, and a brisk wind that whipped the water into tiny waves. Kabaraijian felt good, despite the events of the previous night. Grotto did that to him. Out on the High Lakes, somehow, he felt that he could beat Bartling.

He'd run into similar problems before, on other worlds. Bartling wasn't alone in his hatred. Ever since the first time they'd ripped a man's brain from his skull and replaced it with a dead man's synthabrain,

45

there had been people screaming that the practice was a perversion and the handlers tainted and unclean. He'd gotten used to the prejudice; it was part of corpse handling. And he'd beaten it before. He could beat Bartling now.

The first part of the voyage was the quickest. The two launches streaked over two big local lakes, past shores lined thickly with silver-wood trees and vine-heavy danglers. But then they began to slow, as the lakes grew smaller and choked with life, and the country wilder. Along the banks, the stately silverwoods and curious danglers began to give way to the dense red and black chaos of firebriar brambles, and a species of low, gnarled tree that never had received a proper name. The vegetation grew on ground increasingly hilly and rocky, and finally mountainous.

Then they began to pass through the caves.

There were hundreds of them, literally, and they honeycombed the mountains that circled the settlement on all sides. The caves had never been mapped thoroughly. There were far too many of them, and they all seemed to connect with each other, forming a natural maze of incredible complexity. Most of them were still half-full of water; they'd been carved from the soft mountain rock by the streams and river that still ran through them.

A stranger could easily get lost in the caves, but strangers never came there. And the corpse handlers never got lost. This was their country. This was where the swirlstones waited, cloaked in rock and darkness.

The launches were all equipped with lights. Kabaraijian switched his on as soon as they hit the first cave, and slowed. Cochran, following close behind, did likewise. The channels that ran through the nearer caves were well known, but shallow, and it didn't pay to risk tearing out the bottom of your boat.

The channel was narrow at first, and the glistening, damp walls of soft greenish stone seemed to press in on them from either side. But gradually the walls moved farther and farther back, finally peeling away entirely as the stream carried the two launches into a great vaulted underground chamber. The cavern was as big as a spaceport, its ceiling lost in the gloom overhead. Before long the walls vanished into the dark too, and the launches traveled in two small bubbles of light across the gently stirring surface of a cold black lake.

Then, ahead of them, the walls took form again. But this time, instead of one passage, there were many. The stream had carved one entrance, but a good half-dozen exits.

Kabaraijian knew the cave, however. Without hesitating, he guided his boat into the widest passage, on the extreme right Cochran followed in his wake. Here the waters flowed down an incline, and the boats began to pick up speed again. "Be careful," Kabaraijian warned Cochran at one point. "The ceiling comes down here." Cochran acknowledged the shout with a wave of his hand.

The warning came barely in time. While the walls were increasingly farther apart, the stone roof above them was moving steadily closer, giving the illusion that the waters were rising. Kabaraijian remembered the way he'd sweated the first time he'd taken this passage; the boat had been going too fast, and he'd feared getting pinched in by the ceiling, and overwhelmed by the climbing waters.

But it was an idle fear. The roof sank close enough to scrape their heads, but no closer. And then it began to rise again to a decent height. Meanwhile, the channel widened still more, and soft sand shelves appeared along either wall.

Finally there was a branching in the passage, and this time Kabaraijian chose the left-hand way. It was small and dark and narrow, with barely enough room for the launch to squeeze through. But it was also short, and after a brief journey, it released them to a second great cavern.

They moved across the chamber quickly, and entered its twin under a grotesque stone arch. Then came yet another twisting passage, and more forks and turns. Kabaraijian led them calmly, hardly thinking, hardly having to think. These were his caves; this particular section of undermountain was his domain, where he'd worked and mined for months. He knew where he was going. And finally he got there.

The chamber was big, and haunting. Far above the shallow waters, the roof had been eaten through by erosion, and light poured in from three great gashes in the rock. It gave the cavern a dim greenish glow, as it bounced off the pale green walls and the wide, shallow pool.

The launches spilled from a thin crack in the cave wall, carried by rushes of cold black water. The water turned green when it hit the light, and tumbled and warmed and slowed. The boats slowed, too, and moved leisurely across the huge chamber toward the white sand beaches that lined the sides.

Kabaraijian pulled up by one such beach, and hopped out into the shallow water, dragging his launch up onto the sand. Cochran followed his example, and they stood side by side when both boats were safely beached.

"Yeah," said Cochran, looking around. "It's nice. And it figures. Leave it to you to find a pretty place to work, while the rest of us are up to our ankles in water, clutching lights."

Kabaraijian smiled. "I found it yesterday," he said. "Completely unworked. Look." He pointed at the wall. "I barely started." There was a pile of loose stones in a rough semicircle around the area he'd been working, and a large bite missing from the rock. But most of the wall was untouched, stretching away from them in sheets of shimmering green.

"You sure no one else knows about this place?" Cochran asked.

"Reasonably. Why?"

Cochran shrugged. "When we were coming through the caves, I could have sworn I heard another launch behind us somewhere."

"Probably echoes," Kabaraijian said. He looked toward his launch. "Anyway, we better get going." He hit his corpse controller, and the three still figures in the boat began to move.

He stood stock-still on the sand, watching them. And as he watched, somewhere in the back of his head, he was also watching himself with their eyes. They rose stiffly, and two of them climbed out onto the sand. The third walked to the chest in the front of the launch, and began unloading the equipment; vibrodrills and picks and shovels. Then, his arms full, he climbed down and joined the others.

None of them were really moving, of course. It was all Kabaraijian. It was Kabaraijian who moved their legs, and made their hands clasp and their arms reach. It was Kabaraijian, his commands picked up by controller and magnified by synthabrain, who put life into the bodies of the dead men. The synthabrains kept the automatic functions going, but it was the corpse handler who gave the corpse its will.

It wasn't easy, and it was far from perfect. The sense impressions thrown back to the handler were seldom useful; mostly he had to watch his corpses to know what they were doing. The manipulation was seldom graceful; corpses moved slowly and clumsily, and fine work was beyond them. A corpse could swing a mallet, but even the best handler couldn't make a dead man thread a needle, or speak.

With a bad handler, a corpse could hardly move at all. It took coordination to run even one dead man, if the handler was doing anything himself. He had to keep the commands to the corpse separate from the commands to his own muscles. That was easy enough for most, but the task grew increasingly complex as the crew grew larger. The record for one handler was twenty-six corpses; but all he'd done was march them, in step. When the dead men weren't all doing the same thing, the corpse handler's work became much more challenging.

Kabaraijian had a three-crew; all top meat, corpses in good condition. They'd been big men, and they still were; Kabaraijian paid premiums for food to keep his property in good condition. One had dark hair and a scar along a cheek, another was blond and young and freckled, the third had mousy brown locks. Other than that, they were interchangeable; all about the same height and weight and build. Corpses don't have personality. They lose that with their minds.

Cochran's crew, climbing out onto the sand in compliance with his work orders, was less impressive. There were only two of them, and neither was a grade-one specimen. The first corpse was brawny enough, with wide shoulders and rippling muscles. But his legs were twisted matchsticks, and he stumbled often and walked more slowly than even the average corpse. The second dead man was reedy and middle-aged, bald, and under-muscled. Both were grimy. Cochran didn't believe in taking care of his crew the way Kabaraijian did. It was a bad habit. Cochran had started as a paid handler working someone else's corpses; upkeep hadn't been his concern.

Each of Kabaraijian's crew bent and picked up a vibrodrill from the stack of equipment on the sand. Then, parallel to each other, they advanced on the cave wall. The drills sank humming holes into the porous rock, and from each drill bite a network of thin cracks branched and grew.

The corpses drilled in unison until each drill was sunk nearly to its hilt and the cracks had grown finger wide. Then, almost as one, they withdrew the drills and discarded them in favor of picks. Work slowed. Crack by crack, the corpses attacked the wall, laboriously peeling off a whole layer of greenish stone. They swung the picks carefully, but with bone-jarring force, untiring, relentless. Incapable of pain, their bones could scarce feel the jars.

The dead men did all the work. Kabaraijian stood behind, a slight, dark statue in the sand, with hands on hips and eyes hooded. He did nothing but watch. Yet he did all. Kabaraijian *was* the corpses; the corpses were Kabaraijian. He was one man in four bodies, and it was his hand that guided each blow, though he did not touch a tool.

Forty feet down the cave, Cochran and his crew had unpacked and set to work. But Kabaraijian was barely conscious of them, though he could hear the hum of their vibrodrills and the hammering of their picks. His mind was with his corpses, chipping at his wall, alert for the telltale grayish glitter of a swirlstone node. It was draining work; demanding work; tense and nervous. It was a labor only corpse crews could do with real efficiency.

They'd tried other methods a few short years before, when men had first found Grotto and its caves. The early settlers went after swirlstones with automoles, tractorlike rockeaters that could chew up mountains. Problem was, they also chewed up the fragile, deep-buried swirlstones, which often went unrecognized until too late. The company, discovered that careful hand labor was the only way to keep from chipping or shattering an excessive number of stones. And corpse hands were the cheapest hands you could buy.

Those hands were busy now, tense and sweating as the crew peeled whole sections of rock off the broken wall. The natural cleavage of the stone was vertical, which sped the work. Find a crack — force in a pick — lean back and pull — and, with a snap, a flat chunk of rock came with you. Then find a new crack, and begin again.

Kabaraijian watched unmoving as the wall came down, and the pile of green stone accumulated around the feet of his dead men. Only his eyes moved, flicking back and forth over the rock restlessly, alert for swirlstones but finding nothing. Finally he pulled the corpses back, and approached the wall himself. He touched it, stroked the stone, and frowned. The crew had ripped down an entire layer of rock, and had come up empty.

But that was hardly unusual, even in the best of caves. Kabaraijian walked back to the sand's edge, and sent his crew back to work. They picked up vibrodrills and attacked the wall again.

Abruptly he was conscious of Cochran standing beside him, saying something. He could hardly make it out. It isn't easy to pay close attention when you're running three dead men. Part of his mind detached itself and began to listen.

Cochran was repeating himself. He knew that a handler at work wasn't likely to hear what he said the first time. "Matt," he was saying, "listen. I think I heard something. Faintly, but I heard it. It sounded like another launch."

That was serious. Kabaraijian wrenched his mind loose from the dead men, and turned to give Cochran his full attention. The three vibrodrills died, one by one, and suddenly the soft slap of water against sand echoed loudly around them.

"A launch?"

Cochran nodded.

"You sure?" Kabaraijian said.

"Uh — no," said Cochran. "But I *think* I heard something. Same thing as before, when we were moving through the caves."

"I don't know," Kabaraijian said, shaking his head. "Don't think it's likely, Ed. Why would anyone follow us? The swirlstones are everywhere, if you bother to look."

"Yeah," Cochran said. "But I heard something, and I thought I should tell you."

Kabaraijian nodded. "All right," he said. "Consider me told. If anyone shows up, I'll point out a section of wall and let him work it."

"Yeah," Cochran said again. But somehow he didn't look satisfied. His eyes kept jumping back and forth, agitated. He wheeled and walked back down the sand, to the section of wall where his own corpses stood frozen.

Kabaraijian turned back toward the rock, and his crew came alive again. The drills started humming, and once more the cracks spread out. Then, when the cracks were big enough, picks replaced drills, and another layer of stone started coming down.

But this time, something was behind it.

The corpses were ankle deep in splinters of stone when Kabaraijian saw it; a fist-sized chunk of gray nestled in the green. He stiffened at the sight of it, and the corpses froze in mid-swing. Kabaraijian walked around them, and studied the swirlstone node.

It was a beauty; twice the size of the largest stone he'd ever brought in. Even damaged, it would be worth a fortune. But if he could pry it loose intact, his estimate would set a record. He was certain of that. They'd cut it as one stone. He could almost see it. An egg of crystalline fog, smoky and mysterious, where drifting veils of mist shrouded half-seen colors.

Kabaraijian thought about it, and smiled. He touched the node lightly, and turned to call to Cochran.

That saved his life.

The pick sliced through the air where his head had been and smashed against the wall with awful impact, barely missing the swirl-stone node. Sparks and rock chips flew together. Kabaraijian stood frozen. The corpse drew the pick back over its head for another swing.

Within, Kabaraijian reeled, staggered. The pick swung down. Not at the wall; at him.

Then he moved, barely in time, throwing himself to one side. The blow missed by inches, and Kabaraijian landed in the sand and scrambled quickly to his feet. Crouched and wary, he began to back away.

The corpse advanced on him, the pick held over his head. Kabaraijian could hardly think. He didn't understand. The corpse that moved on him was dark-haired and scarred; his corpse. *HIS* corpse. *HIS CORPSE!*

The corpse moved slowly. Kabaraijian kept a safe distance. Then he looked behind him. His other two dead men were advancing from other directions. One held a pick. The other had a vibrodrill.

Kabaraijian swallowed nervously, and stopped dead. The ring of corpses tightened around him. He screamed.

Down the beach, Cochran was looking at the tableau. He took one step toward Kabaraijian. From behind him, there was a blur of something being swung, and a dull thud. Cochran spun with the blow, and landed face down in the sand. He did not get up. His barrel-chested, gimpy corpse stood over him, pick in hand, swinging again and again. His other corpse was moving down the cave, toward Kabaraijian.

The scream was still echoing in the cave, but now Kabaraijian was silent. He watched Cochran go down, and suddenly he moved, throwing himself at the dark-haired dead man. The pick descended, vicious but clumsy. Kabaraijian dodged it. He bowled into the corpse, and both of them went down. The corpse was much slower getting up. By the time he did rise, Kabaraijian was behind him.

The corpse handler moved back, step by slow step. His own crew was in front of him now, stumbling toward him with weapons raised. It was a chilling sight. Their arms moved, and they walked. But their eyes were blank and their faces were dead — *DEAD!* For the first time, Kabaraijian understood the horror some people felt near dead men.

He looked over his shoulder. Both of Cochran's corpses were heading his way, armed. Cochran still had not risen. He lay with his face in the sand and the waters lapping at his boots.

His mind began to work again, in the short breather he was granted. His hand went to his belt. The controller was still on, still warm and humming. He tested it. He reached out to his corpses, into them. He told them to stand still, to drop their tools, to freeze.

They continued to advance.

Kabaraijian shivered. The controller was still working; he could still feel the echoes in his head. But somehow, the corpses weren't responding. He felt very cold.

And colder when it finally hit him, like ice water. Cochran's corpses hadn't responded either. Both crews had turned on their handlers.

Override!

He'd heard of such things. But he'd never seen one, or dreamt of seeing one. Override boxes were very expensive and even more illegal, contraband on any planet where corpse handling was allowed.

But now he was seeing one in action. Someone wanted to kill him. Someone was trying to do just that. Someone was using his own corpses against him, by means of an override box.

He threw himself at his corpses mentally, fighting for control, grappling for whatever had taken them over. But there was no struggle, nothing to come to grips with. The dead men simply failed to respond.

Kabaraijian bent and picked up a vibrodrill.

He straightened quickly, spinning around to face Cochran's two corpses. The big one with the matchstick legs moved in, swinging its pick. Kabaraijian checked the blow with the vibrodrill, holding it above him as a shield. The dead man brought the pick back again.

Kabaraijian activated the drill and drove it into the corpse's gut. There was an awful second of spurting blood and tearing flesh. There should have been a scream too, and agony. But there wasn't.

And the pick came down anyway.

Kabaraijian's thrust had thrown the corpse's aim off, and the blow was a glancing one, but it still ripped his tunic half off his chest and clawed a bloody path from shoulder to stomach. Reeling, he staggered back against the wall, empty-handed.

The corpse came on, pick swinging up again, eyes blank. The vibrodrill transfixed it, still humming, and the blood came in wet red spurts. But the corpse came on.

No pain, Kabaraijian thought, with the small part of his mind not frozen with terror. The blow wasn't immediately fatal, and the corpse can't feel it. It's bleeding to death, but it doesn't know it, doesn't care. It won't stop till it's dead. *There's no pain!*

The corpse was nearly on top of him. He dropped to the sand, grabbed a hunk of rock, and rolled.

Dead men are slow, woefully slow; their reflexes are long-distance ones. The blow was late and off-target. Kabaraijian rolled into the corpse and knocked it down. Then he was on top of it, the rock clutched in his fist, hammering at the thing's skull, smashing it again and again, breaking through to the synthabrain.

Finally, the corpse stopped moving. But the others had reached him. Two picks swung almost simultaneously. One missed entirely. The other took a chunk out of his shoulder.

He grabbed the second pick, and twisted, fighting to stop it, losing. The corpses were stronger than he was, much stronger. The dead man wrenched the pick free and brought it back for another try.

Kabaraijian got to his feet, smashing into the corpse and sending it flailing. The others swung at him, grabbed at him. He didn't stay to fight He ran. They pursued, slow and clumsy but somehow terrifying.

He reached the launch, seized it with both hands, and shoved. It slid reluctantly across the sand. He shoved again, and this time it moved more easily. He was drenched in blood and sweat, and his breath came in short gasps, but he kept shoving. His shoulder shrieked agony. He let it shriek, putting it to the side of the launch and finally getting the boat clear of the sand.

Then the corpses were on him again, swinging at him even as he climbed into the launch. He started the motor and flipped it to top speed. The boat responded. It took off in a sudden explosion of foam, slicing across the green waters toward the dark slit of safety in the far cavern wall. Kabaraijian sighed ... and the corpse grabbed him.

It was in the boat. Its pick was buried uselessly in the wood, but it still had its hands, and those were enough. It wrapped those hands around his neck, and squeezed. He swung at it madly, smashing at its calm, empty face. It made no effort to ward off the blows. It ignored them. Kabaraijian hit it again and again, poked at the vacant eyes, hammered at its mouth until its teeth shattered.

But the fingers on his neck grew tighter and tighter, and not all his struggling could pry one loose. Choking, he stopped kicking the corpse, and kicked the rudder control.

The launch veered wildly, leaning from side to side. The cave rushed past in a blur, and the walls moved in on them. Then came sudden impact, the shriek of tearing wood, and the short tumble from launch to water. Kabaraijian landed on top, but they both went under. The corpse held its grip through everything, dragging Kabaraijian down with it, still choking the life from his throat.

But Kabaraijian took a deep breath before the green closed over him. The corpse tried to breathe underwater. Kabaraijian helped it. He stuck both hands into its mouth and kept it open, making sure it got a good lungful of water.

The dead man died first. And its fingers weakened.

Finally, his lungs near bursting, Kabaraijian forced his way free, and kicked to the surface. The water was only chest high. He stood on the unmoving corpse, keeping it under while he sucked in great drafts of air.

The launch had impaled itself on a crest of jagged rocks that rose from the water off to one side of the exit. The passage from the cave was still at hand, outlined in shadow a few short feet away. But now, was it safe? Without a launch? Kabaraijian considered making his way out on foot, and gave up the idea instantly. There were too many miles to go before he reached simple daylight, let alone the safety of the river station. It would mean being hunted in the darkness by whatever remained of his corpse crew. The prospect sent a chill down his back. No, better to stay and face his attacker.

He kicked free of the corpse, and moved to the debris of his launch, still hung up on the rocks that had caught it. Shielded by the wreck, he'd be difficult to find, or at least to see. And if his enemy couldn't see him, it would be hard to send the corpses against him.

Meanwhile, maybe he could find his enemy.

His enemy. Who? Bartling, of course. It had to be Bartling, or one of his hirelings. Who else?

But *where?* They had to be close, within sight of the beach. You can't run a corpse by remote control; the sense feedback isn't good enough. The only senses you get are vision and hearing, and them dimly. You have to *see* the corpse, see what it's doing, and what you want it to do. So Bartling's man was around here somewhere. In the cave. But where?

And how? Kabaraijian considered that. It must be the other launch that Cochran had heard. Someone must have been following them, someone with an override box. Maybe Bartling had a tracer put on his launch during the night.

Only how'd he know which *launch* to trace?

Kabaraijian bent slightly so only his head showed above the water, and looked out around the end of the ruined launch. The beach was a white sand smear across the dim green length of the huge cavern. There was no noise but the water slapping the side of the boat. But there was motion. The second launch had been pulled free of the sand, and one of the corpses was climbing on board. The others, moving slowly, were wading out into the underground pool. Their picks rested on their shoulders.

They were coming for him. The enemy suspected he was still here. The enemy was hunting for him. Again, he was tempted to dive toward the exit, to run and swim back toward daylight, out of this awful dimness where his own corpses stalked him with cold faces and colder hands.

He squelched the impulse. He might get a head start while they searched the cavern. But, with the launch, they'd make it up in no time. He could try to lose them in the intricacies of the caves. But if they got ahead of him, they could just wait at caves' end. No, no. He had to stay here and find his enemy.

But *where?* He scanned the cave, and saw nothing. It was a great expanse of murky green, stone and water and beaches. The pool was dotted by a few large rocks rising from the water. A man might be hiding behind them. But not a launch. There was nothing big enough to hide a launch. Maybe the enemy wore aquagear? But Cochran had heard a launch ...

The corpse boat was halfway across the cavern, heading for the exit. It was his dead man seated at the controls, the brown-haired one. The other two corpses trailed, as they walked slowly across the shallow pool in the wake of the launch.

Three dead men, stalking. But somewhere their handler was hiding. The man with the override box. Their mind and their will. But where?

The launch was coming closer. Was it leaving? Maybe they thought he'd run for it? Or ... no, probably the enemy was going to blockade the exit, and *then* search the cave.

Did they see him? Did they know where he was?

Suddenly he remembered his corpse controller, and his hand fumbled under water to make sure it was still intact. It was. And working; controllers were watertight. It no longer controlled. But it still might be useful

Kabaraijian closed his eyes, and tried to shut off his ears. He deliberately blotted his senses, and concentrated on the distant sensory echoes that still murmured in his mind. They were there. Even vaguer than usual, but less confused; there were only two sets of images now. His third corpse floated a few feet from him, and it wasn't sending anything.

He twisted his mind tight, and listened, and tried to see. The blurs began to define themselves. Two pictures, both wavering, took form, superimposed over each other. A sense tangle, but Kabaraijian pulled at the threads. The pictures resolved.

One corpse was waist deep in green water, moving slowly, holding a pick. It could see the shaft of the tool, and the hand wrapped around it, and the gradually deepening water. But it wasn't even looking in Kabaraijian's direction.

The second dead man was in the launch, one hand resting on the controls. It wasn't looking either. It was staring down, at the instruments. It took a lot of concentration for a corpse to run any sort of machine. So the handler was having it keep a firm eye on the engine.

Only it could see more than just the engine. It had a very good view of the entire launch.

And suddenly everything fell into place. Certain now that the wrecked launch hid him from view, Kabaraijian moved farther back into its shadow, then threw a hand over the side and pulled himself on board, crouching so he wouldn't be found. The rocks had torn a hole in the bottom of the boat. But the tool chest was intact. He crawled to it, and flipped It open. The corpses had unpacked most of the mining equipment, but there was still a repair kit. Kabaraijian took out a heavy wrench and a screwdriver. He shoved the screwdriver into his belt, and gripped the wrench tightly. And waited.

The other launch was nearly on top of him, and he could hear the purr of its motor and the water moving around it. He waited until it was next to his boat. Then he stood up suddenly, and jumped.

He landed smack in the middle of the other boat, and the launch rocked under the impact. Kabaraijian didn't give the enemy time to react — at least not the time it takes a corpse. He took a single short step, and brought the wrench around in a vicious backhanded blow to the dead man's head. The corpse slumped back. Kabaraijian bent, grabbed its legs, and lifted. And suddenly the dead, man was no longer in the launch.

And Kabaraijian, wheeling, was looking down at the stunned face of Ed Cochran. He hefted the wrench with one hand even as his other reached for the controls, and upped the speed. The boat accelerated, and dove toward the exit. Cave and corpses vanished behind, and darkness closed in with the rocky walls. Kabaraijian switched on the lights.

"Hello, Ed," he said, hefting the wrench again. His voice was very steady and very cold.

Cochran breathed a noisy sigh of relief. "Matt," he maid. "Thank God, I just came to. My corpses — they — "

Kabaraijian shook his head. "No, Ed, it won't wash. Don't bother me with that, please. Just give me the override box."

Cochran looked scared. Then, fighting, he flashed his grin. "Heh. You gotta be kiddin', right? I don't have no override box. I told you I heard another launch."

'There was no other launch. That was a set-up, in case you failed. So was that blow you took on the beach. I'll bet that was tricky — having your corpse swing the pick so you got hit with the side instead of the point. But it was very well done. My compliments, Ed. That was good corpse handling. As was the rest. It isn't easy to coordinate a five-crew doing different things simultaneously. Very nice, Ed. I underestimated you. Never thought you were that good a handler."

Cochran. stared at him from the floor of the launch, his grin gone. Then his gaze broke, and his eyes went back and forth between the walls that pressed around them.

Kabaraijian waved the wrench again, his palm sweaty where he gripped it. His other hand touched his shoulder briefly. The bleeding had stopped. He sat slowly, and rested his hand on the motor.

"Aren't you going to ask me how I knew, Ed?" Kabaraijian said. Cochran, sullen, said nothing. "I'll tell you anyway," Kabaraijian continued. "I saw you. I looked through the eyes of my corpse, and I saw you huddled here in the boat, lying on the floor and peeking over the side to try and spot me. You didn't look dead at all, but you looked very guilty. And suddenly I got it. *You* were the only one with a clear view of that staff on the beach. *You* were the only one in the cave."

He paused, awkward. His voice broke a little, and softened. "Only — why? *Why*, Ed?"

Cochran looked up at him again. He shrugged. "Money," he said. "Only money, Matt. What else?" He smiled; not his usual grin, but a strained, tight smile. "I like you, Matt."

"You've got a peculiar way of showing it," Kabaraijian told him. He couldn't help smiling as he said it. "Whose money?"

"Bartling's," said Cochran. "I needed money real bad. My estimates were low, I didn't have anything saved. If I had to leave Grotto, that would've meant selling my crew just for passage money. Then I'd be a hired handler again. I didn't want that. I needed money fast."

He shrugged. "I was going to try smuggling some swirlstones, but you didn't make that sound good. And last night I got another idea. I didn't think that crap about organizing us and outbidding Bartling would work, but I figured he'd be interested. So I went to see him after I left the tavern. Thought he might pay a little for the information, and maybe even make an exception, let me stay."

He shook his head dourly. Kabaraijian stayed silent. Finally Cochran resumed. "I got to see him, him with three bodyguards. When I told him, he got hysterical. You'd humiliated him already, and now he thought you were on to something. He — he made me an offer. A lot of money, Matt. A lot of money."

"I'm glad I didn't come cheap."

Cochran smiled. "Nah," he said. "Bartling really wanted you, and I made him pay. He gave me the override box. Wouldn't touch it himself.

He said he'd had it made in case the 'meatminds' and their 'zombies' ever attacked him." Cochran reached into the pocket of his tunic, and took out a small, flat cartridge. It looked like a twin for the controller on his belt. He flipped it lightly through the air at Kabaraijian.

But Kabaraijian made no effort to catch it. The box sailed past his shoulder, and hit the water with a splash.

"Hey," said Cochran. "You shoulda got that. Your corpses won't respond till you turn it off."

"My shoulder's stiff," Kabaraijian started. He stopped abruptly.

Cochran stood up. He looked at Kabaraijian as if he were seeing him for the first time. "Yeah," he said. His fists clenched. "Yeah." He was a full head taller than Kabaraijian, and much heavier. And suddenly he seemed to notice the extent of the other's injuries.

The wrench seemed to grow heavier in Kabaraijian's hand. "Don't," he warned.

"I'm sorry," Cochran said. And he dove forward.

Kabaraijian brought the wrench around at his head, but Cochran caught the blow before it connected. His other hand reached up and wrapped itself around Kabaraijian's wrist, and twisted. He felt his fingers going numb.

There was no thought of fair play, or mercy. He was fighting for his life. His free hand went to his waist and grabbed the screwdriver. He pulled it out, and stabbed. Cochran gasped, and his grip suddenly loosened. Kabaraijian stabbed again, and twisted up and out, ripping a gash in tunic and flesh.

Cochran reeled back, clutching at his stomach. Kabaraijian followed him and stabbed a third time, savagely. Cochran fell.

He tried to rise once, and gave it up, falling heavily back to the floor of the launch. Then he lay there, bleeding.

Kabaraijian went back to the motor, and kept the boat clear of the walls. He guided them down the passages smoothly, through the caves and the tunnels and the deep green pools. And in the harsh boat light, he watched Cochran.

Cochran never moved again, and he spoke only once. Just after they had left the caves and come out into the early afternoon sun of Grotto, he looked up briefly. His hands were wet with blood. And his eyes were wet too. "I'm sorry, Matt," he said. "I'm damn sorry."

"Oh, *God!*" Kabaraijian said, his voice thick. And suddenly he stopped the boat dead in the water, and bent to the supply cache. Then he went to Cochran and dressed and bandaged his injuries.

When he reached the controls again, he flipped the speed up to maximum. The launch streaked across the glittering green lakes.

But Cochran died before they reached the river.

Kabaraijian stopped the boat then, and let it float dead in the water. He listened to the sounds of Grotto around him; the rush of river water pouring into the great lake, the songbirds and the daywings, the ever-active lakeleapers arcing through the air. He sat there until dusk fell, staring upriver, and thinking.

He thought of tomorrow and the day after. Tomorrow he must return to the swirlstone caves. His corpses should have frozen when he moved out of range; they should be salvageable. And one of Cochran's crew was still there, too. Maybe he could still piece together a three-crew, if the corpse he'd pushed overboard hadn't drowned.

And there were swirlstones there, big ones. He'd get that egg of dancing fog, and turn it in, and get a good estimate. Money. He had to have money, all he could scrape together. Then he could start talking to the others. And then ... and then Bartling would have a fight on his hands. Cochran was one casualty, the first. But not the last. He'd tell the others that Bartling had sent a man out with an override box, and that Cochran had been killed because of it. It was true. It was all true.

That night Kabaraijian returned with only one corpse in his launch, a corpse that was strangely still and unmoving. Always his corpses had walked behind him into the office. That night the corpse rode on his shoulder.

Chicago, Illinois
December, 1972

George R.R. Martin

Dark, Dark Were the Tunnels

Greel was afraid.

He lay in the warm, rich darkness beyond the place where the tunnel curved, his thin body pressed against the strange metal bar that ran along the floor. His eyes were closed. He strained to remain perfectly still.

He was armed. A short barbed spear was clenched tightly in his right fist. But that did not lessen his fear.

He had come far, far. He had climbed higher and ranged further than any other scout of the People in long generations. He had fought his way through the Bad Levels, where the worm-things still hunted the People relentlessly. He had stalked and slain the glowing killer mole in the crumbling Middle Tunnels. He had wiggled through dozens of unmapped and unnamed passages that hardly looked big enough for a man to pass.

And now he had penetrated to the Oldest Tunnels, the great tunnels and halls of legend, where the taletellers said the People had come from a million years ago.

He was no coward. He was a scout of the People, who dared to walk in tunnels where men had not trod in centuries.

But he was afraid, and was not ashamed for his fear. A good scout knows when to be afraid. And Greel was a very good scout. So he lay silent in the darkness, and clutched his spear, and thought.

Slowly the fear began to wane. Greel steeled himself, and opened his eyes. Quickly he shut them again.

The tunnel ahead was on fire.

He had never seen fire. But the taletellers had sung of it many times. Hot it was. And bright, so bright it hurt the eyes. Blindness was the lot of those who looked too long.

So Greel kept his eyes shut. A scout needed his eyes. He could not allow the fire ahead to blind him.

Back here, in the darkness beyond the bend of the tunnel, the fire was not so bad. It still hurt the eyes to look at it, as it hung upon the curving tunnel wall. But the pain was one that could be borne.

But earlier, when he had first seen the fire, Greel had been unwise. He had crept forward, squinting, to where the wall curved away. He had touched the fire that hung upon the stone. And then, foolishly, he had peered beyond the curve.

His eyes still ached. He had gotten only one quick glimpse before whirling and scrambling silently back to where he lay. But it was enough. Beyond the bend the fire had been brighter, much brighter, brighter than ever he could have imagined. Even with his eyes closed he could still see it, two dancing, aching spots of horrible intense brightness. They would not go away. The fire had burned part of his eyes, he thought.

But still, when he had touched the fire that hung upon the wall, it had not been like the fire of which the taletellers sing. The stone had felt like all other stone, cool and a little damp. Fire was hot, the taletellers said. But the fire on the stone had not been hot to the touch.

It was not fire, then, Greel decided after thought. What it was he did not know. But it could not be fire if it was not hot.

He stirred slightly from where he lay. Barely moving, he reached out and touched H'ssig in the darkness.

His mind-brother was several yards distant, near one of the other metal bars. Greel stroked him with his mind, and could feel H'ssig quiver in response. Thoughts and sensations mingled wordlessly.

H'ssig was afraid, too. The great hunting rat had no eyes. But his scent was keener than Greel's, and there was a strange smell in the tunnel. His ears were better, too. Through them Greel could pick up more of the odd noises that came from within the fire that was not a fire.

Greel opened his eyes again. Slowly this time, not all at once. Squinting.

The holes the fire had burned in his vision were still there. But they were fading. And the dimmer fire that moved on the curving tunnel wall could be endured, if he did not look directly at it.

Still. He could not go forward. And he must not creep back. He was a scout. He had a duty.

He reached out to H'ssig again. The hunting rat had run with him since birth. He had never failed him. He would not fail him now. The rat had no eyes that could be burned, but his ears and his nose would tell Greel what he must know about the thing beyond the curve.

H'ssig felt the command more than he heard it. He crept forward slowly towards the fire.

"A treasurehouse!"

Ciffonetto's voice was thick with admiration. The layer of protective grease smeared onto his face could hardly hide the grin.

Von der Stadt looked doubtful. Not just his face, but his whole body radiated doubt. Both men were dressed alike, in featureless grey coveralls woven of a heavy metallic cloth. But they could never be mistaken. Von der Stadt was unique in his ability to express doubt while remaining absolutely still.

When he moved, or spoke, he underlined the impression. As he did now.

"Some treasurehouse," he said, simply.

It was enough to annoy Ciffonetto. He frowned slightly at his larger companion. "No, I mean it," he said. The beam from his heavy flashlight sliced through the thick darkness, and played up and down one of the rust-eaten steel pillars that stretched from the platform to the roof. "Look at that," Ciffonetto said.

Von der Stadt looked at it. Doubtfully. "I see it," he said. "So where's the treasure?"

Ciffonetto continued to move his beam up and down. "That's the treasure," he said. "This whole place is a major historical find. I knew this was the place to search. I told them so."

"What's so great about a steel beam, anyway?" Von der Stadt asked, letting his own flash brush against the pillar.

"The state of preservation," Ciffonetto said, moving closer. "Most everything above ground is radioactive slag, even now. But down here we've got some beautiful artifacts. It will give us a much better picture about what the old civilization was like, before the disaster."

"We *know* what the old civilization was like," Von der Stadt protested. "We've got tapes, books, films, everything. All sorts of things. The war didn't even touch Luna."

"Yes, yes, but this is different," Ciffonetto said. "This is reality." He ran his gloved hand lovingly along the pillar. "Look here," he said.

Von der Stadt moved closer.

There was writing carved into the metal. Scratched in, rather. It didn't go very deep, but it could still be read, if but faintly.

Ciffonetto was grinning again. Von der Stadt looked doubtful. "Rodney loves Wanda," he said.

He shook his head. "Shit, Cliff," he said, "you can find the same thing in every public john in Luna City."

Ciffonetto rolled his eyes. "Von der Stadt," he said, "if we found the oldest cave painting in the world, you'd probably say it was a lousy picture of a buffalo." He jabbed at the writing with his free hand. "Don't you understand? This is *old*. It's history. It's the remains of a civilization and a nation and a planet that perished almost half a millennium ago."

Von der Stadt didn't reply, but he still looked doubtful. His flash-light wandered. "There's some more if that's what you're after," he said, holding his beam steady on another pillar a few feet distant.

This time it was Ciffonetto who read the inscription. "Repent or ye are doomed." he said, smiling, after his flash melted into Von der Stadt's.

He chuckled slightly. "The words of the prophets are written on the subway walls," he said softly.

Von der Stadt frowned. "Some prophet," he said. "They must have had one hell of a weird religion."

"Oh, Christ," Ciffonetto groaned. "I didn't mean it literally. I was quoting. A mid-twentieth century poet named Simon. He wrote that only fifty years or so before the great disaster."

Von der Stadt wasn't interested. He wandered away impatiently, his flash darting here and there amid the pitch black ruins of the ancient subway station. "It's hot down here," he complained.

"Hotter up there," Ciffonetto said, already lost in a new inscription.

"Not the same kind of hot," Von der Stadt replied.

Ciffonetto didn't bother to answer. "This is the biggest find of the expedition," he said when he looked up at last. "We've got to get pictures. And get the others down here. We're wasting our time on the surface."

"We'll do better down here?" Von der Stadt said. Doubtfully, of course.

Ciffonetto nodded. "That's what I've said all along. The surface was plastered. It's still a radioactive hell up there, even after all these centuries. If anything survived, it was underground. That's where we should look. We should branch out and explore this whole system of tunnels." His hands swept out expansively.

"You and Nagel have been arguing about that the whole trip," Von der Stadt said. "All the way from Luna City. I don't see that it's done you much good."

"Doctor Nagel is a fool," Ciffonetto said carefully.

"I don't think so," Von der Stadt said. "I'm a soldier, not a scientist. But I've heard his side of the argument, and it makes sense. All this stuff down here is great, but it's not what Nagel wants. It's not what the expedition was sent to Earth to look for."

"I know, I know," Ciffonetto said. "Nagel wants life. Human life, especially. So every day he sends the flyers out further and further. And so far all he's come up with is a few species of insects and a handful of mutated birds."

Von der Stadt shrugged.

"If he'd look down here, he'd find what he's after," Ciffonetto continued. "He doesn't realize how *deep* the cities had dug before the war. There are miles of tunnels under our feet. Level after level. That's where the survivors would be, if there are any survivors."

"How do you figure?" Von der Stadt asked.

"Look, when war hit, the only ones to live through it would be those down in deep shelters. Or in the tunnels beneath the cities. The radioactivity would have prevented them from coming up for years. Hell, the surface still isn't very attractive. They'd be trapped down there. They'd adjust. After a few generations they wouldn't want to come up."

But Von der Stadt's attention had wandered, and he was hardly listening any more. He had walked to the edge of the platform, and was staring down onto the tracks.

He stood there silently for a moment, then reached a decision. He stuffed his flashlight into his belt, and began to climb down. "Come on," he said. 'Let's go look for some of these survivors of yours."

H'ssig stayed close to the metal bar as he edged forward. It helped to hide him, and kept away the fire, so he moved in a little band of almost darkness. Hugging it as best he could, he crept silently around the curve, and halted.

Through him Greel watched: watched with the rat's ears and with his nose.

The fire was talking.

There were two scents, alike but not the same. And there were two voices. Just as there had been two fires. The bright things that had burned Greel's eyes were living creatures of some sort.

Greel listened. The sounds H'ssig heard so clearly were words. A language of some sort. Greel was sure of that. He knew the difference between the roars and grunts of animals and the patterns of speech.

But the fire things were talking in a language he did not know. The sounds meant no more to him than to H'ssig who relayed them.

He concentrated on the scent. It was strange, unlike anything he had encountered before. But somehow it felt like a man-scent, though it could not be that.

Greel thought. An almost man-scent. And words. Could it be that the fire things were men? They would be strange men, much unlike the People. But the taletellers sung of men in ancient times that had strange powers and forms. Might not these be such men? Here, in the Oldest Tunnels, where the legends said the Old Ones had created the People — might not such men still dwell here?

Yes.

Greel stirred. He moved slowly from where he lay, raising himself to a crouching position to squint at the curve ahead. A silent snap brought H'ssig back to safety from the fiery tunnel beyond the curve.

There was one way to make sure, Greel thought. Trembling, he reached out cautiously with his mind.

Von der Stadt had adapted to Earth's gravity a lot more successfully than Ciffonetto. He reached the floor of the tunnel quickly, and waited impatiently while his companion climbed down from the platform.

Ciffonetto let himself drop the last foot or so, and landed with a thud. He looked up at the platform apprehensively. "I just hope I can make it back up," he said.

Von der Stadt shrugged. "You were the one who wanted to explore all the tunnels."

"Yes," said Ciffonetto, shifting his gaze from the platform to look around him. "And I still do. Down here, in these tunnels, are the answers we're seeking."

"That's your theory, anyway," Von der Stadt said. He looked in both directions, chose one at random, and moved forward, his flashlight beam spearing out before him. Ciffonetto followed a half-step behind.

The tunnel they entered was long, straight, and empty.

"Tell me," Von der Stadt said in an offhand manner as they walked, "even if your survivors did make it through the war in shelters, wouldn't they have been forced to surface eventually to survive? I mean — how could anyone actually *live* down here?" He looked around the tunnel with obvious distaste.

"Have you been taking lessons from Nagel or something?" Ciffonetto replied. "I've heard that so often I'm sick of it. I admit it would be difficult. But not impossible. At first, there would be access to large stores of canned goods. A lot of that stuff was kept in basements. You could get to it by tunneling. Later, you could raise food. There are plants that will grow without light. And there would be insects and boring animals too, I imagine."

"A diet of bugs and mushrooms. It doesn't sound too healthy to me."

Ciffonetto stopped suddenly, not bothering to reply. "Look there," he said, pointing with his flashlight.

The beam played over a jagged break in the tunnel wall. It looked as though someone had smashed through the stone a long time ago.

Von der Stadt's flash joined Ciffonetto's to light the area better. There was a passage descending from the break. Ciffonetto moved towards it with a start.

"What the hell do you say to this, Von der Stadt," he asked, grinning. He stuck head and flashlight into the crude tunnel, but re-emerged quickly.

"Not much there," he said. "The passage is caved in after a few feet. But still, it confirms what I've been saying."

Von der Stadt looked vaguely uneasy. His free hand drifted to the holstered pistol at his side. "I don't know," he said.

"No, you don't," said Ciffonetto, triumphantly. "Neither does Nagel. Men have lived down here. They may still live here. We've got to organize a more efficient search of the whole underground system."

He paused, his mind flickering back to Von der Stadt's argument of a few seconds earlier. "As for your bugs and mushrooms, men can learn to live on a lot of things. Men adapt. If men survived the war — and this says they did — then they survived the aftermath, I'll wager."

"Maybe," Von der Stadt said. "I can't see what you are so hot on discovering survivors for anyway, though. I mean, the expedition is important and all that. We've got to re-establish spaceflight, and this is a good test for our new hardware. And I guess you scientists can pick up some good stuff for the museums. But humans? What did Earth ever get us besides the Great Famine?"

Ciffonetto smiled tolerantly. "It's because of the Great Famine that we want to find humans," he said. He paused. "We've got enough to entice even Nagel now. Let's head back."

He started walking back in the direction they had come, and resumed talking. "The Great Famine was an unavoidable result of the war on Earth," he said. "When supplies stopped coming, there was absolutely no way to keep all the people in the lunar colony alive. Ninety per cent starved.

"Luna could be made self-sufficient, but only with a very small population. That's what happened. The population adjusted itself. But we recycled our air and our water, grew foods in hydroponic tanks. We struggled, but we survived. And began to rebuild.

"But we lost a lot. Too many people died. Our genetic pool was terribly small, and not too diverse. The colony had never had a lot of racial diversity to begin with.

"That hasn't helped. Population actually declined for a long time after we had the physical resources to support more people. The idea of in-breeding didn't go over. Now population's going up again, but slowly. We're stagnant, Von der Stadt. It's taken us nearly five centuries to get space travel going again, for example. And we still haven't duplicated many of the things they had back on Earth before the disaster."

Von der Stadt frowned. "Stagnant's a strong word," he said. "I think we've done pretty good."

Ciffonetto dismissed the comment with a wave of his flashlight. "Pretty good," he said. "Not good enough. We're not going anywhere. There's so damn few changes, so little in the way of new ideas. We need fresh viewpoints, fresh genetic stock. We need the stimulation of contact with a foreign culture.

"Survivors would give us that. After all Earth's been through, they'd have to have changed in some ways. And they'd be proof that human life can still flourish on Earth. That's crucial if we're going to establish a colony here."

The last point was tacked on almost as an afterthought, but caught Von der Stadt's approval. He nodded gravely.

They had reached the station again. Ciffonetto headed straight for the platform. "C'mon," he said, "let's get back to base. I can't wait to see Nagel's face drop when I tell him what we've found."

They were men.

Greel was almost sure of it. The texture of their minds was curious, but manlike. Greel was a strong mind-mingler. He knew the coarse, dim feel of an animal's mind, the obscene shadows that were the thoughts of the worm-things. And he knew the minds of men.

They were men.

Yet there was a strangeness. Mind-mingling was true communication only with a mind-brother. But always it was a sharing with other men. A dark and murky sharing, full of clouds and flavors and smells and emotions. But a sharing.

Here there was no sharing. Here it was like mind-mingling with a lower animal. Touch, feel, stroke, savor — all that a strong mind-mingler could do with an animal. But never would he feel a response. Men and mind-brothers responded; animals did not.

These men did not respond. These strange fire-men had minds that were silent and crippled.

In the darkness of the tunnel, Greel straightened from his crouch. The fire had faded suddenly from the wall. The men were going away, down the tunnel away from him. The fire went with them.

He edged forward slowly, H'ssig at his side, spear in hand. Distance made mind-mingling difficult. He must keep them in range. He must find out more. He was a scout. He had a duty.

His mind crept out again, to taste the flavor of the other minds. He had to be sure.

Their thoughts moved around him, swirling chaos shot through with streaks of brightness and emotions and dancing, half-seen concepts. Greel understood little. But here he recognized something. And there something else came to him.

He lingered and tasted fully of their minds, and learned. But still it was like mind-mingling with an animal. He could not make himself felt. He could not get an answer.

Still they moved away, and their thoughts dimmed, and the mind-mingling became harder. Greel advanced. He hesitated when he got to the place where the tunnel curved. But he knew he must go on. He was a scout.

He lowered himself to the floor, squinted, and moved around the curve on hands and knees.

Beyond the curve, he started and gasped. He was in a great hall, an immense cavern with a vaulting roof and giant pillars that held up the sky. And the hall was bright with light, a strange, fiery light that danced over everything.

It was a place of legend. A hall of the Old Ones. It had to be. Never had Greel seen a chamber so vast. And he of all the People had wandered furthest and climbed highest.

The men were not in sight, but their fire danced around the mouth of the tunnel at the other end of the hall. It was intense, but not unbearable. The men had gone around another curve. Greel realized that he looked only at the dim reflection of their fire. So long as he did not see it direct, he was safe.

He moved out into the hall, the scout in him crying to climb the stone wall and explore the upper chamber from which the mighty pillars reared. But no. The fire-men were more important. The hall he could return to.

H'ssig rubbed up against his leg. He reached down and stroked the rat's soft fur reassuringly. His mind-brother could sense the turmoil of his thoughts.

Men, yes, he was sure of that. And more he knew. Their thoughts were not those of the People, but they were man-thoughts, and some he could understand. One of them burned, burned to find other men. They seek the People, Greel thought.

That he knew, He was a scout and a mind-mingler. He did not make mistakes. But what he must do he did not know.

They sought the People. That might be good. When first that concept had touched him, Greel had quivered with joy. These fire-men were like the Old Ones of legend. If they sought the People, he would lead them. There would be rewards, and glory, and the taletellers would sing his name for generations.

More, it was his duty. Things went not well with the People in recent generations. The time of good had ended with the coming of the worm-things, who had driven the People from tunnel after tunnel. Even now, below his feet, the fight went on still in the Bad Levels and the tunnels of the People.

And Greel knew the People were losing.

It was slow. But certain. The worm-things were new to the People. More than animal, but less, less than men. They needed not the tunnels. They stalked through the earth itself, and nowhere were men safe.

The People fought back. Mind-minglers could sense the worm-things, and spears could slay them, and the great hunting rats could rip them to shreds. But always the worm-things fled back into the earth itself. And there were many worm-things, and few People.

But these new men, these fire-men, they could change the war. Legends said the Old Ones had fought with fire and stranger weapons, and these men lived in fire. They could aid the People. They could give mighty weapons to drive the worm-things back into the darkness from which they came.

But.

But these men were not quite men. Their minds were crippled, and much, much of their thought was alien to Greel. Only glimpses of it could he catch. He could not know them as he could know another of the People when they mingled minds.

He could lead them to the People. He knew the way. Back and down, a turn here, a twist there. Through the Middle Tunnels and the Bad Levels.

But what if he led them, and they were enemy to the People? What if they turned on the People with their fire? He feared for what they might do.

Without him, they would never find the People. Greel was certain of that. Only he, in long generations, had come this far. And only with stealth and mind-mingling and H'ssig alongside him. They would never find the ways he had come, the twisting tunnels that led deep, deep into the earth.

So the People were safe if he did not act. But then the worm-things would win, eventually. It might take many generations. But the People could not hold out.

His decision. No mind-mingler could reach a small part of the distance that separated him from the tunnels of the People. He alone must decide.

And he must decide soon. For he realized, with a shock, that the fire-men were coming back. Their odd thoughts grew stronger, and the light in the hall grew more and more intense.

He hesitated, then moved slowly backwards towards the tunnel from which be had come.

"Wait a minute," Von der Stadt said when Ciffonetto was a quarter of the way up the wall. "Let's try the other directions."

Ciffonetto craned his head around awkwardly to look at his companion, gave it up as a bad job, and dropped back to the tunnel floor. He looked disgruntled. "We should get back," he said. "We've got enough."

Von der Stadt shrugged. "C'mon. You're the one wanted to explore down here. So we might as well do a thorough job of it. Maybe we're only a few feet away from another one of your big finds."

"Alright," said Ciffonetto, pulling his flashlight from his belt where he had stashed it for his intended assault on the platform. "I suppose you have a point. It would be tragic if we got Nagel down here and he tripped over something we had missed."

Von der Stadt nodded assent. Their flashlight beams melted together, and they strode quickly towards the deeper darkness of the tunnel mouth.

They were coming. Fear and indecision tumbled in Greel's thoughts. He hugged the tunnel wall. Back he moved, fast and silent. He must keep away from their fire until he could decide what he must do.

But after the first turn, the tunnel ran long and straight. Greel was fast. But not fast enough. And his eyes were incautiously wide when the fire appeared suddenly in full fury.

His eyes burned. He squealed in sudden pain, and threw himself to the ground. The fire refused to go away. It danced before him even with his eyes closed, shifting colors horribly.

Greel fought for control. Still there was distance between them. Still he was armed. He reached out to H'ssig, nearby in the tunnel. The eyeless rat again would be his eyes.

Eyes still shut, Greel began to crawl back, away from the fire. H'ssig remained.

"What the hell was *that?*"

Von der Stadt's whispered question hung in the air for an instant. He was frozen where he had rounded the curve. Ciffonetto, by his side, had also stopped dead at the sound.

The scientist looked puzzled. "I don't know," he said. "It was — odd. Sounded like some sort of animal in pain. A scream, sort of. But as if the screamer were trying to remain silent, almost."

His flashlight darted this way and that, slicing ribbons of light from the velvet darkness, but revealing little. Von der Stadt's beam pointed straight ahead, unmoving.

"I don't like it," Von der Stadt stated doubtfully. "Maybe there is something down here. But that doesn't mean it's friendly." He shifted his flash to his left hand, and drew his pistol. "We'll see," he said.

Ciffonetto frowned, but said nothing. They started forward again.

They were big, and they moved fast. Greel realized with a sick despair that they would catch him. His choice had been made for him.

But perhaps it was right. They were men. Men like the Old Ones. They would help the People against the worm-things. A new age would dawn. The time of fear would pass. The horror would fade. The old glories of which the taletellers sing would return, and once again the People would build great halls and mighty tunnels.

Yes. They had decided for him, but the decision was right. It was the only decision. Man must meet man, and together they would face the worm-things.

He kept his eyes closed. But he stood.

And spoke.

Again they froze in mid-step. This time the sound was no muffled scream. It was soft, almost hissing, but it was too clear to be misunderstood.

Both flash beams swung wildly now, for seconds. Then one froze. The other hesitated, then joined it.

Together they formed a pool of light against a distant part of the tunnel wall. And in the pool stood — what?

"My God," said Von der Stadt. "Cuff, tell me what it is quick, before I shoot it."

"Don't," Ciffonetto replied. "It isn't moving."

"But — what?"

"I don't know." The scientist's voice had a strange, uncertain quiver in it.

The creature in the pool of light was small, barely over four feet. Small and sickening. There was something vaguely manlike about it. but the proportions of the limbs were all wrong, and the hands and feet were grotesquely malformed. And the skin, the skin was a sickly, maggoty white.

But the face was the worst. Large, all out of proportion to the body, yet the mouth and nose could hardly he seen. The head was all eyes. Two great, immense, grotesque eyes, now safely hidden by lids of dead white skin.

Von der Stadt was rock steady, but Ciffonetto shook a bit as he looked at it. Yet he spoke first.

"Look," he said, his voice soft. "In its hand. I think — I think that's a tool."

Silence. Long, strained silence. Then Ciffonetto spoke again. His voice was hoarse.

"I think that's a man."

Greel burned.

The fire had caught him. Even shut tight, his eyes ached, and he knew the horror that lurked outside if he opened them. And the fire had caught him. His skin itched strangely, and hurt. Worse and worse it hurt.

Yet he did not stir. He was a scout. He had a duty. He endured, while his mind mingled with those of the others.

And there, in their minds, he saw fear, but checked fear. In a distorted, blurry way he saw himself through their eyes. He tasted the awe and the revulsion that warred in one. And the unmixed revulsion that churned inside the other.

He angered, but he checked his anger. He must reach them. He must take them to the People. They were blind and crippled and could not help their feelings. But if they understood, they would aid. Yes.

He did not move. He waited. His skin burned, but he waited.

"That," said Von der Stadt. "That *thing* is a man?"

Ciffonetto nodded. "It must be. It carries tools. It spoke." He hesitated. "But — God, I never envisioned anything like this. The tunnels, Von der Stadt. The dark. For long centuries only the dark. I never thought — so much evolution in so little time."

"A *man?*" Still Von der Stadt doubted. "You're crazy. No man could become something like *that.*"

Ciffonetto scarcely heard him. "I should have realized " he mumbled. "Should have guessed. The radiation, of course. It would speed up mutation. Shorter life-spans, probably. You were right. Von der Stadt. Men can't live on bugs and mushrooms. Not men like us. So they adapted. Adapted to the darkness, and the tunnels. It — "

Suddenly he started. "Those eyes," he said. He clicked off his flashlight, and the walls seemed to move closer. "He must be sensitive. We're hurting him. Divert your flash, Von der Stadt."

Von der Stadt gave him a doubtful sidelong glance. "It's dark enough down here already," he said. But he obeyed. His beam swung away.

"History," Ciffonetto said. "A moment that will live in — "

He never finished. Von der Stadt was tense, trigger-edged. As his beam swung away from the figure down the tunnel, he caught another flicker of movement in the darkness. He swung back and forth, found the thing again, pinned it against the tracks with a beam of light.

Almost he had shot before. But he had hesitated, because the manlike figure had been still and unfamiliar.

This new thing was not still. It squealed and scurried. Nor was it unfamiliar. This time Von der Stadt did not hesitate.

There was a roar, a flash. Then a second.

"Got it," said Von der Stadt. "A damn rat."

And Greel screamed.

After the long burning, there had come an instant of relief. But only an instant. Then, suddenly, pain flooded him. Wave after wave after wave. Rolled over him, blotting out the thoughts of the fire-men, blotting out their fear, blotting out his anger.

H'ssig died. His mind-brother died.

The fire-men had killed his mind-brother.

He shrieked in painrage. He darted forward, swung up his spear.

He opened his eyes. There was a flash of vision, then more pain and blindness. But the flash was enough. He struck. And struck again. Wildly, madly, blow after blow, thrust after thrust.

Then, again, the universe turned red with pain, and then again sounded that awful roar that had come when H'ssig died. Something threw him to the tunnel floor, and his eyes opened again, and fire, fire was everywhere.

But only for a while. Only for a while. Then, shortly, it was darkness again for Greel of the People.

The gun still smoked. The hand was still steady. But Von der Stadt's mouth hung open as he looked, unbelieving, from the thing he had blasted across the tunnel, to the blood dripping from his uniform, then back again.

Then the gun dropped, and he clutched at his stomach, clutched at the wounds. His hand came away wet with blood. He stared at it. Then stared at Ciffonetto.

"The rat," he said. There was pain in his voice. "I only shot a rat. It was going for him. Why, Cliff? I — ?"

And he fell. Heavily. His flashlight shattered and went dark.

There was a long fumbling in the blackness. Then, at last, Ciffonetto's light winked on, and the ashen scientist knelt beside his companion.

"Von," he said, tugging at the uniform. "Are you all right?" He ripped away the fabric to expose the torn flesh.

Von der Stadt was mumbling. "I didn't even see him coming. I took my light away, like you said, Cliff. Why? I wasn't going to shoot him. Not if he was a man. I only shot a rat. Only a rat. It was going for him, too."

Ciffonetto, who had stood paralyzed through everything, nodded. "It wasn't your fault, Von. But you must have scared him. You need treating, now, though. He hurt you bad. Can you make it back to camp?"

He didn't wait for an answer. He slipped his arm under Von der Stadt's. and lifted him to his feet, and began to walk him down the tunnel, praying they could make it back to the platform.

"I only shot a rat," Von der Stadt kept saying, over and over, in a dazed voice.

"Don't worry," said Ciffonetto. "It won't matter. We'll find others. We'll search the whole subway system if we have to. We'll find them."

"Only a rat. Only a rat."

They reached the platform. Ciffonetto lowered Von der Stadt back to the ground. "I can't make the climb carrying you, Von," he said. "I'll have to leave you here. Go for help." He straightened, hung the flash from his belt.

"Only a rat," Von der Stadt said again.

"Don't worry," said Ciffonetto. "Even if we don't find them, nothing will be lost. They were clearly sub-human. Men once, maybe. But no more. Degenerated. There was nothing they could have taught us, anyway."

But Von der Stadt was past listening, past hearing. He just sat against the wall, clutching his stomach and feeling the blood ooze from between his fingers, mumbling the same words over and over.

Ciffonetto turned to the wall. A few short feet to the platform, then the old, rusty escalator, and the basement ruins, and daylight. He had to hurry. Von der Stadt wouldn't last long.

He grabbed the rock, pulled himself up, hung on desperately as his other hand scrambled and found a hold. He pulled up again.

He was almost there, almost at the platform level, when his weak Lunar muscles gave out on him. There was a sudden spasm, his hand slipped loose, his other hand couldn't take the weight.

He fell. On the flashlight.

The darkness was like nothing he had ever seen. Too thick, too complete. He fought to keep from screaming.

When he tried to rise again, he did scream. More than the flashlight had broken in the fall.

His scream echoed and re-echoed through the long, black tunnel he could not see. It was a long time dying. When it finally faded, he screamed again. And again.

Finally, hoarse, he stopped. "Von," he said. "Von, can you hear me?" There was no answer. He tried again. Talk, he must talk to hold his sanity. The darkness was all around him, and he could almost hear soft movements a few feet away.

Von der Stadt giggled, sounding infinitely far away.

"It was only a rat," he said. "Only a rat."

Silence. Then, softly, Ciffonetto. "Yes, Von, yes."

"It was only a rat."

"It was only a rat."

"It was only a rat."

Washington, D.C.
May, 1971

The Hero

The city was dead and the flames of its passing spread a red stain across the green-gray sky.

It had been a long time dying. Resistance had lasted almost a week and the fighting had been bitter for a while. But in the end the invaders had broken the defenders, as they had broken so many others in the past. The alien sky with its double sun did not bother them. They had fought and won under skies of azure blue and speckled gold and inky black.

The Weather Control boys had hit first, while the main force was still hundreds of miles to the east. Storm after storm had flailed at the streets of the city, to slow defensive preparations and smash the spirit of resistance.

When they were closer the invaders had sent up howlers. Unending high-pitched shrieks had echoed back and forth both day and night and before long most of the populace had fled in demoralized panic. By then the attackers' main force was in range and launched plague bombs on a steady westward wind.

Even then the natives had tried to fight back. From their defensive emplacements ringing the city the survivors had sent up a hail of atomics, managing to vaporize one whole company whose defensive screens were overloaded by the sudden assault. But the gesture was a feeble one at best. By that time incendiary bombs were raining down steadily upon the city and great clouds of acid-gas were blowing across the plains.

And behind the gas, the dreaded assault squads of the Terran Expeditionary Force moved on the last defenses.

Kagen scowled at the dented plastoid helmet at his feet and cursed his luck. A routine mopping-up detail, he thought. A perfectly routine operation — and some damned automatic interceptor emplacement somewhere had lobbed a low-grade atomic at him.

It had been only a near miss but the shock waves had damaged his hip rockets and knocked him out of the sky, landing him in this godforsaken little ravine east of the city. His light plastoid battle armor had protected him from the impact but his helmet had taken a good whack.

Kagen squatted and picked up the dented helmet to examine it. His long-range com and all of his sensory equipment were out. With his rockets gone, too, he was crippled, deaf, dumb and half-blind. He swore.

A flicker of movement along the top of the shallow ravine caught his attention. Five natives came suddenly into view, each carrying a hair-trigger submachine gun. They carried them at the ready, trained on Kagen. They were fanned out in line, covering him from both right and left. One began to speak.

He never finished. One instant, Kagen's screech gun lay on the rocks at his feet. Quite suddenly it was in his hand.

Five men will hesitate where one alone will not. During the brief flickering instant before the natives' fingers began to tighten on their triggers, Kagen did not pause, Kagen did not hesitate, Kagen did not think.

Kagen killed.

The screech gun emitted a loud, ear-piercing shriek. The enemy squad leader shuddered as the invisible beam of concentrated high-frequency sound ripped into him. Then his flesh began to liquefy. By then Kagen's gun had found two more targets.

The guns of the two remaining natives finally began to chatter. A rain of bullets enveloped Kagen as he whirled to his right and he grunted under the impact as the shots caromed off his battle armor. His screech gun leveled — and a random shot sent it spinning from his grasp.

Kagen did not hesitate or pause as the gun was wrenched from his grip. He bounded to the top of the shallow ravine with one leap, directly toward one of the soldiers.

The man wavered briefly and brought up his gun. The instant was all Kagen needed. With all the momentum of his leap behind it, his right hand smashed the gun butt into the enemy's face and his left, backed by fifteen hundred pounds of force, hammered into the native's body right under the breastbone.

Kagen seized the corpse and heaved it toward the second native, who had ceased fire briefly as his comrade came between himself and Kagen. Now his bullets tore into the airborne body. He took a quick step back, his gun level and firing.

And then Kagen was on him. Kagen knew a searing flash of pain as a shot bruised his temple. He ignored it, drove the edge of his hand into the native's throat. The man toppled, lay still.

Kagen spun, still reacting, searching for the next foe.

He was alone.

Kagen bent and wiped the blood from his hand with a piece of the native's uniform. He frowned in disgust. It was going to be a long trek back to camp, he thought, tossing the blood-soaked rag casually to the ground.

Today was definitely not his lucky day.

He grunted dismally, then scrambled back down into the ravine to recover his screech gun and helmet for the hike.

On the horizon, the city was still burning.

Ragelli's voice was loud and cheerful as it came crackling over the short-range communicator nestled in Kagen's fist.

"So it's you, Kagen," he said laughing. "You signaled just in time. My sensors were starting to pick up something. Little closer and I would've screeched you down."

"My helmet's busted and the sensors are out," Kagen replied. "Damn hard to judge distance. Long-range com is busted, too."

"The brass was wondering what happened to you," Ragelli cut in. "Made 'em sweat a little. But I figured you'd turn up sooner or later."

"Right," Kagen said. "One of these mudworms zapped the hell out of my rockets and it took me a while to get back. But I'm coming in now."

He emerged slowly from the crater he had crouched in, coming in sight of the guard in the distance. He took it slow and easy.

Outlined against the outpost barrier, Ragelli lifted a ponderous silver-gray arm in greeting. He was armored completely in a full duralloy battlesuit that made Kagen's plastoid armor look like tissue paper, and sat in the trigger-seat of a swiveling screech-gun battery. A bubble of defensive screens enveloped him, turning his massive figure into an indistinct blur.

Kagen waved back and began to eat up the distance between them with long, loping strides. He stopped just in front of the barrier, at the foot of Ragelli's emplacement.

"You look damned battered," said Ragelli, appraising him from behind a plastoid visor, aided by his sensory devices. "That light armor doesn't buy you a nickel's worth of protection. Any farm boy with a pea shooter can plug you."

Kagen laughed. "At least I can move. You may be able to stand off an Assault Squad in that duralloy monkey suit, but I'd like to see you do anything on offense, chum. And defense doesn't win wars."

"Your pot," Ragelli said. "This sentry duty is boring as hell." He flicked a switch on his control panel and a section of the barrier winked out. Kagen was through it at once. A split second later it came back on again.

Kagen strode quickly to his squad barracks. The door slid open automatically as he approached it and he stepped inside gratefully. It felt good to be home again and back at his normal weight. These light gravity mudholes made him queasy after awhile. The barracks were artificially maintained at Wellington-normal gravity, twice Earth-normal. It was expensive but the brass kept saying that nothing was too good for the comfort of our fighting men.

Kagen stripped off his plastoid armor in the squad ready room and tossed it into the replacement bin. He headed straight for his cubicle and sprawled across the bed.

Reaching over to the plain metal table alongside his bed, he yanked open a drawer and took out a fat greenish capsule. He swallowed it hastily, and lay back to relax as it took hold throughout his system. The regulations prohibited taking synthastim between meals, he knew, but the rule was never enforced. Like most troopers, Kagen took it almost continuously to maintain his speed and endurance at maximum.

He was dozing comfortably a few minutes later when the com box mounted on the wall above his bed came to sudden life.

"Kagen."

Kagen sat up instantly, wide-awake.

"Acknowledged," he said.

"Report to Major Grady at once."

Kagen grinned broadly. His request was being acted on quickly, he thought. And by a high officer, no less. Dressing quickly in loose-fitting brown fatigues, he set off across the base.

The high officers' quarters were at the center of the outpost. They consisted of a brightly lit, three-story building, blanketed overhead by defensive screens and ringed by guardsmen in light battle armor. One of the guards recognized Kagen and he was admitted on orders.

Immediately beyond the door he halted briefly as a bank of sensors scanned him for weapons. Troopers, of course, were not allowed to bear arms in the presence of high officers. Had he been carrying a screech gun alarms would have gone off all over the building while the tractor beams hidden in the walls and ceilings immobilized him completely.

But he passed the inspection and continued down the long corridor toward Major Grady's office. A third of the way down, the first set of tractor beams locked firmly onto his wrists. He struggled the instant he felt the invisible touch against his skin — but the tractors held him steady. Others, triggered automatically by his passing, came on as he continued down the corridor.

Kagen cursed under his breath and fought with his impulse to resist. He hated being pinned by tractor beams, but those were the rules if you wanted to see a high officer.

The door opened before him and he stepped through. A full bank of tractor beams seized him instantly and immobilized him. A few adjusted slightly and he was snapped to rigid attention, although his muscles screamed resistance.

Major Carl Grady was working at a cluttered wooden desk a few feet away, scribbling something on a sheet of paper. A large stack of papers rested at his elbow, an old-fashioned laser pistol sitting on top of them as a paperweight.

Kagen recognized the laser. It was some sort of heirloom, passed down in Grady's family for generations. The story was that some ancestor of his had used it back on Earth, in the Fire Wars of the early twenty-first century. Despite its age, the thing was still supposed to be in working order.

After several minutes of silence Grady finally set down his pen and looked up at Kagen. He was unusually young for a high officer but his unruly gray hair made him look older than he was. Like all high officers, he was Earth-born; frail and slow before the assault squad troopers from the dense, heavy gravity War Worlds of Wellington and Rommel.

"Report your presence," Grady said curtly. As always, his lean, pale face mirrored immense boredom.

"Field Officer John Kagen, assault squads, Terran Expeditionary Force."

Grady nodded, not really listening. He opened one of his desk drawers and extracted a sheet of paper.

"Kagen," he said, fiddling with the paper, "I think you know why you're here." He tapped the paper with his finger. "What's the meaning of this?"

"Just what it says, Major," Kagen replied. He tried to shift his weight but the tractor beams held him rigid.

Grady noticed and gestured impatiently. "At rest," he said. Most of the tractor beams snapped off, leaving Kagen free to move, if only at half his normal speed. He flexed in relief and grinned.

"My term of enlistment is up within two weeks Major. I don't plan to re-enlist. So I've requested transportation to Earth. That's all there is to it."

Grady's eyebrows arched a fraction of an inch but the dark eyes beneath them remained bored.

"Really?" he asked. "You've been a soldier for almost twenty years now, Kagen. Why retire? I'm afraid I don't understand."

Kagen shrugged. "I don't know. I'm getting old. Maybe I'm just getting tired of camp life, It's all starting to get boring, taking one damn mudhole after another. I want something different. Some excitement."

Grady nodded. "I see. But I don't think I agree with you, Kagen." His voice was soft and persuasive. "I think you're underselling the T.E.F. There is excitement ahead, if you'll only give us a chance." He leaned back in his chair, toying with a pencil he had picked up. "I'll tell you something, Kagen. You know, we've been at war with the Hrangan Empire for nearly three decades now. Direct clashes between us and the enemy have been few and far between up to now. Do you know why?"

"Sure," Kagen said.

Grady ignored him. "I'll tell you why," he continued. "So far each of us has been struggling to consolidate his position by grabbing these little worlds in the border regions. These mudholes, as you call them. But they're very important mudholes. We need them for bases, for their raw materials, for their industrial capacity and for the conscript labor they provide. "That's why we try to minimize damage in our campaigns. And that's why we use psychwar tactics like the howlers. To frighten away as many natives as possible before each attack. To preserve labor."

"I know all that," Kagen interrupted with typical Wellington bluntness. "What of it? I didn't come here for a lecture."

Grady looked up from the pencil. "No," he said. "No, you didn't. So I'll tell you, Kagen. The prelims are over. It's time for the main event. There are only a handful of unclaimed worlds left. Soon now, we'll be coming into direct conflict with the Hrangan Conquest Corps. Within a year we'll be attacking their bases."

The major stared at Kagen expectantly, waiting for a reply. When none came, a puzzled look flickered across his face. He leaned forward again.

"Don't you understand, Kagen?" he asked. "What more excitement could you want? No more fighting these piddling civilians in uniform, with their dirty little atomics and their primitive projectile guns. The Hrangans are a real enemy. Like us, they've had a professional army for generations upon generations. They're soldiers, born and bred. Good ones, too. They've got screens and modem weapons. They'll be foes to give our assault squads a real test."

"Maybe," Kagen said doubtfully. "But that kind of excitement isn't what I had in mind. I'm getting old. I've noticed that I'm definitely slower lately — even synthastim isn't keeping up my speed."

Grady shook his head. "You've got one of the best records in the whole T.E.F., Kagen. You've received the Stellar Cross twice and the World Congress Decoration three times. Every com station on Earth carried the story when you saved the landing party on Torego. Why should you doubt your effectiveness now? We're going to need men like you against the Hrangans. Re-enlist."

"No," said Kagen emphatically. "The regs say you're entitled to your pension after twenty years and those medals have earned me a nice bunch of retirement bonuses. Now I want to enjoy them." He grinned broadly. "As you say, everyone on Earth must know me. I'm a hero. With that reputation, I figure I can have a real screechout."

Grady frowned and drummed on the desk impatiently. "I know what the regulations say, Kagen. But no one ever really retires — you must know that. Most troopers prefer to stay with the front. That's their job. That's what the War Worlds are all about."

"I don't really care, Major," Kagen replied. "I know the regs and I know I have a right to retire on full pension. You can't stop me."

Grady considered the statement calmly, his eyes dark with thought.

"All right," he said after a long pause. "Let's be reasonable about this. You'll retire with full pension and bonuses. We'll set you down on Wellington in a place of your own. Or Rommel if you like. We'll make you a youth barracks director — any age group you like. Or a training camp director. With your record you can start right at the top."

"Uh-uh," Kagen said firmly. "Not Wellington. Not Rommel. Earth."

"But why? You were born and raised on Wellington — in one of the hill barracks, I believe. You've never seen Earth."

"True," said Kagen. "But I've seen it in camp telecasts and flicks. I like what I've seen. I've been reading about Earth a lot lately, too. So now I want to see what it's like." He paused, then grinned again. "Let's just say I want to see what I've been fighting for."

Grady's frown reflected his displeasure. "I'm from Earth, Kagen," he said. "I tell you, you won't like it. You won't fit in. The gravity is too low — and there are no artificial heavy gravity barracks to take shelter in. Synthastim is illegal, strictly prohibited. But War Worlders need it, so you'll have to pay exorbitant prices to get the stuff. Earthers aren't reaction trained, either. They're a different kind of people. Go back to Wellington. You'll be among your own kind."

"Maybe that's one of the reasons I want Earth," Kagen said stubbornly. "On Wellington I'm just one of hundreds of old vets. Hell, every one of the troopers who *does* retire heads back to his old barracks. But on Earth I'll be a celebrity. Why, I'll be the fastest, strongest guy on the whole damn planet. That's got to have some advantages."

Grady was starting to look agitated. "What about the gravity?" he demanded. "The synthastim?"

"I'll get used to light gravity after a while, that's no problem. And I won't be needing that much speed and endurance, so I figure I can kick the synthastim habit."

Grady ran his fingers through his unkempt hair and shook his head doubtfully. There was a long, awkward silence. He leaned across the desk.

And, suddenly, his hand darted towards the laser pistol.

Kagen reacted. He dove forward, delayed only slightly by the few tractor beams that still held him. His hand flashed toward Grady's wrist in a crippling arc.

And suddenly wrenched to a halt as the tractor beams seized Kagen roughly, held him rigid and then smashed him to the floor.

Grady, his hand frozen halfway to the pistol, leaned back in the chair. His face was white and shaken. He raised his hand and the tractor beams let up a bit. Kagen climbed slowly to his feet.

"You see, Kagen," said Grady. "That little test proves you're as fit as ever. You'd have gotten me if I hadn't kept a few tractors on you to slow you down. I tell you, we need men with your training and experience. We need you against the Hrangans. Re-enlist."

Kagen's cold blue eyes still seethed with anger. "Damn the Hrangans," he said. "I'm not re-enlisting and no goddamn little tricks of yours are going to make me change my mind. I'm going to Earth. You can't stop me."

Grady buried his face in his hands and sighed.

"All right, Kagen," he said at last. "You win. I'll put through your request."

He looked up one more time, and his dark eyes looked strangely troubled.

"You've been a great soldier, Kagen. We'll miss you. I tell you that you'll regret this decision. Are you sure you won't reconsider?"

"Absolutely sure," Kagen snapped.

The strange look suddenly vanished from Grady's eyes. His face once more took on the mask of bored indifference.

"Very well," he said curtly. "You are dismissed."

The tractors stayed on Kagen as he turned. They guided him — very firmly — from the building.

"You ready, Kagen?" Ragelli asked, leaning casually against the door of the cubicle.

Kagen picked up his small travel bag and threw one last glance around to make sure he hadn't forgotten anything. He hadn't. The room was quite bare.

"Guess so," he said, stepping through the door

Ragelli slipped on the plastoid helmet that had been cradled under his arm and hurried to catch up as Kagen strode down the corridor.

"I guess this is it," he said as he matched strides.

"Yeah," Kagen replied. "A week from now I'll be taking it easy back on Earth while you're getting blisters on your tail sitting around in that damned duralloy tuxedo of yours."

Ragelli laughed. "Maybe," he said. "But I still say you're nuts to go to Earth of all places, when you could command a whole damned training camp on Wellington. Assuming you wanted to quit at all, which is also crazy — "

The barracks door slid open before them and they stepped through. Ragelli still talking. A second guard flanked Kagen on the other side. Like Ragelli, he was wearing light battle armor.

Kagen himself was in full dress whites, trimmed with gold braid. A ceremonial laser, deactivated, was slung in a black leather holster at his side. Matching leather boots and a polished steel helmet set off the uniform. Azure blue bars on his shoulder signified field officer rank. His medals jangled against his chest as he walked.

Kagen's entire third assault squad was drawn up at attention on the spacefield behind the barracks in honor of his retirement. Alongside the ramp to the shuttlecraft, a group of high officers stood by, cordoned off by defensive screens. Major Grady was in the front row, his bored expression blurred somewhat by the screens.

Flanked by the two guards, Kagen walked across the concrete slowly, grinning under his helmet. Piped music welled out over the field, and Kagen recognized the T.E.F. battle hymn and the Wellington anthem.

At the foot of the ramp he turned and looked back. The company spread out before him saluted in unison on a command from the high officers and held position until Kagen returned the salute. Then one of the squad's other field officers stepped forward, and presented him with his discharge papers.

Jamming them into his belt, Kagen threw a quick, casual wave to Ragelli, then hurried up the ramp. It lifted slowly behind him.

Inside the ship, a crewman greeted him with a curt nod. "Got special quarters prepared for you," he said. "Follow me. Trip should only take about fifteen minutes. Then we'll transfer you to a starship for the Earth trip."

Kagen nodded and followed the man to his quarters. They turned out to be a plain, empty room, reinforced with duralloy plates. A view-screen covered one wall. An acceleration couch faced it.

Alone, Kagen sprawled out on the acceleration couch, clipping his helmet to a holder on the side. Tractor beams pressed down gently, holding him firmly in place for the liftoff.

A few minutes later a dull roar came from deep within the ship and Kagen felt several gravities press down upon him as the shuttlecraft took off. The viewscreen, suddenly coming to life, showed the planet dwindling below.

The viewer blinked off when they reached orbit. Kagen started to sit up but found he still could not move. The tractor beams held him pinned to the couch.

He frowned. There was no need for him to stay in the couch once the craft was in orbit. Some idiot had forgotten to release him.

"Hey," he shouted, figuring there would be a com box somewhere in the room. "These tractors are still on. Loosen the damned things so I can move a little."

No one answered.

He strained against the beams. Their pressure seemed to increase. The blasted things were starting to pinch a little, he thought. Now those morons were turning the knob the wrong way.

He cursed under his breath. "No," he shouted. "Now the tractors are getting heavier. You're adjusting them the wrong way."

But the pressure continued to climb and he felt more beams locking on him, until they covered his body like an invisible blanket. The damn things were really starting to hurt now

"You idiots," he yelled. "You morons. Cut it out, you bastards." With a surge of anger he strained against the beams, cursing. But even

Wellington-bred muscle was no match for tractors. He was held tightly to the couch.

One of the beams was trained on his chest pocket. Its pressure was driving his Stellar Cross painfully into his skin. The sharp edge of the polished medal had already sliced through the uniform and he could see a red stain spreading slowly through the white.

The pressure continued to mount and Kagen writhed in pain, squirming against his invisible shackles. It did no good. The pressure still went higher and more and more beams came on.

"Cut it out!" he screeched. "You bastards, I'll rip you apart when I get out of here. You're killing me, dammit!"

He heard the sharp snap of a bone suddenly breaking under the strain. Kagen felt a stab of intense pain in his right wrist. An instant later there was another snap.

"Cut it out!" he cried, his voice shrill with pain. "You're killing me. Damn you, you're killing me!"

And suddenly he realized he was right.

Grady looked up with a scowl at the aide who entered the office. "Yes? What is it?"

The aide, a young Earther in training for high officer rank, saluted briskly. "We just got the report from the shuttlecraft, sir. It's all over. They want to know what to do with the body."

"Space it," Grady replied. "Good as anything." A thin smile flickered across his face and he shook his head. "Too bad. Kagen was a good man in combat but his psych training must have slipped somewhere. We should send a strong note hack to his barracks conditioner. Though it's funny it didn't show up until now."

He shook his head again. "Earth," he said. "For a moment he even had me wondering if it was possible. But when I tested him with my laser, I knew. No way, no way." He shuddered a little. "As if we'd ever let a War Worlder loose on Earth." Then he turned back to his paperwork.

As the aide turned to leave. Grady looked up again.

"One other thing," he said. "Don't forget to send that PR release back to Earth. Make it War-Hero-Dies-When-Hrangans-Blast-Ship. Jazz it up good. Some of the big com networks should pick it up and it'll make good publicity. And forward his medals to Wellington. They'll want them for his barracks museum."

The aide nodded and Grady returned to his work. He still looked quite bored.

Evanston, Illinois
February, 1969

George R.R. Martin

fta

Hyperspace exists. Of that there can he no doubt. We have proved is mathematically. While we cannot know the laws of hyperspace as yet, we can he certain that they are not the laws of normal space. In hyperspace, there is no reason to suppose that the limiting velocity of light will apply. So all that remains is to find a means of moving from normal space to hyperspace, and back again. Give me the funds to find a hyperdrive, and I will give you the stars!

— Dr. Frederik D. Canferelli,
founder of the FTL Foundation,
addressing the Committee on Technological Assessment,
World Senate, Geneva, May 21, 2016

EVERYONE KNOWS AN ANT CAN'T
MOVE A RUBBER TREE PLANT
— Motto of the FTL Foundation

Kinery entered in a rush, a thick file bulging under his arm. He was an aggressive young man, with short blond hair and a spike beard and a no-nonsense manner. He showed no deference.

Jerome Schechter, the deputy director of the FTL Foundation, watched through tired eyes while Kinery sat down without invitation and slammed his file onto Schechter's cluttered desk.

"Morning, Schechter," Kinery said curtly. "I'm glad I finally broke through your palace guard. You're a very difficult man to get to see, you know that?"

Schechter nodded. "And you're very persistent," he said. The deputy director was a large man, layered in fat, with heavy eyebrows and a shock of thick gray hair.

"One has to be persistent in dealing with you people. Schechter, I'm not going to waste words. I've been getting a runaround from FTL, and I want to know why."

"A runaround?" Schechter smiled. "I don't know what you mean."

"Let's not play games. You and I both know that I'm one of the best damn physicists to come along in many years. You've seen my papers on hyperspace, if you keep up with your specialty at all. You should know that my approach is valid. I've given the field its biggest kick in the pants since Lopez. And he was thirty years ago. I'm on the track of a hyper-drive engine, Schechter. Everybody who knows anything knows that.

"But I need funding. My university can't meet the costs of the equipment I need. So I came to the FTL Foundation. Damn it, Schechter, you people should have been overjoyed to get my application. Instead, I get a year's worth of stalling, then a turndown. And I can't even get an explanation out of anyone. You're always in conference, your assistants hand me doubletalk, and Lopez seems to be on a perma-nent vacation."

Kinery folded his arms and sat back in his seat stiffly. Schechter played with a paperweight, and sighed. "You're angry, Mr. Kinery," he said. "It never pays to get angry."

Kinery leaned forward again. "I have a *right* to be angry. The FTL Foundation was set up for the express purpose of finding a hyperspace drive. I am about to do just that. Yet you won't even give me a hearing, let alone money."

Schechter sighed again. "You're working under several mis-apprehensions. To begin with, the FTL Foundation was created to research a method of faster-than-light travel. A star drive, let us say. Hyperspace is only one avenue toward that end. Right now, we're pursuing other avenues that look more promising. We ... "

"I know all about those other avenues," Kinery interrupted. "Dead ends, all of them. You're wasting the taxpayers money. And my God, some of things you're funding! Allison and his teleportation experi-ments. Claudia Daniels with her nonsense about an esper-engine. And Chung's time-stasis hypothesis! How much are you giving *him?* If you ask me, the FTL Foundation's been mismanaged ever since Canferelli died. The only one who was going in the right direction at all was Lopez, and you loons took him out of the field and made him an administrator."

Schechter looked up and studied his guest. Kinery's face was a trifle flushed, and his lips were pressed tightly together. "I understand you've been to see Senator Markham," the deputy director said. "Do you intend to bring these charges to his attention?"

"Yes," Kinery said sharply. "Unless I get some answers. And I guarantee you that if those answers don't satisfy me, I'm going to see to it that the Senate Technology Committee takes a good look at the FTL Foundation.

Schechter nodded. "Very well," he said. "I'll give you your answers. Kinery, do you have any idea how crowded Earth is right now?"

Kinery snorted. "Of course. I — "

"No," Schechter said. "Don't brush it off. Think about it. It's important. We don't have any *room* left, Kinery. Not here, not anywhere on Earth. And the colonies on Mars and Luna and Callisto are jokes. we both know that. Man's in a dead end. We need the stars for racial survival. The FTL Foundation is the hope of mankind, and thanks to Canferelli, the public sees the Foundation only in terms of hyperspace."

Kinery was not appeased. "Schechter, I've gotten enough bull from your staff during the past year. I don't need any from you."

Schechter just smiled. Then he rose and walked to the window, to look out on the sky-crowding towers of the megalopolis around them. "Kinery," he said without turning, "did you ever wonder why Lopez has not funded a hyperspace research project since he became director? After all, it was his field."

"I ... " Kinery began.

Schechter cut him off. "Never mind," he said. "It isn't important. We fund the crackpot theories that we fund because they're better than nothing. Hyperspace is the dead end, Kinery. We keep the myth alive for the public, but we know better."

Kinery grimaced. "Oh, come, now, Schechter. Take a look at my papers. You give me the funding and I'll give you a hyperspace engine within two years.

Schechter turned to face him. "I'm sure you would," he said, in a voice infinitely weary. "You know, Canferelli once said there was no reason why the limiting velocity of light should apply in hyperspace. He was right. It doesn't.

"I'm sorry, Kinery. Really I am. But Lopez gave us a hyperdrive thirty years ago. That's when we discovered that the limiting velocity in hyperspace is not the speed of light.

"It's slower, Kinery. It's *slower.*"

Chicago, Illinois
June, 1973

Run to Starlight

Hill stared dourly at the latest free-fall football results from the Belt as they danced across the face of the desk console, but his mind was elsewhere. For the seventeenth time that week, he was silently cursing the stupidity and shortsightedness of the members of the Starport City Council.

The damn councilmen persisted in cutting the allocation for an artificial gravity grid out of the departmental budget every time Hill put it in. They had the nerve to tell him to stick to "traditional" sports in planning his recreational program for the year.

The old fools had no idea of the way free-fall football was catching on throughout the system, although he'd tried to explain it to them, God knows how many times. The Belt sport should be an integral part of any self-respecting recreational program. And, on Earth, that meant you had to have a gravity grid. He'd planned on installing it beneath the stadium, but now —

The door to his office slid open with a soft hum. Hill looked up and frowned, snapping off the console. An agitated Jack De Angelis stepped through.

"What is it now?" Hill snapped.

"Uh, Rog, there's a guy here I think you better talk to," De Angelis replied. "He wants to enter a team in the City Football League."

"Registration closed on Tuesday," Hill said. "We've already got twelve teams. No room for any more. And why the hell can't you handle this? You're in charge of the football program.

"This is a special case," De Angelis said.

"Then make an exception and let the team in if you want to," Hill interrupted. "Or don't let them in. It's your program. It's your decision. Must I be bothered with every bit of trivia in this whole damned department?"

"Hey, take it easy, Rog," De Angelis protested. "I don't know what you're so steamed up about. Look, I — hell, I'll show you the problem." He turned and went to the door. "Sir, would you step in here a minute," he said to someone outside.

Hill started to rise from his seat, but sunk slowly back into the chair when the visitor appeared in the doorway.

De Angelis was smiling. "This is Roger Hill, the director of the Starport Department of Recreation," he said smoothly. "Rog, let me introduce Remjhard-nei, the head of the Brish'diri trade mission to Earth."

Hill rose again, and offered his hand numbly to the visitor. The Brish'dir was squat and grotesquely broad. He was a good foot shorter than Hill, who stood six foot four, but still gave the impression of dwarfing the director somehow. A hairless, bullet shaped head was set squarely atop the alien's massive shoulders. His eyes were glittering green marbles sunk in the slick, leathery gray skin. There were no external ears, only small holes on either side of the skull. The mouth was a lipless slash.

Diplomatically ignoring Hill's open-mouthed stare, Remjhard bared his teeth in a quick smile and crushed the director's hand in his own. "I am most pleased to meet you, sir," he said in fluent English, his voice a deep bass growl. "I have come to enter a football team in the fine league your city so graciously runs."

Hill gestured for the alien to take a seat, and sat down himself. De Angelis, still smiling at his boss' stricken look, pulled another chair up to the desk for himself.

"Well, I — " Hill began uncertainly. "This team, is it a — a Brish'diri team?"

Remjhard smiled again. "Yes," he answered. "Your football, it is a fine game. We of the mission have many times watched it being played on the 3V wallscreens your people were so kind as to install. It has fascinated us. And now some of the half-men of our mission desire to try to play it." He reached slowly into the pocket of the black and silver uniform he wore, and pulled out a folded sheet of paper.

"This is a roster of our players," he said, handing it to Hill. "I believe the newsfax said such a list is required to enter your league."

Hill took the paper and glanced down at it uncertainly. It was a list of some fifteen Brish'diri names, neatly typed out. Everything seemed to be in order, but still — "You'll forgive me, I hope," Hill said, "but I'm somewhat unfamiliar with the expressions of your people. You said — half-men? Do you mean children?"

Remjhard nodded, a quick inclination of his bulletlike head. "Yes. Male children, the sons of mission personnel. All are aged either eight or nine Earth seasons."

Hill silently sighed with relief. "I'm afraid it's out of the question, then," he said. "Mr. De Angelis said you were interested in the City League, but that league is for boys aged eighteen and up. Occasionally we'll admit a younger boy with exceptional talent and experience, but never anyone this young." He paused briefly. We do have several leagues for younger boys, but they've already begun play. It's much too late to add another team at this point."

"Pardon, Director Hill, but I think you misunderstand," Remjhard said. "A Brish'dir male is fully mature at fourteen Earth years. In our culture, such a person is regarded as a full adult. A nine-year-old Brish'dir is roughly equivalent to an eighteen-year-old Terran male in terms of physical and intellectual development. That is why our half-men wish to register for this league and not one of the others, you see."

"He's correct. Rog," De Angelis said. "I've read a little about the Brish'diri, and I'm sure of it. In terms of maturity, these youngsters are eligible for the City League."

Hill threw De Angelis a withering glance. if there was one thing he didn't need at the moment, it was a Brish'diri football team in one of his leagues, and Remjhard was arguing convincingly enough without Jack's help.

"Well, all right," Hill said. "Your team may well be of age, but there are still problems. The Rec Department sports program is for local residents only. We simply don't have room to accommodate everyone who wants to participate. And your home planet is, as I understand, several hundred light years beyond the Starport city limits." He smiled.

"True," Remjhard said. "But our trade mission has been in Starport for six years. An ideal location due to your city's proximity to Grissom Interstellar Spaceport, from which most of the Brish'diri traders operate while on Earth. All of the current members of the mission have been here for two Earth years, at least. We are Starport residents, Director Hill. I fail to understand how the location of Brishun enters into the matter at hand."

Hill squirmed uncomfortably in his seat, and glared at De Angelis, who was grinning. "Yes, you're probably right again," he said. "But I'm still afraid we won't be able to help you. Our junior leagues are touch football, but the City League, as you might know, is tackle. It can get quite rough at times. State safety regulations require the use of special equipment. To make sure no one is injured seriously. I'm sure you understand. And the Brish'diri — "

He groped for words, anxious not to offend. "The — uh — physical construction of the Brish'diri is so different from the Terran that our equipment couldn't possibly fit. Chances of injury would be too great, and the department would be liable. No. I'm sure it couldn't be allowed. Too much risk."

"We would provide special protective equipment," Remjhard said quietly. "We would never risk our own offspring if we did not feel it safe."

Hill started to say something, stopped, and looked to De Angelis for help. He had run out of good reasons why the Brish'diri couldn't enter the league.

Jack smiled. "One problem remains, however," he said, coming to the director's rescue. "A bureaucratic snag, but a difficult one. Registration for the league closed on Tuesday. We've already had to turn away several teams, and if we make an exception in your case, well — " De Angelis shrugged. "Trouble. Complaints. I'm sorry, but we must apply the same rule to all."

Remjhard rose slowly from his seat, and picked up the roster from where it lay on the desk. "Of course," he said gravely. "All must follow the regulations. Perhaps next year we will be on time." He made a formal half-bow to Hill, turned, and walked from the office.

When he was sure the Brish'dir was out of earshot, Hill gave a heartfelt sigh and swiveled to face De Angelis. "That was close," he said. "Christ, a Baldy football team. Half the people in this town lost sons in the Brish'diri War, and they still hate them. I can imagine the complaints."

Hill frowned. "And you! Why couldn't you just get rid of him right away instead of putting me through that?"

De Angelis grinned. "Too much fun to pass up," he said. "I wondered if you'd figure out the right way to discourage him. The Brish'diri have an almost religious respect for laws, rules, and regulations. They wouldn't think of doing anything that would force someone to break a rule. In their culture, that's just as bad as breaking a rule yourself."

Hill nodded. "I would have remembered that myself if I wasn't so paralyzed at the thought of a Brish'diri football team in one of our leagues," he said limply. "And now that that's over with, I want to talk to you about that gravity grid. Do you think there's any way we could rent one instead of buying it outright? The Council might go for that. And I was thinking — "

A little over three hours later, Hill was signing some equipment requisitions when the office door slid open to admit a brawny. dark-haired man in a nondescript gray suit.

"Yes?" the director said, a trifle impatiently. "Can I help you?"

The dark-haired man flashed a government ID as he took a seat. "Maybe you can. But you certainly haven't so far, I'll tell you that much. My name's Tomkins. Mac Tomkins. I'm from the Federal E.T. Relations Board."

Hill groaned. "I suppose it's about that Brish'diri mess this morning," he said, shaking his head in resignation.

"Yes," Tomkins cut in at once. "We understand that the Brish'diri wanted to register some of their youngsters for a local football league. You forbade it on a technicality. We want to know why."

"Why?," said Hill incredulously, staring at the government man. "*Why?* For God sakes, the Brish'diri War was only over seven years ago. Half of those boys on our football teams had brothers killed by the Bulletbrains. Now you want me to tell them to play football with the subhuman monsters of seven years back? They'd run me out of town."

Tomkins grimaced, and looked around the room. "Can that door be locked?" he asked, pointing to the door he had come in by.

"Of course," Hill replied, puzzled.

"Lock it then," Tomkins said. Hill adjusted the appropriate control on his desk.

"What I'm going to tell you should not go beyond this room," Tomkins began.

Hill cut him off with a snort. "Oh, come now, Mr. Tomkins. I may be only a small-time sports official, but I'm not stupid. You're hardly about to import some galaxy-shattering top secret to a man you met a few seconds ago.

Tomkins smiled. "True. The information's not secret, but it is a little ticklish. We would prefer that every Joe in the street doesn't know about it."

"Alright, I'll buy that for now. Now what's this all about? I'm sorry if I've got no patience with subtlety, but the most difficult problem I've handled in the last year was the protest in the championship game in the Class B Soccer League. Diplomacy just isn't my forte."

"I'll be brief," Tomkins said. "We — E.T. Relations, that is — we want you to admit the Brish'diri team into your football league."

"You realize the furor it would cause?" Hill asked.

"We have some idea. In spite of that, we want them admitted."

"Why, may I ask?"

"Because of the furor if they aren't admitted." Tomkins paused to stare at Hill for a second, then apparently reached a decision of some sort and continued. "The Earth-Brishun War was a ghastly, bloody deadlock, although our propaganda men insist on pretending it was a great victory. No sane man on either side wants it resumed. But not everyone is sane."

The agent frowned in distaste. "There are elements among us who regard the Brish'diri — or the Bulletbrains, or Baldies, or what ever you want to call them — as monsters, even now, seven years after the killing has ended."

"And you think a Brish'diri football team would help to overcome the leftover hates?" Hill interrupted.

"Partially. But that's not the important part. You see, there is also an element among the Brish'diri that regards humans as subhuman — vermin to be wiped from the galaxy. They are a very virile, competitive race. Their whole culture stresses combat. The dissident element I mentioned will seize on your refusal to admit a Brish'diri team as a sign of fear, an admission of human inferiority. They'll use it to agitate for a resumption of the war. We don't want to risk giving them a propaganda victory like that. Relations are too strained as it is."

"But the Brish'dir I spoke to — " Hill objected. "I explained it all to him. A rule. Surely their respect for law — "

"Remjhard-nei is a leader of the Brish'diri peace faction. *He* personally will defend your position. But he and his son were disappointed by the refusal. They will talk. They already have been talking. And that means that eventually the war faction will get ahold of the story and turn it against us."

"I see. But what can I do at this point? I've already told Remjhard that registration closed Tuesday. If I understand correctly, his own morality would never permit him to take advantage of an exception now."

Tomkins nodded. "True. You can't make an exception. Just change the rule. Let in all the teams you refused. Expand the league."

Hill shook his head, wincing. "But our budget — it couldn't take it. We'd have more games. We'd need more time, more referees, more equipment."

Tomkins dismissed the problem with a wave of his hand. "The government is already buying the Brish'diri special football uniforms. We'd be happy to cover all your extra costs. You'd get a better recreational program for all concerned."

Hill still looked doubtful. "Well — "

"Moreover," Tomkins said, "we might be able to arrange a government grant or two to holster other improvements in your program. Now how about it?"

Hill's eyes sparkled with sudden, interest. "A grant? How big a grant? Could you swing a gravity grid?"

"No problem," said Tomkins. A slow grin spread across his face.

Hill returned the grin. "Then, mister, Starport's got itself a Brish'diri football team. But, oh, are they going to scream!" He flicked on the desk intercom. "Get Jack De Angelis in here," he ordered. "I've got a little surprise for him."

The sky above Starport Municipal Stadium was bleak and dreary on a windy Saturday morning a week later, but Hill didn't mind it at all. The Stadium force bubble kept out the thin, wet drizzle that had soaked him to the bones on the way to the game, and the weather fitted his mood beautifully.

Normally, Hill was far too busy to attend any of his department's sporting events. Normally *everyone* was too busy to attend the department's sporting events. The Rec Department leagues got fairly good coverage in the local newspaper, but they seldom drew many spectators. The record was something like 400 people for a championship game a few years ago.

Or rather, that *was* the record, Hill reminded himself. No more. The Stadium was packed today, in spite of the hour, the rain, and everything else. Municipal Stadium was never packed except for the traditional Thanksgiving Day football game between Starport High and its archrival Grissom City Prep. But today it was packed.

Hill knew why. It had been drilled into him the hard way after he had made the damn fool decision to let the Brish'diri into the league. The whole city was up in arms. Six local teams had withdrawn from the City League rather than play with the "inhuman monsters." The office switchboard had been flooded with calls daily, the vast majority of them angry denunciations of Hill. A city council member had called for his resignation.

And that, Hill reflected glumly, was probably what it would come to in the end. The local newspaper, which had always been hard-line conservative on foreign affairs, was backing the drive to force Hill out of office. One of its editorials had reminded him gleefully that Starport Municipal Stadium was dedicated to those who had given their lives in the Brish'diri War, and had screamed about "desecration." Meanwhile, on its sports pages, the paper had taken to calling the Brish'diri team "the Baldy Eagles."

Hill squirmed uncomfortably in his seat on the 50 yard line, and prayed silently that the game would begin, He could feel the angry stares on the back of his neck, and he had the uneasy impression that he was going to be hit with a rock any second now.

Across the field, he could see the camera installation of one of the big 3V networks. All five of them were here, of course; the game had gotten planetwide publicity. The newsfax wires had also sent reporters, although they had seemed a little confused about what kind of a story this was. One had sent a political reporter, the other a sportswriter.

Out on the Stadium's artificial grass, the human team was running through a few plays and warming up. Their bright red uniforms were emblazoned with **KEN'S COMPUTER REPAIR** in white lettering, and they wore matching white helmets. They looked pretty good, Hill decided from watching them practice. Although they were far from championship caliber. Still, against a team that had never played football before, they should mop up.

De Angelis, wearing a pained expression and a ref's striped shirt, was out on the field talking to his officials. Hill was taking no chances with bad calls in this game. He made sure the department's best men were on hand to officiate.

Tomkins was also there, sitting in the stands a few sections away from Hill. But the Brish'diri were not. Remjhard wanted to attend, but E.T. Relations, on Hill's advice, had told him to stay at the mission. Instead, the game was being piped to him over closed circuit 3V.

Hill suddenly straightened in his seat. The Brish'diri team, which called itself the Kosg-Anjehn after a flying carnivore native to Brishun, had arrived, and the players were walking slowly out onto the field.

There was a brief instant of silence, and then someone in the crowd started booing. Others picked it up. Then others. The Stadium was filled with the boos. Although, Hill noted with relief, not everyone was joining in. Maybe there were some people who saw things his way.

The Brish'diri ignored the catcalls. Or seemed to, at any rate. Hill had never seen an angry Brish'dir, and was unsure how one would go about showing his anger.

The Kosg-Anjehn wore tight-fitting black uniforms, with odd-looking elongated silver helmets to cover their bullet-shaped heads. They looked like no football team Hill had ever seen. Only a handful of them stood over five feet, but they were all as squat and broad as a tackle for the Packers. Their arms and legs were thick and stumpy, but rippled with muscles that bulged in the wrong places. The helmeted heads, however, gave an impression of frailty, like eggshells ready to shatter at the slightest impact.

Two of the Brish'diri detached themselves from the group and walked over to De Angelis. Evidently they felt they didn't need a warm-up, and wanted to start immediately. De Angelis talked to them for an instant, then turned and beckoned to the captain of the human team.

"How do you think it'll go?"

Hill turned. It was Tomkins. The E.T. agent had struggled through the crowd to his side.

"Hard to say." the director replied. "The Brish'diri have never really played football before, so the odds are they'll lose. Being from a heavy gravity planet, they'll be stronger than the humans, so that might give them an edge. But they're also a lot slower from what I hear."

"I'll have to root them home," Tomkins said with the smile. "Bolster the cause of interstellar relations and all that."

Hill scowled. "*You* root them home if you like. I'm pulling for the humans. Thanks to you, I'm in enough trouble already. If they catch me rooting for the Brish'diri they'll tear me to shreds."

He turned his attention back to the field. The Computer-men had won the toss, and elected to receive. One of the taller Brish'diri was going back to kick off.

"Tuhgayh-dei," Tomkins provided helpfully. "The son of the mission's chief linguist." Hill nodded.

Tuhgayh-dei ran forward with a ponderous, lumbering gallop, nearly stopped when he finally reached the football, and slammed his foot into it awkwardly but hard. The ball landed in the upper tier of the stands, and a murmur went through the crowd.

"Pretty good," Tomkins said. "Don't you think?"

"Too good," replied Hill. He did not elaborate.

The humans took the ball on their twenty. The Computer-men went into a huddle, broke it with a loud clap, and ran to their positions. A ragged cheer went up from the stands.

The humans went down into the three-point stance. Their Brish'diri opponents did not. The alien linemen just stood there, hands dangling at their sides, crouching a little.

"They don't know much about football," Hill said. "But after that kickoff, I wonder if they have to."

The ball was snapped, and the quarterback for Ken's Computer Repair, a rangy ex-high school star named Sullivan, faded back to pass. The Brish'diri rushed forward in a crude blitz, and crashed into the human linemen.

An instant later, Sullivan was laying face-down in the grass, buried under three Brish'diri. The aliens had blown through the offensive line as if it didn't exist.

That made it second-and-fifteen. The humans huddled again, came out to another cheer, not quite so loud as the first one. The ball was snapped. Sullivan handed off to a beefy fullback, who crashed straight ahead.

One of the Brish'diri brought him down before he went half a yard. It was a clumsy tackle, around the shoulders. But the force of the contact knocked the fullback several yards in the wrong direction.

When the humans broke from their huddle for the third time the cheer could scarcely be heard. Again Sullivan tried to pass. Again the Brish'diri blasted through the line en masse. Again Sullivan went down for a loss.

Hill groaned. "This looks worse every minute," he said.

Tomkins didn't agree. "I don't think so. They're doing fine. What difference does it make who wins?"

Hill didn't bother to answer that.

There was no cheering when the humans came out in punt formation. Once more the Brish'diri put on a strong rush, but the punter got the ball away before they reached him.

It was a good, deep kick. The Kosg-Anjehn took over on their own twenty-five yard line. Marhdaln-nei, Remjhard's son, was the Brish'diri quarterback. On the first play from scrimmage, he handed off to a halfback, a runt built like a tank.

The Brish'diri blockers flattened their human opponents almost effortlessly, and the runt ploughed through the gaping hole, ran over two would-be tacklers, and burst into the clear. He was horribly slow, however, and the defenders finally brought him down from behind after a modest thirty-yard gain. But it took three people to stop him.

On the next play, Marhdaln tried to pass. He got excellent protection, but his receivers, trudging along at top speed, had defensemen all over them. And the ball, when thrown, went sizzling over the heads of Brish'diri and human alike.

Marhdaln returned to the ground again after that, and handed off to a runt halfback once more. This time he tried to sweep around end, but was hauled to the ground after a gain of only five yards by a quartet of human tacklers.

That made it third-and-five. Marhdaln kept to the ground. He gave the ball to his other halfback, and the brawny Brish'dir smashed up the middle. He was a little bit faster than the runt. When he got in the clear, only one man managed to catch him from behind. And one wasn't enough. The alien shrugged off the tackle and lumbered on across the goal line.

The extra point try went under the crossbar instead of over it. But it still nearly killed the poor guy in the stands who tried to catch the ball.

Tomkins was grinning. Hill shook his head in disgust. "This isn't the way it's supposed to go," he said, "They'll kill us if the Brish'diri win."

The kickoff went out of the stadium entirely this time. On the first play from the twenty, a Brish'diri lineman roared through the line and hit Sullivan just as he was handing off. Sullivan fumbled.

Another Brish'dir picked up the loose ball and carried it into the end zone while most of the humans were still lying on the ground.

"My god," said Hill, feeling a bit numb. "They're too strong. They're too damn strong. The humans can't cope with their strength. Can't stop them,"

"Cheer up," said Tomkins. "It can't get much worse for your side."

But it did. It got a lot worse.

On offense, the Brish'diri were well-nigh unstoppable. Their runners were all short on speed, but made up for it with muscle. On play after play, they smashed straight up in the middle behind a wall of blockers, flicking tacklers aside like bothersome insects.

And then Marhdaln began to hit on his passes. Short passes, of course. The Brish'diri lacked the speed to cover much ground. But they could outjump any human, and they snared pass after pass in the air. There was no need to worry about interceptions. The humans simply couldn't hang on to Marhdaln's smoking pitches.

On defense, things were every bit as bad. The Computer-men couldn't run against the Brish'diri line. And Sullivan seldom had time to complete a pass, for the alien rushers were unstoppable. The few passes he did hit on went for touchdowns; no Brish'diri could catch a human from behind. But those were few and far between.

When Hill fled the Stadium in despair at the half, the score was Kosg-Anjehn — 37, Ken's Computer Repair — 7.

The final score was 57-14. The Brish'diri had emptied their bench in the second half.

Hill didn't have the courage to attend the next Brish'diri game later in the week. But nearly everyone else in the city showed up to see if the Kosg-Anjehn could do it again.

They did. In fact, they did even better. They beat Anderson's Drugs by a lop-sided 61-9 score.

After the Brish'diri won their third contest, 43-17, the huge crowds began tapering off. The Starport Municipal Stadium was only three-quarters full when the Kosg-Anjehn rolled over the Stardusters, 38-0, and a mere handful showed up on a rainy Thursday afternoon to see the aliens punish the United Veterans Association, 51-6. And no one came after that.

For Hill, the Brish'diri win over the UVA-Sponsored team was the final straw. The local paper made a heyday out of that, going on and on about the "ironic injustice" of having the UVA slaughtered by the Brish'diri in a stadium dedicated to the dead veterans of the Brish'diri War. And Hill, of course, was the main villain in the piece.

The phone calls had finally let up by that point. But the mail had been flowing into his office steadily, and most of it was not very comforting. The harassed Rec director got a few letters of commendation and support, but the bulk of the flood speculated crudely about his ancestry or threatened his life and property.

Two more city councilmen had come out publicly in favor of Hill's dismissal after the Brish'diri defeated UVA. Several others on the council were wavering, while Hill's supporters, who backed him strongly in private, were afraid to say anything for the record. The municipal elections were simply too close, and none were willing to risk their political skins.

And of course the assistant director of recreation, next in line for Hill's Job, had wasted no time in saying *he* would certainly never have done such an unpatriotic thing.

With disaster piling upon disaster, it was only natural that Hill reacted with something less than enthusiasm when he walked into his office a few days after the fifth Kosg-Anjehn victory and found Tomkins sitting at his desk waiting for him.

"And what in the hell do you want now?" Hill roared at the E.T. Relations man.

Tomkins looked slightly abashed, and got up from the director's. chair. He had been watching the latest free-fall football results on the desk console while waiting for Hill to arrive.

"I've got to talk to you," Tomkins said. "We've got a problem."

"We've got lots of problems," Hill replied. He strode angrily to his desk, sat down, flicked off the console, and pulled a sheaf of papers from a drawer.

"This is the latest of them." he continued, waving the papers at Tomkins. "One of the kids broke his leg in the Starduster game. It happens all the time. Football's a rough game. You can't do anything to prevent it. On a normal case, the department would send a letter of apology to the parents, our insurance would pay for it, and everything would be forgotten.

"But not in this case. Oh, no. This injury was inflicted while the kid was playing against the Brish'diri. So his parents are charging negligence on our part and some the city. So our insurance company refuses to pay up. It claims the policy doesn't cover damage by inhuman, super-strong, alien monsters. Bah! How's that for a problem, Mr. Tomkins? Plenty more where that came from."

Tomkins frowned. "Very unfortunate. But my problem is a lot more serious than that. I — "Hill started to interrupt, but the E.T. Relations man waved him down. "No, please, hear me out. This is very important."

He looked around for a seat, grabbed the nearest chair, and pulled it up to the desk. "Our plans have backfired badly," he began. There has been a serious miscalculation — our fault entirely, I'm afraid. E.T. Relations failed to consider *all* the ramifications of this Brish'diri football team."

Hill fixed him with an iron stare. 'What's wrong now?"

"Well," Tomkins said awkwardly, "we knew that refusal to admit the Kosg-Anjehn into your league would be a sign of human weakness and fear to the Brish'diri war faction. But once you admitted them, we thought the problem was solved.

"It wasn't. We went wrong when we assumed that winning or losing would make no difference to the Brish'diri. To us, it was just a game. Didn't matter who won. After all, Brish'diri and Terrans would be getting to know each other, competing harmlessly on even terms. Nothing but good could come from it, we felt."

"So?" Hill interrupted. "Get to the point."

Tomkins shook his head sadly. "The point is, we didn't know the Brish'diri would win so *big*. And so *regularly*." He paused. "We — uh — we got a transmission late last night from one of our men on Brishun. It seems the Brish'diri war faction is using the one-sided football scores as propaganda to prove the racial inferiority of humans. They seem to be getting a lot of mileage out of it."

Hill winced. "So it was all for nothing. So I've subjected myself to all this abuse and endangered my career for absolutely nothing. Great! That was all I needed, I tell you."

"We still might be able to salvage something," Tomkins said. "That's why I came to see you. If you can arrange it for the Brish'diri to *lose*, it would knock holes in that superiority yarn and make the war faction look like fools. It would discredit them for quite awhile."

"And just how am I supposed to *arrange* for them to lose, as you so nicely put it? What do you think I'm running here anyway, professional wrestling?"

Tomkins just shrugged lamely. "I was hoping you'd have some ideas," he said.

Hill leaned forward, and flicked on his intercom. "Is Jack out there?" he asked. "Good. Send him in."

The lanky sports official appeared less than a minute later. "You're on top of this City football mess," Hill said. "What's the chances the Kosg-Anjehn will lose?"

De Angelis looked puzzled. "Not all that good, offhand," he replied. "They've got a damn fine team."

He reached into his back pocket and pulled out a notebook. "Let me check their schedule," he continued, thumbing through the pages. He stopped when he found the place.

"Well, the league's got a round-robin schedule, as you know. Every team plays every other team once, best record is champion. Now the Brish'diri are currently 5-0, and they've beaten a few of the better teams. We've got ten teams left in the league, so they've got four games left to play. Only two of those are with the weakest teams in the league, and the third opponent is only mediocre."

"And the fourth?," Hill said hopefully.

"That's your only chance. An outfit sponsored by a local tavern, the Blastoff Inn. Good team. Fast, strong. Plenty of talent. They're also 5-0, and should give the Brish'diri some trouble." De Angelis frowned. "But, to be frank, I've seen both teams, and I'd still pick the Brish'diri. That ground game of theirs is just too much." He snapped the notebook shut and pocketed it again.

"Would a close game be enough?" Hill said, turning to Tomkins again.

The E.T. Relations man shook his head. "No. They have to be beaten. If they lose, the whole season's meaningless. Proves nothing but that the two races can compete on roughly equal terms. But if they win, it looks like they're invincible, and our stature in Brish'diri eyes takes a nosedive."

"Then they'll have to lose, I guess," Hill said. His gaze shifted back to De Angelis. "Jack, you and me are going to have to do some hard thinking about how the Kosg-Anjehn can be beaten. And then we're going to call up the manager of the Blastoff Inn team and give him a few tips. You have any ideas?"

De Angelis scratched his head thoughtfully. "Well — " he began. "Maybe we — "

During the two weeks that followed, De Angelis met with the Blastoff Inn coach regularly to discuss plans and strategy, and supervised a few practice sessions. Hill, meanwhile, was fighting desperately to keep his job, and jotting down ideas on how to beat the Brish'diri during every spare moment.

Untouched by the furor, the Kosg-Anjehn won its sixth game handily, 40-7, and then rolled to devastating victories over the circuit's two cellar-dwellers. The margins were 73-0 and 62-7. That gave them an unblemished 8-0 ledger with one game left to play.

But the Blastoff inn team was also winning regularly, although never as decisively. It too would enter the last game of the season undefeated.

The local paper heralded the showdown with a sports page streamer on the day before the game. The lead opened, "The stakes will be high for the entire human race tomorrow at Municipal Stadium, when Blastoff Inn meets the Brish'diri Baldy Eagles for the championship of the Department of Recreation City Football League."

The reporter who wrote the story never dreamed how close to the truth he actually was.

The crowds returned to the Stadium for the championship game, although they fell far short of a packed house. The local paper was there too. But the 3V networks and the newsfax wires were long gone. The novelty of the story had worn off quickly.

Hill arrived late, just before game time. and joined Tomkins on the 50-yard line. The E.T. agent seemed to have cheered up somewhat. "Our guys looked pretty good during the warm-up," he told the director. "I think we've got a chance."

His enthusiasm was not catching, however. "Blastoff Inn might have a chance, but I sure don't," Hill said glumly. "The city council is meeting tonight to consider a motion calling for my dismissal. I have a strong suspicion that it's going to pass, no matter who wins this afternoon."

"Hmmmmm," said Tomkins. for want of anything better to say. "Just ignore the old fools. Look, the game's starting."

Hill muttered something under his breath and turned his attention back to the field. The Brish'diri had lost the toss once more, and the kickoff had once again soared out of the stadium. It was first-and-ten for the Blastoff Inn on its own twenty.

And at that point the script suddenly changed.

The humans lined up for their first play of the game but with a difference. Instead of playing immediately in back of the center, the Blastoff quarterback was several yards deep, in a shotgun formation.

The idea, Hill recalled, was to take maximum advantage of human speed, and mount a strong passing offense. Running against the Brish'diri was all but impossible, he and De Angelis had concluded after careful consideration. That meant an aerial attack, and the only way to provide that was to give the Blastoff quarterback time to pass. Ergo, the shotgun formation.

The hike from center was dead on target and the Blastoff receivers shot off downfield, easily outpacing the ponderous Brish'diri defensemen. As usual, the Kosg-Anjehn crashed through the line en masse, but they had covered only half the distance to the quarterback before he got off the pass.

It was a long bomb, a psychological gambit to shake up the Brish'diri by scoring on the first play of the game. Unfortunately, the pass was slightly overthrown.

Hill swore.

It was now second-and-ten. Again the humans lined up in a shotgun offense, and again the Blastoff quarterback got off the pass in time. It was a short, quick pitch to the sideline, complete for a nine yard gain. The crowd cheered lustily.

Hill wasn't sure what the Brish'diri would expect on third-and-one. But whatever it was, they didn't get it. With the aliens still slightly off balance, Blastoff went for the bomb again.

This time it was complete. All alone in the open, the fleet human receiver snagged the pass neatly and went all the way in for the score. The Brish'diri never laid a hand on him.

The crowd sat in stunned silence for a moment when the pass was caught. Then. when it became clear that there was no way to prevent the score, the cheering began, and peaked slowly to an ear-splitting roar. The stadium rose to its feet as one, screaming wildly.

For the first time all season, the Kosg-Anjehn trailed. A picture perfect place kick made the score 7-0 in favor of Blastoff Inn.

Tomkins was on his feet, cheering loudly. Hill, who had remained seated, regarded him dourly. "Sit down," he said. "The games not over yet."

The Brish'diri soon underlined that point. No sooner did they take over the ball then they came pounding back upfield, smashing into the line again and again. The humans alternated between a dozen different defensive formations. None of them seemed to do any good. The Brish'diri steamroller ground ahead inexorably.

The touchdown was an anticlimax. Luckily, however, the extra point try failed. Tuhgayh-dei lost a lot of footballs, but he had still not developed a knack for putting his kicks between the crossbars.

The Blastoff offense took the field again. They looked determined. The first play from scrimmage was a short pass over the middle, complete for fifteen yards. Next came a tricky double pass. Complete for twelve yards.

On the following play, the Blastoff fullback tried to go up the middle. He got creamed for a five yard loss.

"If they stop our passing, we're dead," Hill said to Tomkins, without taking his eyes off the field.

Luckily, the Blastoff quarterback quickly gave up on the idea of establishing a running game. A prompt return to the air gave the humans another first down. Three plays later, they scored. Again the crowd roared.

Trailing now 14-6, the Brish'diri once more began to pound their way upfield. But the humans, elated by their lead, were a little tougher now. Reading the Brish'diri offense with confident precision, the defensemen began gang-tackling the alien runners.

The Kosg-Anjehn drive slowed down, then stalled. They were forced to surrender the ball near the 50-yard line.

Tomkins started pounding Hill on the back. "You did it," he said. "We stopped them on offense too. We're going to win."

"Take it easy," Hill replied. 'That was a fluke. Several of our men just happened to be in the right place at the right time. It's happened before. No one ever said the Brish'diri scored every time they got the ball. Only most of the time."

Back on the field, the Blastoff passing attack was still humming smoothly. A few accurate throws put the humans on the Kosg-Anjehn's thirty.

And then the aliens changed formations. They took several men off the rush, and put them on pass defense. They started double-teaming the Blastoff receivers. Except it wasn't normal double-teaming. The second defender was playing far back of the line of scrimmage. By the time the human had outrun the first Brish'diri, the second would be right on top of him.

"I was afraid of something like this," Hill said. "We're not the only ones who can react to circumstances."

The Blastoff quarterback ignored the shift in the alien defense, and stuck to his aerial game plan. But his first pass from the thirty, dead on target, was batted away by a Brish'dir defender who happened to be right on top of the play.

The same thing happened on second down. That made it third-and-ten. The humans called time out. There was a hurried conference on the sidelines.

When action resumed, the Blastoff offense abandoned the shotgun formation. Without the awesome Brish'diri blitz to worry about, the quarterback was relatively safe in his usual position.

There was a quick snap, and the quarterback got rid of the ball equally quickly, an instant before a charging Brish'dir bore him to the ground. The halfback who got the handoff streaked to the left in an end run.

The other Brish'diri defenders lumbered towards him en masse to seal shut the sideline. But just as he reached the sideline, still behind the line of scrimmage, the Blastoff halfback handed off to a teammate streaking right.

A wide grin spread across Hill's face. A reverse!

The Brish'diri were painfully slow to change directions. The human swept around right end with ridiculous ease and shot upfield, surrounded by blockers. The remaining Brish'diri closed in. One or two were taken out by team blocks. The rest found it impossible to lay their hands on the swift, darting runner. Dodging this way and that, he wove a path neatly between them and looped into the endzone.

Once more the stadium rose to its feet. This time Hill stood up, too.

Tomkins was beaming again. "Ha!" he said. "I thought you were the one who said we couldn't run against them."

"Normally we can't," the director replied. "There's no way to run over or through them, so runs up the middle are out. End runs are better, but if they're in their normal formation, that too is a dreary prospect. There is no way a human runner can get past a wall of charging Brish'diri.

"However, when they spread out like they just did, they give us an open field to work with. We can't go over or through them, no, but we sure as hell can go *between* them when they're scattered all over the field. And Blastoff Inn has several excellent open-field runners."

The crowd interrupted him with another roar to herald a successful extra point conversion. It was now 21-6.

The game was far from over, however. The human defense was not nearly as successful on the next series of downs. Instead of relying exclusively on the running game, Marhdaln-nei kept his opponents guessing with some of his patented short, hard pop passes.

To put on a more effective rush, the Blastoff defense spread out at wide intervals. The offensive line thus opened up, and several humans managed to fake out slower Brish'diri blockers and get past them to the quarterback. Marhdaln was even thrown for a loss once.

But the Blastoff success was short-lived. Marhdaln adjusted quickly. The widely spread human defense, highly effective against the pass, was a total failure against the run. The humans were too far apart to gang-tackle. And there was no way short of mass assault to stop a Brish'dir in full stride.

After that there was no stopping the Kosg-Anjehn, as Marhdaln alternated between the pass and the run according to the human defensive formation. The aliens marched up-field quickly for their second touchdown.

This time, even the extra point was on target.

The Brish'diri score had taken some of the steam out of the crowd, but the Blastoff Inn offense showed no signs of being disheartened when they took the field again. With the aliens back in their original blitz defense, the human quarterback fell back on the shotgun once more.

His first pass was overthrown, but the next three in a row were dead on target and moved Blastoff to the Kosg-Anjehn forty. A running play, inserted to break the monotony, ended in a six yard loss. Then came another incomplete pass. The toss was perfect, but the receiver dropped the ball.

That made it third-and-ten, and a tremor of apprehension went through the crowd. Nearly everyone in the stadium realized that the humans had to keep scoring to stay in the game.

The snap from center was quick and clean. The Blastoff quarterback snagged the ball, took a few unhurried steps backward to keep at a safe distance from the oncoming Brish'diri rushers, and tried to pick out a receiver. He scanned the field carefully. Then he reared back and unleashed a bomb.

It looked like another touchdown. The human had his alien defender beaten by a good five yards and was still gaining ground. The pass was a beauty.

But then, as the ball began to spiral downward, the Brish'diri defender stopped suddenly in mid-stride. Giving up his hopeless chase, he craned his head around to look for the ball, spotted it, braced himself — and jumped.

Brish'diri leg muscles, evolved for the heavy gravity of Brishun, were far more powerful than their human counterparts. Despite their heavier bodies, the Brish'diri could easily outjump any human. But so far they had only taken advantage of that fact to snare Marhdaln's pop passes.

But now, as Hill blinked in disbelief the Kosg-Anjehn defenseman leaped at least five feet into the air to meet the descending ball in mid-air and knock it aside with a vicious backhand slap.

The stadium moaned.

Forced into a punting situation, Blastoff Inn suddenly seemed to go limp. The punter fumbled the snap from center, and kicked the ball away when he tried to pick it up. The Brish'dir who picked it up got twenty yards before be was brought down.

The human defense this time put up only token resistance as Marhdaln led his team downfield on a series of short passes and devastating runs.

It took the Brish'diri exactly six plays to narrow the gap to 21-19. Luckily, Tuhgayh missed another extra point.

There was a loud cheer when the Blastoff offense took the field again. But right from the first play after the kickoff, it was obvious that something had gone out of them.

The human quarterback, who had been giving a brilliant performance, suddenly became erratic. To add to his problems, the Brish'diri were suddenly jumping all over the field.

The alien kangaroo pass defense had several severe limitations. It demanded precise timing and excellent reflexes on the part of the jumpers, neither of which was a Brish'diri forte. But it was a disconcerting tactic that the Blastoff quarterback had never come up against before. He didn't know quite how to cope with it.

The humans drove to their own forty, bogged down, and were forced to punt. The Kosg-Anjehn promptly marched the ball back the other way and scored. For the first time in the game, they led.

The next Blastoff drive was a hit more successful, and reached the Brish'diri twenty before it ground to a halt. The humans salvaged the situation with a field goal.

The Kosg-Anjehn rolled up another score, driving over the goal line just seconds before the half ended.

The score stood at 31-24 in favor of the Brish'diri.

And there was no secret about the way the tide was running.

It had grown very quiet in the stands.

Tomkins, wearing a worried expression, turned to Hill with a sigh, "Well, maybe we'll make a comeback in the second half. We're only down seven. That's not so bad."

"Maybe," Hill said doubtfully. "But I don't think so. They've got all the momentum. I hate to say so, but I think we're going to get run out of the stadium in the second half."

Tomkins frowned. "I certainly hope not. I'd hate to see what the Brish'diri war faction would do with a really lopsided score. Why, they'd — " He stopped, suddenly aware that Hill wasn't paying the slightest hit of attention. The director's eyes had wandered back to the field.

"Look," Hill said, pointing. "By the gate. Do you see what I see?"

"It looks like a car from the trade mission," the E.T. agent said, squinting to make it out.

"And who's that getting out?"

Tomkins hesitated. "Remjhard-nei," he said at last.

The Brish'dir climbed smoothly from the low-slung black vehicle, walked a short distance across the stadium grass, and vanished through the door leading to one of the dressing rooms.

"What's he doing here?" Hill asked. "Wasn't he supposed to stay away from the games?"

Tomkins scratched his head uneasily. "Well, that's what we advised. Especially at first, when hostility was at its highest. But he's not a *prisoner*, you know. There's no way we could force him to stay away from the games if he wants to attend."

Hill was frowning. "Why should he take your advice all season and suddenly disregard it now?"

Tomkins shrugged. "Maybe he wanted to see his son win a championship."

"Maybe. But I don't think so. There's something funny going on here."

By the time the second half was ready to begin, Hill was feeling even more apprehensive. The Kosg-Anjehn had taken the fields a few minutes earlier, but Remjhard had not reappeared. He was still down in the alien locker room.

Moreover, there was something subtly different about the Brish'diri as they lined up to receive the kickoff. Nothing drastic. Nothing obvious. But somehow the atmosphere was changed. The aliens appeared more carefree, more relaxed. Almost as if they had stopped taking their opponents seriously.

Hill could sense the difference. He'd seen other teams with the same sort of attitude before, in dozens of other contests. It was the attitude of a team that already knows how the game is going to come out. The attitude of a team that knows it is sure to win — or doomed to lose.

The kickoff was poor and wobbly. A squat Brish'dir took it near the thirty and headed upfield. Two Blastoff tacklers met him at the thirty-five.

He fumbled.

The crowd roared. For a second the ball rolled loose on the stadium grass. A dozen hands reached for it, knocking it this way and that. Finally, a brawny Blastoff lineman landed squarely on top of it and trapped it beneath him.

And suddenly the game turned around again.

"I don't believe it," Hill said. "That was it. The break we needed. After that touchdown pass was knocked aside, our team just lost heart. But now, after this, look at them. We're back in this game."

The Blastoff offense raced onto the field, broke their huddle with an enthusiastic shout, and lined up. It was first-and-ten from the Brish'diri twenty-eight.

The first pass was deflected off a bounding Brish'dir. The second, however, went for a touchdown.

The score was tied.

The Kosg-Anjehn held onto the kickoff this time. They put the ball in play near the twenty-five.

Marhdaln opened the series of downs with a pass. No one, human or Brish'diri, was within ten yards of where it came down. The next play was a run. But the Kosg-Anjehn halfback hesitated oddly after he took the handoff. Given time to react, four humans smashed into him at the line of scrimmage. Marhdaln went back to the air. The pass was incomplete again.

The Brish'diri were forced to punt.

Up in the stands, Tomkins was laughing wildly. He began slapping Hill on the back again. "Look at that! Not even a first down. We held them. And you said they were going to run us out of the stadium."

A strange half-smile danced across the director's face. "Ummm," he said. "So I did." The smile faded.

It was a good, solid punt, but Blastoff's deep man fielded it superbly and ran it back to the fifty. From there, it took only seven plays for the human quarterback, suddenly looking cool and confident again, to put the ball in the end zone.

Bouncing Brish'diri had evidently ceased to disturb him. He simply threw the ball through spots where they did not happen to be bouncing.

This time the humans missed the extra point. But no one cared. The score was 37-31. Blastoff Inn was ahead again.

And they were ahead to stay. No sooner had the Kosg-Anjehn taken over again then Marhdaln threw an interception. It was the first interception he had thrown all season.

Naturally, it was run back for a touchdown.

After that, the Brish'diri seemed to revive a little. They drove three-quarters of the way down the field, but then they bogged down as soon as they got within the shadow of the goalposts. On fourth-and-one from the twelve yard line, the top Brish'dir runner slipped and fell behind the line of scrimmage.

Blastoff took over. And scored.

From then on, it was more of the same.

The final score was 56-31. The wrong team had been run out of the stadium.

Tomkins, of course, was in ecstasy. "We did it. I knew we could do it. This is perfect, just perfect. We humiliated them. The war faction will be totally discredited now. They'll never be able to stand up under the ridicule." He grinned and slapped Hill soundly on the back once again.

Hill winced under the blow, and eyed the E.T. man dourly. "There's something funny going on here. If the Brish'diri had played all season the way they played in the second half, they never would have gotten this far. Something happened in that locker room during the halftime."

Nothing could dent Tomkins' grin, however. "No, no," he said. "It was the fumble. That was what did it. It demoralized them, and they fell apart. They just clutched, that's all. It happens all the time."

"Not to teams this good it doesn't," Hill replied. But Tomkins wasn't around to hear. The E.T. agent had turned abruptly and was weaving his way through the crowd, shouting something about being right back.

Hill frowned and turned back to the field. The stadium was emptying quickly. The Rec director stood there for a second, still looking puzzled. Then suddenly he vaulted the low fence around the field, and set off across the grass.

He walked briskly across the stadium and down into the visitor's locker room. The Brish'diri were changing clothes in sullen silence, and filing out of the room slowly to the airbus that would carry them back to the trade mission.

Remjhard-nei was sitting in a corner of the room.

The Brish'dir greeted him with a slight nod. "Director Hill. Did you enjoy the game? It was a pity our half-men failed in their final test. But they still performed creditably, do you not think?"

Hill ignored the question. "Don't give me the bit about failing, Remjhard. I'm not as stupid as I look. Maybe no one else in the stadium realized what was going on out there this afternoon, but I did. You didn't lose that game. You threw it deliberately. And I want to know why!"

Remjhard stared at Hill for a long minute. Then, very slowly, he rose from the bench on which he was seated. His face was blank and expressionless, but his eyes glittered in the dim light.

Hill suddenly realized that they were alone in the locker room. Then he remembered the awesome Brish'diri strength, and took a hasty step backwards away from the alien.

"You realize," Remjhard said gravely, "that it is a grave insult to accuse a Brish'dir of dishonorable conduct?"

The emissary took another careful look around the locker room to make sure the two of them were alone. Then he took another step towards Hill.

And broke into a wide smile when the director, edging backwards, almost tripped over a locker.

"But, of course, there is no question of dishonor here," the alien continued. "Honor is too big for a half-man's play. And, to be sure, in the rules that you furnished us, there was no provision requiring partic-ipants to — " He paused " — to play at their best, shall we say?" .

Hill, untangling himself from the locker, sputtered. "But there are unwritten rules, traditions. This sort of thing simply is not sportin'."

Remjhard was still smiling. "To a Brish'dir, there is nothing as meaningless as an unwritten rule. It is a contradiction in terms, as you say."

"But *why!*" said Hill. "That's what I can't understand. Everyone keeps telling me that your culture is virile, competitive, proud. Why should you throw the game? Why should you make yourselves look bad? *Why?*"

Remjhard made an odd gurgling noise. Had he been a human, Hill would have thought he was choking. Instead, he assumed he was laughing.

"Humans amuse me," the Brish'dir said at last. "You attach a few catch phrases to a culture, and you think you understand it. And, if something disagrees with your picture, you are shocked.

"I am sorry, Director Hill. Cultures are not that simple. They are very complex mechanisms. A word like pride does not describe everything about the Brish'diri.

"Oh, we are proud. Yes. And competitive. Yes. But we are also intelligent. And our values are flexible enough to adjust to the situation at hand."

Remjhard paused again, and looked Hill over carefully. Then he decided to continue. "This football of yours is a fine game, Director Hill. I told you that once before. I mean it. It is very enjoyable, a good exercise of mind and body.

"But it is only a game. Competing in games is important, of course. But there are larger competitions. More important ones. And I am intelligent enough to know which one gets our first priority.

"I received word from Brishun this afternoon about the use to which the Kosg-Anjehn victories were being put. Your friend from Extraterrestrial Relations must have told you that I rank among the leaders of the Brish'diri Peace Party. I would not be here on Earth otherwise. None of our opponents are willing to work with humans whom they consider animals.

"Naturally I came at once to the stadium and informed our halfmen that they must lose. And they, of course, complied. They too realize that some competitions are more important than others.

"For in losing, we have won. Our opponents on Brishun will not survive this humiliation. In the next Great Choosing many will turn against them. And I, and others at the mission, will profit. And the Brish'diri will profit.

"Yes, Director Hill," Remjhard concluded, still smiling. "We are a competitive race. But competition for control of a world takes precedence over a football game."

Hill was smiling himself by now. Then be began to laugh. "Of course," he said. "And when I think of the ways we pounded our heads out to think of strategies to beat you. When all we had to do was tell you what was going on." He laughed again.

Remjhard was about to add something when suddenly the locker room door swung open and Tomkins stalked in. The E.T. agent was still beaming.

"Thought I'd find you here, Hill," he began. "Still trying to investigate those conspiracy theories of yours, eh?" He chuckled and winked at Remjhard.

"Not really," Hill replied. "It was a harebrained theory. Obviously it was the fumble that did it."

"Of course," Tomkins said. "Glad to hear it. Anyway, I've got good news for you."

"Oh? What's that? That the world is saved? Fine. But I'm still out of a job come tonight."

"Not at all," Tomkins replied. "That's what my call was about. We've got a job for you. We want you to join E.T. Relations."

Hill looked dubious. "Come now," he said. "Me? An E.T. agent? I don't know the first thing about it. I'm a small-time local bureaucrat and sports official. How am I supposed to fit into E.T. Relations?"

"As a sports director," Tomkins replied. "Ever since this Brish'diri thing broke, we've been getting dozens of requests from other alien trade missions and diplomatic stations on Earth. They all want a crack at it too. So, to promote good will and all that, we're going to set up a program. And we want you to run it. At double your present salary, of course."

Hill thought about the difficulties of running a sports program for two dozen wildly different types of extraterrestrials.

Then he thought about the money he'd get for doing it.

Then he thought about the Starport City Council.

"Sounds like a fine idea," he said. "But tell me. That gravity grid you were going to give to Starport — is that transferable too?"

"Of course," Tomkins said.

"Then I accept." He glanced over at Remjhard. "Although I may live to regret it when I see what the Brish'diri can do on a basketball court."

Evanston, Illinois
December, 1970

George R.R. Martin

The Exit to San Breta

It was the highway that first caught my attention. Up to that night, it had been a perfectly normal trip. It was my vacation, and I was driving to L.A. through the Southwest, taking my own sweet time about it. That was nothing new, I'd done it several times before.

Driving is my hobby. Or cars in general, to be precise. Not many people take the time to drive anymore. It's just too slow for most. The automobile's been pretty much obsolete since they started mass-producing cheap copters back in '93. And whatever life it had left in it was knocked out by the invention of the personal gravpak.

But it was different when I was a kid. Back then, everybody had a car, and you were considered some sort of a social freak if you didn't get your driver's license as soon as you were old enough. I got interested in cars when I was in my late teens, and have stayed interested ever since.

Anyway, when my vacation rolled around, I figured it was a chance to try out my latest find. It was a great car, an English sports model from the late '70s. Jaguar XKL. Not one of the classics, true, but a nice car all the same. It handled beautifully.

I was doing most of my traveling at night, as usual. There's something special about night driving. The old, deserted highways have an atmosphere about them in the starlight, and you can almost see them as they once were — vital and crowded and full of life, with cars jammed bumper to bumper as far as the eye could see.

Today, there's none of that. Only the roads themselves are left, and most of them are cracked and overgrown with weeds. The states can't bother taking care of them anymore — too many people objected to the waste of tax money. But ripping them up would be too expensive. So they just sit, year after year, slowly falling apart. Most of them are still driveable, though; they built their roads well back in the old days.

There's still some traffic. Car nuts like me, of course. And the hovertrucks. They can ride over just about anything, but they can go faster over flat surfaces. So they stick to the old highways pretty much.

It's kind of awesome whenever a hovertruck passes you at night. They do about two hundred or so, and no sooner do you spot one in your rear-view mirror then it's on top of you. You don't see much — just a long silver blur, and a shriek as it goes by. And then you're alone again.

Anyway, I was in the middle of Arizona, just outside San Breta, when I first noticed the highway. I didn't think much of it then. Oh, it was unusual all right, but not that unusual.

The highway itself was quite ordinary. It was an eight-lane freeway, with a good, fast surface, and it ran straight from horizon to horizon. At night, it was like a gleaming black ribbon running across the white sands of the desert.

No, it wasn't the highway that was unusual. It was its condition. At first, I didn't really notice. I was enjoying myself too much. It was a clear, cold night, and the stars were out, and the Jag was riding beautifully.

Riding *too* beautifully. That's when it first dawned on me. There were no bumps, no cracks, no potholes. The road was in prime condition, almost as if it had just been built. Oh, I'd been on good roads before. Some of them just stood up better than others. There's a section outside Baltimore that's superb, and parts of the L.A. freeway system are quite good.

But I'd never been on one this good. It was hard to believe a road could be in such good shape, after all those years without repair.

And then there were the lights. They were all on, all bright and clear. None of them were busted. None of them were out, or blinking. Hell, none of them were even dim. The road was beautifully lighted.

After that, I began to notice other things. Like the traffic signs. Most places, the traffic signs are long gone, removed by souvenir hunters or antique collectors as a reminder of an older, slower America. No one replaces them — they aren't needed. Once in awhile you'll come across one that's been missed, but there's never anything left but an oddly shaped, rusted hunk of metal.

But this highway had traffic signs. Real traffic signs. I mean, ones you could read. Speed limit signs, when no one's observed a speed limit in years. Yield signs, when there's seldom any other traffic to yield to. Turn signs, exit signs, caution signs — all kinds of signs. And all as good as new.

But the biggest shock was the lines. Paint fades fast, and I doubt that there's a highway in America where you could still make out the white lines in a speeding car. But you could on this one. The lines were sharp and clear, the paint fresh, the eight lanes clearly marked.

Oh, it was a beautiful highway all right. The kind they had back in the old days. But it didn't make sense. No road could stay in this condition all these years. Which meant someone had to be maintaining it. But who? Who would bother to maintain a highway that only a handful of people used each year? The cost would be enormous, with no return at all.

I was still trying to puzzle it out when I saw the other car.

I had just flashed by a big red sign marking Exit 76, the exit to San Breta, when I saw it. Just a white speck on the horizon, but I knew it had to be another motorist. It couldn't be a hovertruck, since I was plainly gaining on it. And that meant another car, and a fellow aficionado.

It was a rare occasion. It's damn seldom you meet another car on the open road. Oh, there are regular conventions, like the Fresno Festival on Wheels and the American Motoring Association's Annual Trafficjam. But they're too artificial for my tastes. Coming across another motorist on the highway is something else indeed.

I hit the gas, and speeded up to around one-twenty. The Jag could do better, but I'm not a nut on speed like some of my fellow drivers. And I was picking up ground fast. From the way I was gaining, the other car couldn't have been doing better than seventy.

When I got within range, I let go with a blast on my horn, trying to attract his attention. But he didn't seem to hear me. Or at least he didn't show any sign. I honked again.

And then, suddenly, I recognized the make.

It was an Edsel.

I could hardly believe it. The Edsel is one of the real classics, right up there with the Stanley Steamer and the Model T.

The few that are left sell for a rather large fortune nowadays.

And this was one of the rarest, one of those original models with the funny noses. There were only three or four like it left in the world, and those were not for sale at any price. An automotive legend, and here it was on the highway in front of me, as classically ugly as the day it came off the Ford assembly line.

I pulled alongside, and slowed down to keep even with it. I couldn't say that I thought much of the way the thing had been kept up. The white paint was chipped, the car was dirty, and there were signs of body rust on the lower part of the doors. But it was still an Edsel, and it could easily be restored. I honked again to get the attention of the driver, but he ignored me. There were five people in the car from what I could see, evidently a family on an outing. In the back, a heavy-set woman was trying to control two small kids who seemed to be fighting. Her husband appeared to be soundly asleep in the front seat, while a younger man, probably his son, was behind the wheel.

That burned me. The driver was very young, probably only in his late teens, and it irked me that a kid that age should have the chance to drive such a treasure. I wanted to be in his place.

I had read a lot about the Edsel; books of auto lore were full of it. There was never anything quite like it. It was the greatest disaster the field had ever known. The myths and legends that had grown up around its name were beyond number.

All over the nation, in the scattered dingy garages and gas depots where car nuts gather to tinker and talk, the tales of the Edsel are told to this day. They say they built the car too big to fit in most garages. They say it was all horsepower, and no brake. They call it the ugliest machine ever designed by man. They retell the old jokes about its name. And there's one famous legend that when you got it going fast enough, the wind made a funny whistling noise as it rushed around that hood.

All the romance and mystery and tragedy of the old automobile was wrapped up in the Edsel. And the stories about it are remembered and retold long after its glittering contemporaries are so much scrap metal in the junk yards.

As I drove along beside it, all the old legends about the Edsel came flooding back to me, and I was lost in my own nostalgia. I tried a few more blasts on my horn, but the driver seemed intent on ignoring me, so I soon gave up. Besides, I was listening to see if the hood really did whistle in the wind.

I should have realized by then how peculiar the whole thing was — the road, the Edsel, the way they were ignoring me. But I was too enraptured to do much thinking. I was barely able to keep my eyes on the road.

I wanted to talk to the owners, of course. Maybe even borrow it for a little while. Since they were being so damned unfriendly about stopping, I decided to follow them for a bit, until they pulled in for gas or food. So I slowed and began to tail them. I wanted to stay fairly close without tailgating, so I kept to the lane on their immediate left.

As I trailed them, I remember thinking what a thorough collector the owner must be. Why, he had even taken the time to hunt up some rare, old style license plates. The kind that haven't been used in years. I was still mulling over that when we passed the sign announcing Exit 77.

The kid driving the Edsel suddenly looked agitated. He turned in his seat and looked back over his shoulder, almost as if he was trying to get another look at the sign we had already left behind. And then, with no warning, the Edsel swerved right into my lane.

I hit the brakes, but it was hopeless, of course. Everything seemed to happen at once. There was a horrible squealing noise, and I remember getting a brief glimpse of the kid's terrified face just before the two cars made impact. Then came the shock of the crash.

The Jag hit the Edsel broadside, smashing into the driver's compartment at seventy. Then it spun away into the guard rail, and came to a stop. The Edsel, hit straight on, flipped over on its back in the center of the road. I don't recall unfastening my seat belt or scrambling out of my car, but I must have done so, because the next thing I remember I was crawling on the roadway, dazed but unhurt.

I should have tried to do something right away, to answer the cries for help that were coming from the Edsel. But I didn't. I was still shaken, in shock. I don't know how long I lay there before the Edsel exploded and began to burn. The cries suddenly became screams. And then there were no cries.

By the time I climbed to my feet, the fire had burned itself out, and it was too late to do anything. But I still wasn't thinking very clearly. I could see lights in the distance, down the road that led from the exit ramp. I began to walk towards them.

That walk seemed to take forever. I couldn't seem to get my bearings, and I kept stumbling. The road was very poorly lighted, and I could hardly see where I was going. My hands were scraped badly once when I fell down. It was the only injury I suffered in the entire accident.

The lights were from a small cafe, a dingy place that had marked off a section of the abandoned highway as its airlot. There were only three customers inside when I stumbled through the door, but one of them was a local cop.

"There's been an accident," I said from the doorway. "Somebody's got to help them."

The cop drained his coffee cup in a gulp, and rose from his chair. "A copter crash, mister?" he said. "Where is it?"

I shook my head. "N-no. No. Cars. A crash, a highway accident. Out on the old interstate." I pointed vaguely in the direction I had come.

Halfway across the room, the cop stopped suddenly and frowned. Everybody else laughed. "Hell, no one's used that road in twenty years, you sot." a fat man yelled from the corner of the room. "It's got so many potholes we use it for a golf course," he added, laughing loudly at his own joke.

The cop looked at me doubtfully. "Go home and sober up, mister," he said. "I don't want to have to run you in." He started back towards his chair.

I took a step into the room. "Dammit, I'm telling the truth," I said, angry now more than dazed. "And I'm not drunk. There's been a collision on the interstate, and there's people trapped up there in ... " My voice trailed off as it finally struck me that any help I could bring would be far too late.

The cop still looked dubious. "Maybe you ought to go check it out," the waitress suggested from behind the counter. "He might be telling the truth. There was a highway accident last year, in Ohio somewhere. I remember seeing a story about it on 3V."

"Yeah, I guess so," the cop said at last. "Let's go, buddy. And you better be telling the truth."

We walked across the airlot in silence, and climbed into the four-man police copter. As he started up the blades, the cop looked at me and said, "You know, if you're on the level, you and that other guy should get some kind of medal."

I stared at him blankly.

"What I mean, is you're probably the only two cars to use that road in ten years. And you still manage to collide. Now that had to take some doing, didn't it?" He shook his head ruefully. "Not everybody could pull off a stunt like that. Like I said, they ought to give you a medal."

The interstate wasn't nearly as far from the cafe as it had seemed when I was walking. Once airborne, we covered the distance in less than five minutes. But there was something wrong. The highway looked somehow different from the air.

And suddenly I realized why. It was darker. Much darker.

Most of the lights were out, and those that weren't were dim and flickering.

As I sat there stunned, the copter came down with a thud in the middle of a pool of sickly yellow light thrown out by one of the fading lamps. I climbed out in a daze, and tripped as I accidentally stepped into one of the potholes that pockmarked the road. There was a big clump of weeds growing in the bottom of this one, and a lot more rooted in the jagged network of cracks that ran across the highway.

My head was starting to pound. This didn't make sense. None of it made sense. I didn't know what the hell was going on.

The cop came around from the other side of the copter, a portable med sensor slung over one shoulder on a leather strap. "Let's move it," he said. "Where's this accident of yours?"

"Down the road, I think," I mumbled, unsure of myself. There was no sign of my car, and I was beginning to think we might be on the wrong road altogether, although I didn't see how that could be.

It was the right road, though. We found my car a few minutes later, sitting by the guard rail on a pitch black section of highway where all the lights had burnt out. Yes, we found my car all right.

Only there wasn't a scratch on it. And there was no Edsel.

I remembered the Jaguar as I had left it. The windshield shattered. The entire front of the car in ruins. The right fender smashed up where it had scraped along the guard rail. And here it was, in mint condition.

The cop, scowling, played the med sensor over me as I stood there staring at my car. "Well, you're not drunk," he said at last, looking up. "So I'm not going to run you in, even though I should. Here's what you're going to do, mister — you're going to get in that relic, and turn around, and get out of here as fast as you can. 'Cause if I *ever* see you around here again, you might have a real accident. Understand?"

I wanted to protest, but I couldn't find the words. What could I say that would possibly make sense? Instead, I nodded weakly. The cop turned with disgust, muttering something about practical jokes, and stalked back to his copter.

When he was gone, I walked up to the Jaguar and felt the front of it incredulously, feeling like a fool. But it was real. And when I climbed in and turned the key in the ignition, the engine rumbled reassuringly, and the headlights speared out into the darkness. I sat there for a long time before I finally swung the car out into the middle of the road, and made a U turn.

The drive back to San Breta was long and rough. I was constantly bouncing in and out of potholes. And thanks to the poor lighting and the treacherous road conditions, I had to keep my speed at a minimum.

The road was lousy. There was no doubt about that. Usually I went out of my way to avoid roads that were this bad. There was too much chance of blowing a tire.

I managed to make it to San Breta without incident, taking it slow and easy. It was two a.m. before I pulled into town. The exit ramp, like the rest of the road, was cracked and darkened. And there was no sign to mark it.

I recalled from previous trips through the area that San Breta boasted a large hobbyist garage and gas depot, so I headed there and checked my car with a bored young night attendant. Then I went straight to the nearest motel. A night's sleep, I thought, would make everything make sense.

But it didn't. I was every bit as confused when I woke up in the morning. More so, even. Now something in the back of my head kept telling me the whole thing had been a bad dream. I swatted down that tempting thought out of hand, and tried to puzzle it out.

I kept puzzling through a shower and breakfast, and the short walk back to the gas depot. But I wasn't making any progress. Either my mind had been playing tricks on me, or something mighty funny had been going on last night. I didn't want to believe the former, so I made up my mind to investigate the latter.

The owner, a spry old man in his eighties, was on duty at the gas depot when I returned. He was wearing an old-fashioned mechanic's coverall, a quaint touch. He nodded amiably when I checked out the Jaguar.

"Good to see you again," he said. "Where you headed this time?"

"L.A. I'm taking the interstate this time."

His eyebrows rose a trifle at that. "The interstate? I thought you had more sense than that. That road's a disaster. No way to treat a fine piece of machinery like that Jaguar of yours."

I didn't have the courage to try to explain, so I just grinned weakly and let him go get the car. The Jag had been washed, checked over, and gassed up. It was in prime shape.

I took a quick look for dents, but there were none to be found.

"How many regular customers you get around here?" I asked the old man as I was paying him. "Local collectors, I mean, not guys passing through."

He shrugged. "Must be about a hundred in the state. We get most of their business. Got the best gas and the only decent service facilities in these parts."

"Any decent collections?"

"Some," he said. "One guy comes in all the time with a Pierce-Arrow. Another fellow specializes in the forties. He's got a really fine collection. In good shape, too."

I nodded. "Anybody around here own an Edsel?" I asked.

"Hardly," he replied. "None of my customers have that kind of money. Why do you ask?"

I decided to throw caution on the road, so to speak. "I saw one last night on the road. Didn't get to speak to the owner, though. Figured it might be somebody local."

The old man's expression was blank, so I turned to get into the Jag. "Nobody from around here," he said as I shut the door. "Must've been another guy driving through. Funny meeting him on the road like that, though. Don't often get — "

Then, just as I was turning the key in the ignition, his jaw dropped about six feet. "Wait a minute!" he yelled. "You said you were driving on the old interstate. You saw an Edsel on the interstate?"

I turned the motor off again. "That's right," I said.

"Christ," he said. "I'd almost forgotten, it's been so long. Was it a white Edsel? Five people in it?"

I opened the door and got out again. "Yeah," I said. "Do you know something about it?"

The old man grabbed my shoulders with both hands. There was a funny look in his eyes. "You just saw it?" he said, shaking me. "Are you sure that's all that happened?"

I hesitated a moment, feeling foolish. "No," I finally admitted. "I had a collision with it. That is, I thought I had a collision with it. But then — " I gestured limply towards the Jaguar.

The old man took his hands off me, and laughed. "Again," he muttered. "After all these years."

"What do you know about this?" I demanded. "What the hell went on out there last night?"

He sighed. "C'mon," he said. "I'll tell you all about it."

"It was over forty years ago," he told me over a cup of coffee in a cafe across the street. "Back in the '70s. They were a family on a vacation outing. The kid and his father were taking shifts behind the wheel. Anyway, they had hotel reservations at San Breta. But the kid was driving, and it was late at night, and somehow he missed his exit. Didn't even notice it.

"Until he hit Exit 77, that is. He must've been really scared when he saw that sign. According to people who knew them, his father was a real bastard. The kind who'd give him a real hard time over something like that. We don't know what happened, but they figure the kid panicked. He'd only had his license about two weeks. Of all things, he tried to make a U turn and head back towards San Breta.

"The other car hit him broadside. The driver of that car didn't have his seat belt on. He went through the windshield, hit the road, and was killed instantly. The people in the Edsel weren't so lucky. The Edsel turned over and exploded, with them trapped inside. All five were burned to death."

I shuddered a little as I remembered the screams from the burning car. "But that was forty years ago, you said. How does that explain what happened to me last night?"

. "I'm getting to that," the old man said. He picked up a donut, dunked it into his coffee, and chewed on it thoughtfully. "Next thing was about two years later," he said at last. "Guy reported a collision to the cops. Collision with a Edsel. Late at night. On the interstate. The way he described it, it was an instant replay of the other crash. Only, when they got there, his car wasn't even dented. And there was no sign of the other car.

"Well, that guy was a local boy, so it was dismissed as a publicity stunt of some sort. But then, a year later, still another guy came in with the same story. This time he was from the east, couldn't possibly have heard of the first accident. The cops didn't know what to make of it.

"Over the years it happened again and again. There were a few things common to all the incidents. Each time it was late at night. Each time the man involved was alone in his car, with no other cars in sight. There were never any witnesses, as there had been for the first crash, the real one. All the collisions took place just beyond Exit 77, when the Edsel swerved and tried to make a U turn.

"Lots of people tried to explain it. Hallucinations, somebody said. Highway hypnosis, claimed somebody else. Hoaxes, one guy argued. But only one explanation ever made sense, and that was the simplest. The Edsel was a ghost. The papers made the most of that. 'The haunted highway,' they called the interstate."

The old man stopped to drain his coffee, and then stared into the cup moodily. "Well, the crashes continued right up through the years whenever the conditions were right. Until '93. And then traffic began slacking off. Fewer and fewer people were using the interstate. And there were fewer and fewer incidents." He looked up at me. "You were the first one in more than twenty years. I'd almost forgotten." Then he looked down again, and fell silent.

I considered what he had said for a few minutes. "I don't know," I said finally, shaking my head. "It all fits. But a ghost? I don't think I believe in ghosts. And it all seems so out of place.

"Not really," said the old man, looking up. "Think back on all the ghost stories you read as a kid. What did they all have in common?"

I frowned. "Don't know."

"Violent death, that's what. Ghosts were the products of murders and of executions, debris of blood and violence. Haunted houses were all places where someone had met a grisly end a hundred years before. But in twentieth century America, you didn't find the violent death in mansions and castles. You found it on the highways, the bloodstained highways where thousands died each year. A modern ghost wouldn't live in a castle or wield an axe. He'd haunt a highway, and drive a car. What could be more logical?"

It made a certain amount of sense. I nodded. "But why this highway? Why this car? So many people died on the roads. Why is this case special?"

The old man shrugged. "I don't know. What made one murder different from another? Why did only some produce ghosts? Who's to say? But I've heard theories. Some said the Edsel is doomed to haunt the highway forever because it is, in a sense, a murderer. It caused the accident, caused those deaths. This is a punishment."

"Maybe," I said doubtfully. "But the whole family? You could make a case that it was the kid's fault. Or even the father's, for letting him drive with so little experience. But what about the rest of the family? Why should they be punished?"

"True, true," the old man said. "I never bought that theory myself. I've got my own explanation." He looked me straight in the eye.

"I think they're lost," he said.

"Lost?" I repeated, and he nodded.

"Yes," he said. "In the old days, when the roads were crowded, you couldn't just turn around when you missed an exit. You had to keep going, sometimes for miles and miles, before you could find a way to get off the road and then get back on. Some of the cloverleafs they designed were so complicated you might never find your way back to your exit.

"And that's what happened to the Edsel, I think. They missed their exit, and now they can't find it. They've got to keep going. Forever." He sighed. Then he turned, and ordered another cup of coffee.

We drank in silence, then walked back to the gas depot. From there, I drove straight to the town library. It was all there, in the old newspapers on file. The details of the original accident, the first incident two years later, and the others, in irregular sequence. The same story, the same crash, over and over. Everything was identical, right down to the screams.

The old highway was dark and unlit that night when I resumed my trip. There were no traffic signs or white lines, but there were plenty of cracks and potholes. I drove slowly, lost in thought.

A few miles beyond San Breta I stopped and got out of the car. I sat there in the starlight until it was nearly dawn, looking and listening. But the lights stayed out, and I saw nothing.

Yet, around midnight, there was a peculiar whistling sound in the distance. It built quickly, until it was right on top of me, and then faded away equally fast.

It could have been a hovertruck off over the horizon somewhere, I suppose. I've never heard a hovertruck make that sort of noise, but still, it might have been a hovertruck.

But I don't think so.

I think it was the wind whistling through the nose of a rusty white ghost car, driving on a haunted highway you won't find on any road maps. I think it was the cry of a little lost Edsel, searching forever for the exit to San Breta.

Evanston, Illinois
April, 1970

Slide Show

Becker was the second speaker on the program. So he waited patiently.

The man who preceded him was a doctor, the head of some sort of charity clinic in one of the undercities. Tall, gaunt, and elderly, he spoke in a droning monotone, and kept running his fingers nervously through his sparse gray hair. The audience, some thirty-odd plump upperlevel matrons, was trying hard to pay attention, but Becker could sense their restlessness.

He didn't blame them. The presentation wasn't very effective. The doctor was telling medical horror stories, of undercity kids too poor to get decent hospital care, of needless deaths, and of long-cured diseases that still flourished down below. But his voice and his manner drained the punch from his words. And his slides, as well as being of the old-fashioned flat kind, were woefully ill chosen. Instead of moving photos of sick kids and undercity squalor, there were tedious pictures of the clinic and its staff, and then even blueprints of the proposed expansion.

Becker fought to stifle his own yawns. He felt a little bit sorry for the doctor. But only a little bit. Mostly he was still feeling sorry for himself.

Finally the doctor concluded his presentation with a halting, self-conscious plea for funds. The ladies gave him a round of polite applause. Then the chairwoman turned to Becker. "Any time you're ready to begin, Commander," she said pleasantly.

Becker rose from his contour chair and flashed a plastic smile. "Thank you," he said, as he made his way to the front of the plushly furnished living room. He waited a moment while the doctor cleared the old slide projector from the speaker's table, then swung up his portable holocaster to take its place. "You can take down the screen, ladies," he said. "My machine doesn't need it. And clear a circle around — oh — there." He pointed.

The women hastened to comply. Becker watched them and smiled at them. But inside, as usual, he felt only a vague distaste for the whole thing.

Even in the darkened living room, he cut a much more imposing figure than the doctor, and he knew it. He was big and broad of shoulder, and the soft gray uniform he wore hinted at his athletic build. He had a classic profile, a decisive chin, and thick black hair with just a touch of gray at the temples. And his steel-blue eyes were perfectly matched by the leather of his boots and belt, and the scarf that was casually knotted about his neck, under the open collar.

He looked very much like a SPACE recruiting poster. Of late, he'd regretted that. There were times, in recent years, when he'd have given anything for a hook nose, or a weak chin, or a receding hairline.

The holocaster was set up and humming, and the audience was waiting. Becker pushed his thoughts aside and thumbed the first slide.

In the circle the women had cleared, a cube of deeper darkness appeared. Darkness touched by stars. In one corner of the cube, Earth floated in silent blue-green majesty. But the center of the holograph was occupied by the ship. A fat silver cigar with a pot belly. Or a pregnant torpedo. There were many ways to describe it, and most of them had been used at one time or other.

Appreciative murmurs sounded from the audience. The holoslide was very real, and very striking. Becker, smiling, began smoothly. "This is the *Starwind*, one of the four SPACE starcruisers. The cruisers are stellar exploration ships, each with a crew of more than a hundred. Antispace jump-generators give them speeds many times that of light. These four frail ships, even as I speak, are carrying out the destiny of our race, and making man's age-old dream a reality. They are giving man the stars."

A practiced note of warm fondness crept into his voice, and he gestured at the silver shape afloat in the cube of black. "The *Starwind* was my ship," he said. "I was one small member of its crew during its last voyage. The slides you are about to see were taken during that voyage, a voyage that must rank among the most eventful in history. At least I'd say so." He smiled. "But then, I'm prejudiced."

His voice went on, detailing the size, design, and capabilities of the starcruiser and its crew. But he never got too technical, and there were always human touches and even hints of poetry to spice the presentation. Becker was too good at his job to bore *his* audience.

But even as his tongue went through its familiar paces, his mind was elsewhere. Out with the *Starwind*, in the sunless void of antispace. Out among the stars.

Where is she now? he thought. it's been almost a year now since she left. On this new trip. Without me. God knows what new worlds they've found while I'm stuck back here, feeding slick crap to little old ladies.

And there was an old bitterness to his thoughts, and an old longing in his stomach. And he grew aware, for the millionth time, of how much he hated what his life had become. But no hint of that crept into his smooth and warm and very professional speech.

He thumbed the holocaster, and the slide changed. Now the cube was blinding white, flecked with pits of pulsing black. And in the center of the projection was a thing that looked like a floating black octopus with glowing crimson veins.

"This is antispace," Becker said simply. "Or at least, this is how human eyes perceive antispace. The mathematicians are still trying to figure out its true nature. But when our jump-generators are on, this is how we see it. Almost like a photographic negative: white darkness, and sparkling black stars."

He paused, waiting for the inevitable question. And, as always, it came. "Commander," one of the women said, "what's that — that *thing* in the middle?"

He smiled. "You're not the only one who'd like to know," he said. "Whatever it is, it has no counterpart in normal space. Or at least, none that we can see. But it and things like it have been sighted several times by starcruisers in antispace. This slide, taken by the *Starwind* on its last voyage, is the best picture we've ever gotten of one. The creature — if it is a creature, which is still only a guess — is larger than a ship. By a good deal. But it seems to be harmless."

His voice was reassuring. His mind wondered. *Seems to be harmless, he thought. Yeah. But this one seemed to be after the ship. There are still arguments about whether it could have done anything if it caught us.*

Maybe this time it did. Maybe it got them this trip. I always said it was possible. Although the brass doesn't like to admit it. They're afraid that there'll be more budget cuts if they admit the program is dangerous. So they pretend that everything is safe and sane and bland out there, just like Earth. But it isn't, It isn't. Earth died of dullness years ago. Out there a man can still live, and feel, and dream.

He finished his spiel on antispace. His thumb moved. The cube of white vanished. Instead, a huge red globe burned in the center of the room.

"The *Starwind's* first stop was this red giant, still unnamed," Becker. told the women. "The crew nicknamed it Red Light. Because it stopped us. And because it is a red light, rather obviously. There were no planets, but we circled this star for a month, taking readings and sending in probes. The information we gathered should tell us a lot about stellar evolution."

I remember the first time I saw it, he was thinking as he spoke. *God! What a sight! My first star — Sol doesn't count. Wilson was on watch with me, but he was so damned busy taking readings he hardly bothered to look. Yet now he's out there again. And I'm here. There's no justice.*

A new slide. This time a mottled globe of orange and blue floated in the cube. Behind it, a bright yellow sun only slightly smaller than Sol.

Becker's voice became solemn. "Our first planetfall," he said. "And one of the greatest moments in human history. That is the planet we named Anthill. I'm sure you've read all about it by now, and seen the holoshows. But remember, for us it was new and strange and unexpected. This was humanity's first contact with another sentient race."

He thumbed for the next slide, one of the big ones. And when it flashed into view, there were the expected gasps of awe and admiration. The audience held its collective breath.

There was a vast, dark plain in the center of the cube, under a blood-red sky where scuttling black clouds obscured the alien sun. And rising from the plain, the towers. Thin and black and twining, twisting around each other, branching together and splitting again as they rose. They rose for nearly a mile, and all around them were the fragile web-like bridges that linked each to its brothers to make an intricate whole. A river ran through the middle of the city, and gave a clue to the vast size of the structure.

"One of their cities," Becker said. And the slight note of awe in his voice was real. "The home of more than a million of them, by our estimate. We called the builders Spiderants. Because there was something of the spider web in the cities that they built. And because — well, look."

The city vanished. The new slide was a closeup. A thick black strand looping through the cube. From it hung what looked like a four-foot-long ant. But appearances were deceiving.

There were a few murmurs of revulsion, even though most of the audience had probably seen photos before. Becker quelled them quickly. "Don't be fooled," he cautioned. "Despite what your eyes tell you, that's not a big ant. It's not even an insect. No exoskeleton, for example, although it looks like one at first glance. And that bug, we think, is quite intelligent. Their culture is very different from ours. But they have their own sense of beauty. Look at their city again."

He touched his holocaster. The hanging Spiderant vanished, and again the towers rose amid the carpet. The same angle. But this time, night. And it made a difference.

For the towers glowed.

Black in the reddish daylight, now they shone with a soft green light. A gorgeous glowing tracery against the darkness, they rose and rose and twisted, and every loop and web had a soft radiance all its own. Unbelievably intricate.

Becker, despite himself, still shivered at the slide. As he had shivered the first time he had seen it. In person. The holo woke dreams and memories, and made him hate his reality all the more.

They've taken this away from me, he thought. Forever. And given me — what? Nothing. Nothing I want, anyway.

But he said only, "And when the dawn comes ... " And the slide changed.

Now a reddish-yellow glow suffused the horizon behind the city, and the radiance of the towers was paler and dying. But something new, and just as awesome, had been added. For now the web of the city was aswarm with life. From each branch and strand and loop, Spiderants hung. Dangling even from the highest towers, nearly a mile above the ground. Clustered together, crawling over each other, yet somehow orderly. The whole city.

"They do this every dawn," Becker said. "And as their sun rises, they sing to it."

If you can call it song, he thought. *To my ears, that first night outside the landing craft, it was moaning. But weird. Rising and falling, up and down, for hours and hours. Even Wilson was awestruck. A million beings moaning together. Moaning a hymn to their sun.*

His thumb flicked down and up, and suddenly they were looking at a closeup of a web strand, laden heavily with Spiderants. Then it moved once more, and there was another view of the city. And after a while still another, and another. And all the time his voice went on, telling of this curious race and the little they had learned about it.

"The *Starwind* lay off Anthill for more than six months, sending down landing craft regularly," he said. "But the Spiderants are yet a race of unanswered questions. We still have not cracked their language, or determined how intelligent they really are. They seem to have no technology, as we know it. But they have — well — something else."

More views of the city came and went. And then of other, like cities. And some not so like — one that rose from the planet's brackish sea, and another where the towers jutted sideways to join two mountains in a twisted embrace.

"We had been there nearly a month before we were allowed up in the towers," Becker continued. "And even then it took us a while before we realized that the cities of the Spiderants were not built, but grown. Those towers are not buildings at all. They are plants: huge, incredibly hardy, incredibly complex. But, for all that, plants."

Lawrence was the first one to find that out, he remembered. *He was so damned excited when he got back that he was incoherent. But he had a right to be. It was our first clue. Before that, nothing made sense. Mile-high towers without machines were especially nonsensical. At least I thought so. Hell. I wonder where Lawrence is now.*

"When we discovered that, we began to wonder whether the Spiderants were intelligent after all. We got our answer when we branched out from the original landing site. This was one of the things we saw."

Red-black gloom suddenly filled the cube. Through it flapped something huge and green and triangular. Airborne and manta-like, with a long tail that split in half over and over again until it was a trail of thin, whiplike tendrils.

Far below it, a city. On top, Spiderants.

"This is a domesticated flying creature, almost as big as a Jet. It has to stay low, of course. And it doesn't have anything like an airplane's speed. But then, it doesn't pollute, either. And it gets around."

We got around faster, though, he thought. *I remember that afternoon I trailed one with a flyer. God, but those things are slow. Still, sort of majestic. And when those incredible wings flap with that funny rippling motion, it's something to see. Of course, that ass Donway had to try buzzing it. At least he's down, too. I couldn't stand it if he had gone out again.*

"What it is, of course," he was saying, "is another plant. A mobile, flying plant. When it's not transporting Spiderants, it flies up high to catch the sun. And it takes in nourishment through that tail structure, which is actually a root of sorts. A lot more complicated than anything any Earth plant has, of course."

He went through several more slides, showing other mantas, and then several of them in formation. "We think that these things were bred deliberately by the Spiderants. As were the towers. If the theory is right, then we've stumbled across the greatest biological engineers you could ever want. There's a lot to he learned from them, if we can crack the communications barrier. Anthill will be a regular stop for our starcruisers from now on."

Including the Starwind, *of course. She was scheduled to visit there again this mission. Maybe she's there now. Maybe Lawrence and Wilson and the rest are listening to the Spiderants right this moment. While I talk. Or sing. My performance doesn't much compare to theirs.*

He paused. "We spent more than six months on Anthill, and had to cut out much of our scheduled mission because of the overstay. But I think you'll agree that it was worth it" — with a smile, and the ladies in the audience mumbled agreement. "Finally, however, we had to move on. There was still time for one more stop before we turned around and began to jump for home."

He hit the button, and the last view of Anthill died. The halo that was born in its stead was spectacular. The matrons greeted it with gasps. They'd seen it before, on magazine covers and news broadcasts. But the holoslide captured more, much more.

"The world we called Storm," Becker said. Very softly. And then fell silent while they looked.

A surly green sea was wrestling the wind. From it rose the volcano: a trident in bluish-black stone whose triple peaks dripped fire. Smoke whipped up to mix with the glowering sky, lava coiled down to stream hissing into the ocean.

And *above* the volcano, literally leaning over it, a foam-flecked wall of green. Tidal wave? No. The Earth term didn't apply. This was bigger. More spectacular. Looming larger than the mountain itself, caught just seconds before impact.

"We couldn't land on Storm," Becker said. "There was no safe place to put down. But we sent manned probes into the atmosphere. This slide was taken by one of those probes." He smiled again and put a note of pride into his voice. But in with the pride, just barely, was a taste of anger. "I'm happy to tell you that it was my probe."

At least they can't take that away from me, he thought. They took away my stars, but they can't take Storm. I captured it with this picture. The essence of a planet. The soul. There, in a holocube. And it's mine.

And I was the only one to see the rest. Seconds after. When the wild-wave hit, and the volcano broke and shattered under the blow, and the world was full of storm and steam and fire. And I was the only one to watch ...

His voice was going on smoothly without him. "Storm is a young world," it was saying. "Still very much a toddler on the celestial scale. But it's a lusty kid. It's mostly water, and what land there is is still volcanic. Earthquakes and eruptions are daily events — and they give birth to things like the wildwave you see in the cube. Winds average hundreds of miles an hour, and the electrical displays make common Earth lightning look pale and weak. Look."

The trident and the wildwave vanished, and a skyscape took their place. There was ball lightning everywhere, and massive bolts that crackled and joined in a blinding net.

You can almost hear the thunder just looking at it. But on Storm, I didn't just hear. I felt it. It was all around me, and the ship shook to it, and I was scared shitless. But at least I was alive. What am I now?

His thumb moved of its own volition, and a new view of Storm came on cube. And his voice continued its glib narration. But the rest of him was millions of miles away, lost in a land of lightning and wild-waves.

Storm was my favorite, his thought ran. *Red Light was a heart-stopping first, and Anthill was haunting and puzzling and magical. But them I shared. Storm was almost my own. Only a handful of us got to swoop down, after Ainslie got careless and let his probe get blown against a mountain. But I was one of the handful. They can't take that away, either.*

His mind wandered. But all the while new vistas came and went in the cube, and his voice went on, and the ladies ooohed and aahed on schedule. And, finally, the end approached. And jerked him back to reality.

The next-to-last slide was the same as the first; the *Starwind*, in orbit around Earth. Waiting for new supplies, and new funding, and a new mission. And a few new men.

The last slide was an address. Glowing red letters floated in the white cube. And Becker, hating it, provided the narration.

"Space exploration is the greatest adventure in man's history," he said, smiling his plastic smile and talking with a plastic-pleasant tongue. "And the stars are our joy and our destiny. Not everyone can go to the stars, of course. But all those who want to can share in the adventure, and help to build the destiny. Worldgov has many expenses, and many causes crying for priority. It can only fund a small part of the budget needed to operate the starcruisers. The rest, as you know, is provided by interested citizens.

"If you share our dreams, we ask you to join the fight. For only a hundred credits a year, you can become members of the Friends of SPACE. You'll receive membership credentials, of course. And a complimentary subscription to *Starflight*, the official SPACE magazine. And you'll be giving a gift to your children. *All* your children, and all the children of man. You'll be giving them the stars."

"For a gift like that, the price tag is pretty low." He pointed at the address floating in the holocube. "If you'd like to help, send your contributions there — to SPACE, Box 27, Worldgov Center, Geneva."

His smile broadened. "And, of course, all contributions are tax deductible." He bowed silently, and flicked off the holocaster. "Whether you care to contribute or not, I hope you enjoyed the show."

Then the audience started applauding, and the lights came on, and the chairwoman rose to announce that refreshments would be served. While they were getting the food, a steady stream of women flowed up to Becker and thanked him effusively for his presentation and promised him support. He acknowledged their praise with nods and laughter and pleasant smiles.

And despised them, all the while. *God,* he thought, I *hate this. They've taken away my stars and given me chattering fat ladies and phony upperlevel parlors. And I hate it. And it isn't fair. Hell, it isn't even life.*

They gave him synthetic coffee and protein cookies. And he took them with a smile. And hated them. But he ate them, and stayed, and made small talk. That was SPACE policy. Finally, the audience began to break up and leave, one by one.

Just as Becker was beginning to think of leaving, the doctor drifted up, holding his coffee limply. He didn't seem quite as old with the lights on. But he looked very tired.

"That was quite a show, Commander," he said with a wan smile. "I'm afraid you blitzed me. I have a hunch you'll be getting all the contributions."

Becker returned a professional smile. "Well, your own presentation was very interesting, Doctor. And there's certainly a need for your kind of work down in the undercities. I wouldn't be so pessimistic."

The doctor frowned slightly, sipped his coffee, and shook his head. "Come, Commander. Don't humor me. I'm new at this game and I did very badly. And you're good enough to know that."

Becker, who was busy packing up his holocaster, gave the doctor a sharp glance and a genuine grin. He looked around to make sure none of the women were in range of the conversation, then nodded quickly. "You're sharp. And right — your show was third-rate. But you'll get better with time. And then the contributions will start to come in."

"Hmmmmm. Yes." The doctor looked at him hard, paused. Then he seemed to make up his mind about something. And he continued. "Meanwhile, of course, thousands of kids down in the undercities are hungry and sick, And they stay that way. And maybe die. Why? Because I'm not as slick as you." His mouth set in a hard line. "Tell me honestly, Commander — don't you ever feel guilty?"

The case on the holocaster snapped up with a sharp click, and Becker's grin died. "No," he said. There was a bite in his tone suddenly. "Doctor, you know that there are four star-cruisers. There could be forty. Or four hundred. There should be. But Worldgov won't give us the money. Comments like you just made are costing us the stars."

Are costing me the stars, he was saying to himself, his mind seething. *So few ships, so many volunteers. And that damned waiting list ...*

What was it that General Henderson had said? Thousands, wasn't it? Yes, "Commander, there are thousands of applicants for every starcruiser berth. And your performance on your first voyage was ... well, adequate. But not outstanding. I'm afraid I'm going to have to turn down your application for permanent crew status. I'm sorry."

And I said ... what? I said, "You're taking away my stars." For the first time, if not the last.

"I'm sorry" he said. That bastard. He never flew on a starcruiser in his life. That bastard would never leave Earth. "There's nothing I can do. However, Commander, there's still a place for you. You're good-looking and articulate, and you believe in what we're doing. SPACE needs men like you. We're moving you to public relations. Without which, I might add, the starcruisers would be impossible."

"I'm as compassionate as anyone, Becker said, slinging the holo-caster under an arm. "I think your work is vital. I feel for those kids. But you should try some empathy too. And try to understand what we're doing."

"What you're doing is a luxury when kids are hungry on Earth," the doctor said.

Becker shook his head. "No. There has to be room for both. Say you save a kid from death, Doctor. Fine. But what kind of life are you giving him? A pretty drab one, without the stars. And a hopeless one, in the long run. Maybe man can survive on Earth, alone. I think he could. But his dreams can't, and his myths can't. There are too many people, and they've crowded out all the dreams. And there's no life left for anyone. Just day-to-day survival."

He paused there. It was good speech, his own restatement of arguments he had heard hundreds of times in SPACE headquarters. It was enough. But he wanted to add more. He was angry and resentful, and he went on.

"I'll tell you something else, Doctor. I think we need both your work and mine, both Earth and the stars. But I think the balance is wrong. I think we need more stars."

He slapped the holocaster with his free hand. "You think I *like* this sort of shit? I hate it. Doctor. Just like you'd hate it if you did it all the time. I've dreamed of the stars all my life, and now they tell me I'm not good enough to get a permanent berth on a starcruiser. Not that I'm bad, mind you. I'm just not outstanding enough. And there's so little room.

"Tell me, Doctor, how would you feel if Worldgov suddenly announced that only the *best* four hundred doctors in the world would be allowed to practice medicine? Would you make the grade? What would you do? Can you imagine what it'd be like? Going through life, day to day, knowing what you wanted to do — and knowing that it was denied to you, maybe forever. Try to imagine that, if you can. Try to taste it. That's what it's like for me, you see.

"You can't *live* on Earth, Doctor. I can't, anyway. I can exist, but I don't call it living. I've seen the wildwaves of Storm and listened to the Spiderants sing their dawn. Am I supposed to content myself with mindspin trips and football games?" He snorted.

The doctor had calmly continued to sip his coffee during Becker's outburst. Now he lowered his cup, sighed, and gave another tired shake of his head.

"Commander, I feel sorry for you," he said. "You sound very bitter. Like you've been cheated. But you've been so incredibly lucky. And you don't realize it. You've done things most people only dream of, yet you complain of an empty life. I don't buy that. You've flown on a star-cruiser, even if it was only once. Commander, let me tell you something. Down in the undercity I've got patients who've never even seen the stars, and you've been there."

Becker, his anger subsided, gave a wistful smile that seemed somehow out of character. But very genuine.

"I've thought of that, he said sadly. "Sometimes. Maybe you're right. But it doesn't help, Doctor. I wish it did. But it doesn't." He thought a minute. "I'm sorry for your patients who've never seen the stars," he said when he resumed. "You know, I think that's almost worse than hunger. Although that's not fair for me to say, since I've never really been hungry. I hope someday you take your kids to the upper-levels, so they get a glimpse through the smog."

Becker shrugged then. "They're not the only ones I'm sorry for, though. I'm sorry for everyone who has seen the stars and can't go there. And most of all I'm sorry for me, who's been there. And can't go back. I guess that makes me selfish. But that's the way it is, I'm afraid. And I try to live with it.

"And I do sort of believe in what I do. Maybe someday Worldgov will change its mind and we'll get more starcruisers. And I can go out again. And take some of your kids with me, who knows? It's for them too, you know."

Becker wanted to end it there. But the doctor, still unconvinced, came back again. "That's big of you," he said. "But before you give them the stars, try giving them some food, or a healthy environment."

Becker glanced around the room. It was very late, and most of the audience had gone home. *Time to break it off,* he thought. *Another damned show tomorrow.*

"I could answer that," he said. "I won't, I'm not going to convince you, Doctor. And you're not come to convince me, either, I'm afraid. So let's call it a night. Peace?"

He smiled and offered his hand. The doctor shook it. Then Becker turned to the chairwoman and the few matrons who remained, and bade them good night. And left.

It was cold outside on the upperlevels, and there was a brisk night wind whistling down the street between the tower-tops. Becker stopped briefly on his way to the interlevel tubes and looked up. But the smog was heavy, and he could not see the stars.

And maybe that was just as well.

Chicago, Illinois
July, 1972

George R.R. Martin

A Song for Lya

The cities of the Shkeen are old, older far than man's, and the great rust-red metropolis that rose from their sacred hill country had proved to be the oldest of them all. The Shkeen city had no name. It needed none. Though they built cities and towns by the hundreds and the thousands, the hill city had no rivals. It was the largest in size and population, and it was alone in the sacred hills. It was their Rome, Mecca, Jerusalem; all in one. It was *the* city, and all Shkeen came to it at last, in the final days before Union.

That city had been ancient in the days before Rome fell, had been huge and sprawling when Babylon was still a dream. But there was no feel of age to it. The human eye saw only miles and miles of low, red-brick domes; small hummocks of dried mud that covered the rolling hills like a rash. Inside they were dim and nearly airless. The rooms were small and the furniture crude.

Yet it was not a grim city. Day after day it squatted in those scrubby hills, broiling under a hot sun that sat in the sky like a weary orange melon; but the city teemed with life: smells of cooking, the sounds of laughter and talk and children running, the bustle and sweat of brickmen repairing the domes, the bells of the Joined ringing in the streets. The Shkeen were a lusty and exuberant people, almost childlike. Certainly there was nothing about them that told of great age or ancient wisdom. This is a young race, said the signs, this is a culture in its infancy.

But that infancy had lasted more than fourteen thousand years.

The human city was the real infant, less than ten Earth years old. It was built on the edge of the hills, between the Shkeen metropolis and the dusty brown plains where the spaceport had gone up. In human terms, it was a beautiful city: open and airy, full of graceful archways and glistening fountains and wide boulevards lined by trees. The buildings were wrought of metal and colored plastic and native woods, and most of them were low in deference to Shkeen architecture. Most of them ... the Administration Tower was the exception, a polished blue steel needle that split a crystal sky.

You could see it for miles in all directions. Lyanna spied it even before we landed, and we admired it from the air. The gaunt sky-scrapers of Old Earth and Baldur were taller, and the fantastic webbed cities of Arachne were far more beautiful — but that slim blue Tower was still imposing enough as it rose unrivaled to its lonely dominance above the sacred hills.

The spaceport was in the shadow of the Tower, easy walking distance. But they met us anyway. A low-slung scarlet aircar sat purring at the base of the ramp as we disembarked, with a driver lounging against the stick. Dino Valcarenghi stood next to it, leaning on the door and talking to an aide.

Valcarenghi was the planetary administrator, the boy wonder of the sector. Young, of course, but I'd known that. Short, and good-looking, in a dark, intense way, with black hair that curled thickly against his head and an easy, genial smile.

He flashed us that smile then, when we stepped off the ramp, and reached to shake hands. "Hi," he began, "I'm glad to see you." There was no nonsense with formal introductions. He knew who we were, and we knew who he was, and Valcarenghi wasn't the kind of man who put much stock in ritual.

Lyanna took his hand lightly in hers, and gave him her vampire look: big, dark eyes opened wide and staring, thin mouth lifted in a tiny faint smile. She's a small girl, almost waiflike, with short brown hair and a child's figure. She can look very fragile, very helpless. When she wants to. But she rattles people with that look. If they know Lya's a telepath, they figure she's poking around amid their innermost secrets. Actually she's playing with them. When Lyanna is *really* reading, her whole body goes stiff and you can almost see her tremble. And those big, soul-sucking eyes get narrow and hard and opaque.

But not many people know that, so they squirm under her vampire eyes and look the other way and hurry to release her hand. Not Valcarenghi, though. He just smiled and stared back, then moved on to me.

I *was* reading when I took his hand — my standard operating procedure. Also a bad habit, I guess, since it's put some promising friendships into an early grave. My talent isn't equal to Lya's. But it's not as demanding, either. I read emotions. Valcarenghi's geniality came through strong and genuine. With nothing behind it, or at least nothing that was close enough to the surface for me to catch.

We also shook hands with the aide, a middle-aged blond stork named Nelson Gourlay. Then Valcarenghi ushered everybody into the aircar and we took off. "I imagine you're tired," he said after we were airborne, "so we'll save the tour of the city and head straight for the Tower. Nelse will show you your quarters, then you can join us for a drink, and we'll talk over the problem. You've read the materials I sent?"

"Yes," I said. Lya nodded. "Interesting background, but I'm not sure why we're here."

"We'll get to that soon enough," Valcarenghi replied. "I ought to be letting you enjoy the scenery." He gestured toward the window, smiled, and fell silent.

So Lya and I enjoyed the scenery, or as much as we could enjoy during the five-minute flight from spaceport to tower. The aircar was whisking down the main street at treetop level, stirring up a breeze that whipped the thin branches as we went by. It was cool and dark in the interior of the car, but outside the Shkeen sun was riding toward noon, and you could see the heat waves shimmering from the pavement. The population must have been inside huddled around their air-conditioners, because we saw very little traffic.

We got out near the main entrance to the Tower and walked through a huge, sparkling-clean lobby. Valcarenghi left us then to talk to some underlings. Gourlay led us into one of the tubes and we shot up fifty floors. Then we waltzed past a secretary into another, private tube, and climbed some more.

Our rooms were lovely, carpeted in cool green, and paneled with wood. There was complete library there, mostly Earth classics bound in synthaleather, with a few novels from Baldur, our home world. Somebody had been researching our tastes. One of the walls of the bedroom was tinted glass, giving a panoramic view of the city far below us, with a control that could darken it for sleeping.

Gourlay showed it to us dutifully, like a dour bellhop. I read him briefly though, and found no resentment. He was nervous, but only slightly. There was honest affection there for someone. Us? Valcarenghi?

Lya sat down on one of the twin beds. "Is someone bringing our luggage?' she asked.

Gourlay nodded. "You'll be well taken care of," he said. "Anything you want, ask."

"Don't worry, we will," I said. I dropped to the second bed, and gestured Gourlay To a chair. "How long you been here?"

"Six years," he said, taking the chair gratefully and sprawling out all over it. "I'm one of the veterans. I've worked under four administrators now. Dino, and Stuart before him, and Gustaffson before *him*. I was even under Rockwood a few months."

Lya perked up, crossing her legs under her and leaning forward. "That was all Rockwood lasted, wasn't it?"

"Right," Gourlay said. "He didn't like the planet, took a quick demotion to assistant administrator someplace else. I didn't care much, to tell the truth. He was the nervous type, always giving orders to prove who was boss."

"And Valcarenghi?" I asked.

Gourlay made a smile look like a yawn. "Dino? Dino's OK, the best of the lot. He's good, knows he's good. He's only been here two months, but he's gotten a lot done, and he's made a lot of friends. He treats the staff like people, calls everybody by his first name, all that stuff. People like that."

I was reading, and I read sincerity. It was Valcarenghi that Gourlay was affectionate toward, then. He believed what he was saying.

I had more questions, but I didn't get to ask them. Gourlay got up suddenly. "I really shouldn't stay," he said. "You want to rest, right? Come up to the top in about two hours and we'll go over things with you. You know where the tube is?"

We nodded, and Gourlay left. I turned to Lyanna. "What do you think?"

She lay back on the bed and considered the ceiling. "I don't know," she said. "I wasn't reading. I wonder why they've had so many administrators. And why they wanted us."

"We're Talented," I said, smiling. With the capital, yes. Lyanna and I have been tested and registered as psi Talents, and we have the licenses to prove it.

"Uh-huh," she said, turning on her side and smiling back at me. Not her vampire half-smile this time. Her sexy little girl smile.

"Valcarenghi wants us to get some rest," I said. "It's probably not a bad idea."

Lya bounced out of bed. "OK," she said, "but these twins have got to go."

"We could push them together."

She smiled again. We pushed them together.

And we *did* get some sleep. Eventually.

Our luggage was outside the door when we woke. We changed into fresh clothes, old casual stuff, counting on Valcarenghi's notorious lack of pomp. The tube took us to the top of the Tower.

The office of the planetary administrator was hardly an office. There was no desk, none of the usual trappings. Just a bar and lush blue carpets that swallowed us ankle high, and six or seven scattered chairs. Plus lots of space and sunlight, with Shkea laid out at our feet beyond the tinted glass. All four walls this time.

Valcarenghi and Gourlay were waiting for us, and Valcarenghi did the bartending chores personally. I didn't recognize the beverage, but it was cool and spicy and aromatic, with a real sting to it. I sipped it gratefully. For some reason I felt I needed a lift.

"Shkeen wine," Valcarenghi said, smiling, in answer to an unasked question. "They're got a name for it, but I can't pronounce it yet. But give me time. I've only been here two months, and the language is rough."

"You're learning Shkeen?" Lya asked, surprised. I knew why. Shkeen is rough on human tongues, but the natives learned Terran with stunning ease. Most people accepted that happily, and just forgot about the difficulties of cracking the alien language.

"It gives me an insight into the way they think," Valcarenghi said. "At least that's the theory." He smiled.

I read him again, although it was more difficult. Physical contact makes things sharper. Again, I got a simple emotion, close to the surface — pride this time. With pleasure mixed in. I chalked that up to the wine. Nothing beneath.

"However you pronounce the drink, I like it," I said.

"The Shkeen produce a wide variety of liquors and foodstuffs," Gourlay put in. "We've cleared many for export already, and we're checking others. Market should be good."

"You'll have a chance to sample more of the local produce this evening," Valcarenghi said. "I've set up a tour of the city, with a stop or two in Shkeentown. For a settlement of our size, our night life is fairly interesting. I'll be your guide."

"Sounds good," I said. Lya was smiling too. A tour was unusually considerate. Most Normals feel uneasy around Talents, so they rush us in to do whatever they want done, then rush us out again as quickly as possible. They certainly don't socialize with us.

"Now — the problem," Valcarenghi said, lowering his drink and leaning forward in the chair. "You read about the Cult of the Union?"

"A Shkeen religion," Lya said.

"*The* Shkeen religion," corrected Valcarenghi. "Every one of them is a believer. This is a planet without heretics."

"We read the materials you sent on it," Lya said. "Along with everything else."

"What do you think?"

I shrugged. "Grim. Primitive. But no more than any number of others I've read about. The Shkeen aren't very advanced, after all. There were religions on Old Earth that included human sacrifice."

Valcarenghi shook his head, and looked toward Gourlay.

"No, you don't understand," Gourlay started, putting his drink down on the carpet. "I've been studying their religion for six years. It's like no other in history. Nothing on Old Earth like it, no sir. Nor in any other race we've encountered.

"And Union, well, it's wrong to compare it to human sacrifice, just wrong. The Old Earth religions sacrificed one or two unwilling victims to appease their gods. Killed a handful to get mercy for the millions. And the handful generally protested. The Shkeen don't work it that way. The Greeshka takes everyone. And they go willingly. Like lemmings they march off to the caves to be eaten alive by those parasites. *Every* Shkeen is Joined at forty, and goes to Final Union before he's fifty."

I was confused. "All right," I said. "I see the distinction, I guess. But so what? Is this the problem? I imagine that Union is rough on the

Shkeen, but that's their business. Their religion is no worse than the ritual cannibalism of the Hrangans, is it?"

Valcarenghi finished his drink and got up, heading for the bar. As he poured himself a refill, he said, almost casually, "As far as I know, Hrangan cannibalism has claimed no human converts."

Lya looked startled. I felt startled. I sat up and stared. "What?"

Valcarenghi headed back to his seat, glass in hand. "Human converts have been joining the Cult of the Union. Dozens of them are already Joined. None of them have achieved full Union yet, but that's only a question of time." He sat down, and looked at Gourlay. So did we.

The gangling blond aide picked up the narrative. "The first convert was about seven years ago. Nearly a year before I got here, two and a half after Shkea was discovered and the settlement built. Guy named Magly. Psi-psych, worked closely with the Shkeen. He was it for two years. Then another in '08, more the next year. And the rate's been climbing ever since. There was one big one. Phil Gustaffson."

Lya blinked. "The planetary administrator?"

"The same," said Gourlay. "We've had a lot of administrators; Gustaffson came in after Rockwood couldn't stand it. He was a big, gruff old guy. Everybody loved him. He'd lost his wife and kids on his last assignment, but you'd never have known it. He was always hearty, full of fun. Well, he got interested in the Shkeen religion, started talking to them. Talked to Magly and some of the other converts too. Even went to see a Greeshka. That shook him up real bad for a while. But finally he got over it, went back to his researches. I worked with him, but I never guessed what he had in mind. A little over a year ago, he converted. He's Joined now. Nobody's ever been accepted that fast. I hear talk in Shkeentown that he may even be admitted to Final Union, rushed right in. Well, Phil was administrator here longer than anybody else. People liked him, and when he went over, a lot of his friends followed. The rate's way up now."

"Not quite one percent, and rising," Valcarenghi said. "That seems low, but remember what it means. One percent of the people in my settlement are choosing a religion that includes a very unpleasant form of suicide."

Lya looked from him to Gourlay and back again. "Why hasn't this been reported?"

163

"It should have been," Valcarenghi said. "But Stuart succeeded Gustaffson, and he was scared stiff of a scandal. There's no law against humans adopting an alien religion, so Stuart defined it as a non-problem. He reported the conversion rate routinely, and nobody higher up ever bothered to make the correlation and remember just what all these people were converting *to*."

I finished my drink, set it down. "Go on," I said to Valcarenghi.

"I define the situation as a problem," he said. "I don't care how few people are involved, the idea that human beings would allow the Greeshka to consume them alarms me. I've had a team of psychs on it since I took over, but they're getting nowhere. I needed Talent. I want you two to find out *why* these people are converting. Then I'll be able to deal with the situation."

The problem was strange, but the assignment seemed straightforward enough. I read Valcarenghi to be sure. His emotions were a bit more complex this time, but not much. Confidence above all: he was sure we could handle the problem. There was honest concern there, but no fear, and not even a hint of deception. Again, I couldn't catch anything below the surface. Valcarenghi kept his hidden turmoil well hidden, if he had any.

I glanced at Lyanna. She was sitting awkwardly in her chair, and her fingers were wrapped very tightly around her wine glass. Reading. Then she loosened up and looked my way and nodded.

"All right," I said. "I think we can do it."

Valcarenghi smiled. "That I never doubted," he said. "It was only a question of whether you *would*. But enough of business for tonight. I've promised you a night on the town, and I always try to deliver on my promises. I'll meet you downstairs in the lobby in a half-hour."

Lya and I changed into something more formal back in our room. I picked a dark blue tunic, with white slacks and a matching mesh scarf. Not the height of fashion, but I was hoping that Shkea would be several months behind the times. Lya slipped into a silky white skintight with a tracery of thin blue lines that flowed over her in sensuous patterns in response to her body heat. The lines were definitely lecherous, accentuating her thin figure with a singleminded determination. A blue rain-cape completed the outfit.

"Valcarenghi's funny," she said as she fastened it.

"Oh?" I was struggling with the sealseam on my tunic, which refused to seal. "You catch something when you read him?'

"No," she said. She finished attaching the cape and admired herself in the mirror. Then she spun toward me, the cape swirling behind her. "That's it. He was thinking what he was saying. Oh, variations in the wording, of course, but nothing important. His mind was on what we were discussing, and behind that there was only a wall." She smiled. "Didn't get a single one of his deep dark secrets."

I finally conquered the sealseam. "Tsk," I said. "Well, you get another chance tonight."

That got me a grimace. "The hell I do. I don't read people on off-time. It isn't fair. Besides, it's such a strain. I wish I could catch thoughts as easily as you do feelings."

"The price of Talent," I said. "You're more Talented, your price is higher." I rummaged in our luggage for a raincape, but I didn't find anything that went well, so I decided not to wear one. Capes were out, anyway. "I didn't get much on Valcarenghi either. You could have told as much by watching his face. He must be a very disciplined mind. But I'll forgive him. He serves good wine."

Lya nodded. "Right! That stuff did me good. Got rid of the headache I woke up with."

"The altitude," I suggested. We headed for the door.

The lobby was deserted, but Valcarenghi didn't keep us waiting long. This time he drove his own aircar, a battered black job that had evidently been with him for a while. Gourlay wasn't the sociable type, but Valcarenghi had a woman with him, a stunning auburn-haired vision named Laurie Blackburn. She was even younger than Valcarenghi — midtwenties, by the look of her.

It was sunset when we took off. The whole far horizon was a gorgeous tapestry in red and orange, and a cool breeze was blowing in from the plains. Valcarenghi left the coolers off and opened the car windows, and we watched the city darken into twilight as we drove.

Dinner was at a plush restaurant with Baldurian decor — to make us feel comfortable, I guessed. The food, however, was very cosmopolitan. The spices, the herbs, the *style* of cooking were all Baldur. The meats and vegetables were native. It made for an interesting combination. Valcarenghi ordered for all four of us, and we wound up sampling about a dozen different dishes. My favorite was a tiny Shkeen bird that they cooked in sourtang sauce. There wasn't very much of it, but what there was tasted great. We also polished off three bottles of wine during the meal: more of the Shkeen stuff we'd sampled that afternoon, a flask of chilled Veltaar from Baldur, and some real Old Earth Burgundy.

The talk warmed up quickly; Valcarenghi was a born storyteller and an equally good listener. Eventually, of course, the conversation got around to Shkea and the Shkeen. Laurie led it there. She'd been on Shkea for about six months, working toward an advanced degree in extee anthropology. She was trying to discover why the Shkeen civilization had remained frozen for so many millennia.

"They're older than we are, you know," she told us. "They had cities before men were using tools. It should have been space-traveling Shkeen that stumbled on primitive men, not the other way around."

"Aren't there theories on that already?" I asked.

"Yes, but none of them are universally accepted," she said. "Cullen cites a lack of heavy metals, for example. A factor, but is it the *whole* answer? Von Hamrin claims the Shkeen didn't get enough competition. No big carnivores on the planet, so there was nothing to breed aggressiveness into the race. But he's come under a lot of fire. Shkea isn't all *that* idyllic; if it were, the Shkeen never would have reached their present level. Besides, what's the Greeshka if not a carnivore? It *eats* them, doesn't it?"

"What do you think?" Lya asked.

"I think it had something to do with the religion, but I haven't worked it all out yet. Dino's helping me talk to people and the Shkeen are open enough, but research isn't easy." She stopped suddenly and looked at Lya hard. "For me, anyway. I imagine it'd be easier for you."

We'd heard that before. Normals often figure that Talents have unfair advantages, which is perfectly understandable. We do. But Laurie wasn't resentful. She delivered her statement in a wistful, speculative tone, instead of etching it in verbal acid.

Valcarenghi leaned over and put an arm around her. "Hey," he said. "Enough shop talk. Robb and Lya shouldn't be worrying about the Shkeen until tomorrow."

Laurie looked at him, and smiled tentatively. "OK," she said lightly. "I get carried away. Sorry."

"That's OK," I told her. "It's an interesting subject. Give us a day and we'll probably be getting enthusiastic too."

Lya nodded agreement, and added that Laurie would be the first to know if our work turned up anything that would support her theory. I was hardly listening. I know it's not polite to read Normals when you're out with them socially, but there are times I can't resist. Valcarenghi had his arm around Laurie and had pulled her toward him gently. I was curious.

So I took a quick, guilty reading. He was very high — slightly drunk, I guess, and feeling very confident and protective. The master of the situation. But Laurie was a jumble — uncertainty, repressed anger, a vague fading hint of fright. And love, confused but very strong. I doubted that it was for me or Lya. She loved Valcarenghi.

I reached under the table, searching for Lya's hand, and found her knee. I squeezed it gently and she looked at me and smiled. She wasn't reading, which was good. It bothered me that Laurie loved Valcarenghi, though I didn't know why, and I was just as glad that Lya didn't see my discontent.

We finished off the last of the wine in short order, and Valcarenghi took care of the whole bill. Then he rose. "Onward!" he announced. "The night is fresh, and we've got visits to make."

So we made visits. No holoshows or anything that drab, although the city had its share of theaters. A casino was next on the list. Gambling was legal on Shkea, of course, and Valcarenghi would have legalized it if it weren't. He supplied the chips and I lost some for him, as did Laurie. Lya was barred from playing; her Talent was too strong. Valcarenghi won big; he was a superb mindspin player, and pretty good at the traditional games too.

Then came a bar. More drinks, plus local entertainment which was better than I would have expected.

It was pitch black when we got out, and I assumed that the expedition was nearing its end. Valcarenghi surprised us. When we got back to the car, he reached under the controls, pulled out a box of sober-ups, and passed them around.

"Hey," I said. "You're driving. Why do I need this? I just barely got up here."

"I'm about to take you to a genuine Shkeen cultural event, Robb," he said. "I don't want you making rude comments or throwing up on the natives. Take your pill."

I took my pill, and the buzz in my head began to fade. Valcarenghi already had the car airborne. I leaned back and put my arm around Lya, and she rested her head on my shoulder. "Where are we going?" I asked.

"Shkeentown," he replied, never looking back, "to their Great Hall. There's a Gathering tonight, and I figured you'd be interested."

"It will be in Shkeen, of course," Laurie said, "but Dino can translate for you. I know a little of the language too, and I'll fill in whatever he misses."

Lya looked excited. We'd read about Gatherings, of course, but we hardly expected to go see one on our first day on Shkea. The Gatherings were a species of religious rite; a mass confessional of sorts for pilgrims who were about to be admitted to the ranks of the Joined. Pilgrims swelled the hill city daily, but Gatherings were conducted only three or four times a year when the numbers of those-about-to-be-Joined climbed high enough.

The aircar streaked almost soundlessly through the brightly lit settlement, passing huge fountains that danced with a dozen colors and pretty ornamental arches that flowed like liquid fire. A few other cars were airborne, and here and there we flew above pedestrians strolling the city's broad malls. But most people were inside, and light and music flooded from many of the homes we passed.

Then, abruptly, the character of the city began to change. The level ground began to roll and heave, hills rose before us and the behind us, and the lights vanished. Below, the malls gave way to unlit roads of crushed stone and dust, and the domes of glass and metal done in fashionable mock-Shkeen yielded to their older brick brothers. The Shkeen city was quieter than its human counterpart; most of the houses were darkly silent.

Then, ahead of us, a hummock appeared that was larger than the others — almost a hill in itself, with a big arched door and a series of slitlike windows. And light leaked from this one, and noise, and there were Shkeen outside.

I suddenly realized that, although I'd been on Shkea for nearly a day, this was the first sight I'd caught of the Shkeen. Not that I could see them all that clearly from an aircar at night. But I did see them. They were smaller than men — the tallest was around five feet — with big eyes and long arms. That was all I could tell from above.

Valcarenghi put the car down alongside the Great Hall, and we piled out. Shkeen were trickling through the arch from several directions, but most of them were already inside. We joined the trickle, and nobody even looked twice at us, except for one character who hailed Valcarenghi in a thin, squeaky voice and called him Dino. He had friends even here.

The interior was one huge room, with a great crude platform built in the center and an immense crowd of Shkeen circling it. The only light was from torches that were stuck in grooves along the walls, and on high poles surrounding the platform. Someone was speaking, and every one of those great, bulging eyes was turned his way. We four were the only humans in the Hall.

The speaker, outlined brightly by the torches, was a fat, middle-aged Shkeen who moved his arms slowly, almost hypnotically, as he talked. His speech was a series of whistles, wheezes, and grunts, so I didn't listen very closely. He was much too far away to read. I was reduced to studying his appearance, and that of other Shkeen near me. All of them were hairless, as far as I could see, with softish-looking orange skin that was creased by a thousand tiny wrinkles.

They wore simple shifts of crude, multicolored cloth, and I had difficulty telling male from female.

Valcarenghi leaned over toward me and whispered, careful to keep his voice low. "The speaker is a farmer," he said. "He's telling the crowd how far he's come, and some of the hardships of his life."

I looked around. Valcarenghi's whisper was the only sound in the place. Everyone else was dead quiet, eyes riveted on the platform, scarcely breathing. "He's saying that he has four brothers," Valcarenghi told me. "Two have gone on to Final Union, one is among the Joined. The other is younger than himself, and now owns the farm." He frowned. "The speaker will never see his farm again," he said, more loudly, "but he's happy about it."

"Bad crops?" asked Lya, smiling irreverently. She'd been listening to the same whisper. I gave her a stern look.

The Shkeen went on. Valcarenghi stumbled after him. "Now he's telling his crimes, all the things he's done that he's ashamed of, his blackest soul-secrets. He's had a sharp tongue at times, he's vain, once be actually struck his younger brother. Now he speaks of his wife, and the other women he has known. He has betrayed her many times, copulating with others. As a boy, he mated with animals for he feared females. In recent years he has grown incapable, and his brother has serviced his wife."

On and on and on it went, in incredible detail, detail that was both startling and frightening. No intimacy went untold, no secret was left undisturbed. I stood and listened to Valcarenghi's whispers, shocked at first, finally growing bored with the squalor of it all. I began to get restless. I wondered briefly if I knew any human half so well as I now knew this great fat Shkeen. Then I wondered whether Lyanna, with her Talent, knew anyone half so well. It was almost as if the speaker wanted all of us to live through his life right here and now.

His speech lasted for what seemed hours, but finally it began to wind up. "He speaks now of Union," Valcarenghi whispered. "He will be Joined, he is joyful about it, he has craved it for so long. His misery is at an end, his aloneness will cease, soon he shall walk the streets of the sacred city and peal his joy with the bells. And then Final Union, in the years to come. He will be with his brothers in the afterlife."

"No, Dino." This whisper was Laurie. "Quit wrapping human phrases around what he says. He will be his brothers, he says. The phrase also implies they will be him."

Valcarenghi smiled. "OK, Laurie. If you say so ... "

Suddenly the fat farmer was gone from the platform. The crowd rustled, and another figure took his place: much shorter, wrinkled excessively, one eye a great gaping hole. He began to speak, haltingly at first, then with greater skill.

"This one is a brickman, he has worked many domes, he lives in the sacred city. His eye was lost many years ago, when he fell from a dome and a sharp stick poked into him. The pain was very great, but he returned to work within a year, he did not beg for premature Union, he was very brave, he is proud of his courage. He has a wife, but they never had offspring, he is sad of that, he cannot talk to his wife easily, they are apart even when together and she weeps at night, he is sad of that too, but he has never hurt her and ... "

It went on for hours again. My restlessness stirred again, but I cracked down on it — this was too important. I let myself get lost in Valcarenghi's narration, and the story of the one-eyed Shkeen. Before long, I was riveted as closely to the tale as the aliens around me. It was hot and stuffy and all but airless in the dome, and my tunic was getting sooty and soaked by sweat, some of it from the creatures who pressed around me. But I hardly noticed.

The second speaker ended as had the first, with a long praise of the joy of being Joined and the coming of Final Union. Toward the end, I hardly even needed Valcarenghi's translation — I could hear the happiness in the voice of the Shkeen, and see it in his trembling figure. Or maybe I was reading, unconsciously. But I can't read at that distance — unless the target is emoting very hard.

A third speaker ascended the platform, and spoke in a voice louder than the others. Valcarenghi kept pace. "A woman this time," he said. "She has carried eight children for her man, she has four sisters and three brothers, she has farmed all her life, she ... "

Suddenly her speech seemed to peak, and she ended a long sequence with several sharp, high whistles. Then she fell silent. The crowd, as one, began to respond with whistles of their own. An eerie, echoing music filled the Great Hall, and the Shkeen around us all began to sway and whistle. The woman looked out at the scene from a bent and broken position.

Valcarenghi started to translate, but he stumbled over something. Laurie cut in before he could backtrack. "She has now told them of great tragedy," she whispered. "They whistle to show their grief, their oneness with her pain."

"Sympathy, yes," said Valcarenghi, taking over again. "When she was young, her brother grew ill, and seemed to be dying. Her parents told her to take him to the sacred hills, for they could not leave the younger children. But she shattered a wheel on her cart through careless driving, and her brother died upon the plains. He perished without Union. She blames herself."

The Shkeen had begun again. Laurie began to translate, leaning close to us and using a soft whisper. "Her brother died, she is saying again. She faulted him, denied him Union, now he is sundered and alone and gone without ... without ... "

"Afterlife," said Valcarenghi. "Without afterlife."

"I'm not sure that's entirely right," Laurie said. "That concept is ... "

Valcarenghi waved her silent. "Listen," he said. He continued to translate.

We listened to her story, told in Valcarenghi's increasingly hoarse whisper. She spoke longest of all, and her story was the grimmest of the three. When she finished, she too was replaced. But Valcarenghi put a hand on my shoulder and beckoned toward the exit.

The cool night air hit like ice water, and I suddenly realized that I was drenched with sweat. Valcarenghi walked quickly toward the car. Behind us, the speaking was still in progress, and the Shkeen showed no signs of tiring.

"Gatherings go on for days, sometimes weeks," Laurie told us as we climbed inside the aircar. "The Shkeen listen in shifts, more or less — they try terribly to hear every word, but exhaustion gets to them sooner or later and they retire for brief rests, then return for more. It is a great honor to last through an entire Gathering without sleep."

Valcarenghi shot us aloft. "I'm going to try that someday," he said. "I've never attended for more than a couple of hours, but I think I could make it if I fortified myself with drugs. We'll get more understanding between human and Shkeen if we participate more fully in their rituals."

"Oh," I said. "Maybe Gustaffson felt the same way."

Valcarenghi laughed lightly. "Yes, well, I don't intend to participate *that* fully."

The trip home was a tired silence. I'd lost track of time but my body insisted that it was almost dawn. Lya, curled up under my arm, looked drained and empty and only half-awake. I felt the same way.

We left the aircar in front of the Tower, and took the tubes up. I was past thinking. Sleep came very, very quickly.

I dreamed that night. A good dream, I think, but it faded with the coming of the light, leaving me empty and feeling cheated. I lay there, after waking, with my arm around Lya and my eyes on the ceiling, trying to recall what the dream had been about. But nothing came.

Instead, I found myself thinking about the Gathering, running it through again in my head. Finally I disentangled myself and climbed out of bed. We'd darkened the glass, so the room was still pitch black. But I found the controls easily enough, and let through a trickle of late morning light.

Lya mumbled some sort of sleepy protest and rolled over, but made no effort to get up. I left her alone in the bedroom and went out to our library, looking for a book on the Shkeen — something with a little more detail than the material we'd been sent. No luck. The library was meant for recreation, not research.

I found a viewscreen and punched up to Valcarenghi's office. Gourlay answered. "Hello," he said. "Dino figured you'd be calling. He's not here right now. He's out arbitrating a trade contract. What do you need?"

"Books," I said, my voice still a little sleepy. "Something on the Shkeen."

"That I can't do," Gourlay said. "Are none, really. Lots of papers and studies and monographs, but no full-fledged books. I'm going to write one, but I haven't gotten to it yet. Dino figured I could be your resource, I guess."

"Oh."

"Got any questions?"

I searched for a question, found none. "Not really," I said, shrugging. "I just wanted general background, maybe some more information on Gatherings."

"I can talk to you about that later," Gourlay said. "Dino figured you'd want to get to work today. We can bring people to the Tower, if you'd like, or you can get out to them."

"We'll go out," I said quickly. Bringing subjects in for interviews fouls up everything. They get all anxious, and that covers up any emotions I might want to read, and they *think* on different things, too, so Lyanna has trouble.

"Fine" said Gourlay. "Dino put an aircar at your disposal. Pick it up down in the lobby. Also, they'll have some keys for you, so you can come straight up here to the office without bothering with the secretaries and all."

"Thanks," I said. "Talk to you later." I flicked off the viewscreen and walked back to the bedroom.

Lya was sitting up, the covers around her waist. I sat down next to her and kissed her. She smiled, but didn't respond. "Hey," I said. "What's wrong?"

"Headache," she replied. "I thought sober-ups were supposed to get rid of hangovers."

"That's the theory. Mine worked pretty well." I went to the closet and began looking for something to wear. "We should have headache pills around here someplace. I'm sure Dino wouldn't forget anything that obvious."

"Umpf. Yes. Throw me some clothes."

I grabbed one of her coveralls and tossed it across the room. Lya stood up and slipped into it while I dressed, then went off to the wash-room.

"Better," she said. "You're right, he didn't forget medicines."

"He's the thorough sort."

She smiled. "I guess. Laurie knows the language better, though. I read her. Dino made a couple of mistakes in that translation last night."

I'd guessed at something like that. No discredit to Valcarenghi; he was working on a four-month handicap, from what they'd said. I nodded. "Read anything else?"

"No. I tried to get those speakers, but the distance was too much." She came up and took my hand. "Where are we going today?"

"Shkeentown," I said. "Let's try to find some of these Joined. I didn't notice any at the Gathering."

"No. Those things are for Shkeen about-to-be-Joined."

"So I hear. Let's go.

We went. We stopped at the fourth level for a late breakfast in the Tower cafeteria, then got our aircar pointed out to us by a man in the lobby. A sporty green four-seater, very common, very inconspicuous.

I didn't take the aircar all the way into the Shkeen city, figuring we'd get more of the feel of the place if we went through on foot. So I dropped down just beyond the first range of hills, and we walked.

The human city had seemed almost empty, but Shkeentown lived. The crushed-rock streets were full of aliens, hustling back and forth busily, carrying loads of bricks and baskets of fruit and clothing. There were children everywhere, most of them naked; fat balls of orange energy that ran around us in circles, whistling and grunting and grin-ning, tugging at us every once in a while. The kids looked different from the adults. They had a few patches of reddish hair, for one thing, and their skins were still smooth and unwrinkled. They were the only ones who really paid any attention to us. The adult Shkeen just went about their business, and gave us an occasional friendly smile. Humans were obviously not all that uncommon in the streets of Shkeentown.

Most of the traffic was on foot. but small wooden carts were also common. The Shkeen draft animal looked like a big green dog that was about to be sick. They were strapped to the carts in pairs, and they whined constantly as they pulled. So, naturally, men called them whiners. In addition to whining, they also defecated constantly. That, with odors from the food peddled in baskets and the Shkeen themselves, gave the city a definite pungency.

There was noise too, a constant clamor. Kids whistling, Shkeen talking loudly with grunts and whimpers and squeaks, whiners whining and their carts rattling over the rocks. Lya and I walked through it all silently, hand in hand, watching and listening and smelling and ... reading.

I was wide open when I entered Shkeentown, letting everything wash over me as I walked, unfocused but receptive. I was the center of a small bubble of emotion — feelings rushed up at me as Shkeen approached, faded as they walked away, circled around and around with the dancing children. I swam in a sea of impressions. And it startled me.

It startled me because it was all so familiar. I'd read aliens before. Sometimes it was difficult, sometimes it was easy, but it was never pleasant. The Hrangans have sour minds, rank with hate and bitterness, and I feel unclean when I come out. The Fyndii feel emotions so palely that I can scarcely read them at all. The Damoosh are ... *different*. I read them strongly, but I can't find names for the feelings I read.

But the Shkeen — it was like walking down a street on Baldur. No, wait — more like one of the Lost Colonies, when a human settlement has fallen back into barbarism and forgotten its origins. Human emotions rage there, primal and strong and real, but less sophisticated than on Old Earth or Baldur. The Shkeen were like that: primitive, maybe, but very understandable. I read joy and sorrow, envy, anger, whimsy, bitterness, yearning, pain. The same heady mixture that engulfs me everywhere, when I open myself to it.

Lya was reading, too. I felt her hand tense in mine. After a while, it softened again. I turned to her, and she saw the question in my eyes.

"They're people," she said. "They're like us."

I nodded. "Parallel evolution, maybe. Shkea might be an older Earth, with a few minor differences. But you're right. They're more human than any other race we've encountered in space." I considered that. "Does that answer Dino's question? If they're like us, it follows that their religion would be more appealing than a *really* alien one."

"No, Robb," Lya said. "I don't think so. Just the reverse. If they're like us, it doesn't make sense that *they'd* go off so willingly to die. See?"

She was right, of course. There was nothing suicidal in the emotions I'd read, nothing unstable, nothing really abnormal. Yet every one of the Shkeen went off to Final Union in the end.

"We should focus on somebody," I said. "This blend of thought isn't getting us anywhere." I looked around to find a subject, but just then I heard the bells begin.

They were off to the left somewhere, nearly lost in the city's gentle roar. I tugged Lya by the hand, and we ran down the street to find them, turning left at the first gap in the orderly row of domes.

The bells were still ahead, and we kept running, cutting through what must have been somebody's yard, and climbing over a low bush fence that bristled with sweethorns. Beyond that was another yard, a dung pit, more domes, and finally a street. It was there we found the bell-ringers.

There were four of them, all Joined, wearing long gowns of bright red fabric that trailed in the dust, with great bronze bells in either hand. They rang the bells constantly, their long arms swinging back and forth, the sharp, clanging notes filling the street. All four were elderly, as Shkeen go — hairless and pinched up with a million tiny wrinkles. But they smiled very widely, and the younger Shkeen that passed smiled at them.

On their heads rode the Greeshka.

I'd expected to find the sight hideous. I didn't. It was faintly disquieting, but only because I knew what it meant. The parasites were bright blobs of crimson goo, ranging in size from a pulsing wart on the back of one Shkeen skull to a great sheet of dripping, moving red that covered the head and shoulders of the smallest like a living cowl. The Greeshka lived by sharing the nutrients in the Shkeen bloodstream, I knew.

And also by slowly — oh so slowly — consuming its host.

Lya and I stopped a few yards from them, and watched them ring. Her face was solemn, and I think mine was. All of the others were smiling, and the songs that the bells sang were songs of joy. I squeezed Lyanna's hand tightly. "Read," I whispered.

We read.

Me: I read bells. Not the sound of bells, no, no, but the *feel* of bells, the *emotion* of bells, the bright clanging joy, the hooting-shouting-ringing loudness, the song of the Joined, the togetherness and the sharing of it all. I read what the Joined felt as they pealed their bells, their happiness and anticipation, their ecstasy in telling others of their clamorous contentment. And I read love, coming from them in great hot waves, passionate possessive love of a man and woman together, not the weak watery affection of the human who "loves" his brothers. This was real and fervent and it burned almost as it washed over me and surrounded me. They loved themselves, and they loved all Shkeen, and they loved the Greeshka, and they loved each other, and they loved us. They loved us. They loved *me* as hotly and wildly as Lya loved me. And with love I read belonging, and sharing. They four were all apart, all distinct, but they thought as one almost, and they belonged to the Greeshka, and they were all *together* and linked although each was still himself and none could read the others as I read them.

And Lyanna? I reeled back from them, and shut myself off, and looked at Lya. She was white-faced, but smiling. "They're beautiful," she said, her voice very small and soft and wondering. Drenched in love, I still remembered how much I loved *her*, and how I was part of her and her of me.

"What — what did you read?" I asked, my voice fighting the continued clangor of the bells.

She shook her head, as if to clear it. "They love us," she said. You must know that, but oh, I felt it, they *do* love us. And it's so deep. Below that love there's more love, and below that more, and on and on forever. Their minds are so *deep*, so open. I don't think I've ever read a human that deeply. Everything is right at the surface, right there, their whole lives and all their dreams and feelings and memories and oh — I just took it in, swept it up with a reading, a glance. With men, with humans, it's so much work. I have to dig, I have to fight, and even then I don't get down very far. You know, Robb, you know. Oh, *Robb!*" And she came to me and pressed tight against me, and I held her in my arms. The torrent of feeling that had washed over me must have been a tidal wave for her. Her Talent was broader and deeper than mine, and now she was shaken. I read her as she clutched me, and I read love, great love, and wonder and happiness, but also fear, nervous fear swirling through it all.

Around us, the ringing suddenly stopped. The bells one by one, ceased to swing, and the four Joined stood in silence for a brief second. One of the other Shkeen nearby came up to them with a huge, cloth-covered basket. The smallest of the Joined threw back the cloth, and the aroma of hot meatrolls rose in the street. Each of the Joined took several from the basket, and before long they were all crunching away happily, and the owner of the rolls was grinning at them. Another Shkeen, a small nude girl, ran up and offered them a flask of water, and they passed it around without comment.

"What's going on?" I asked Lya. Then, even before she told me, I remembered. Something from the literature that Valcarenghi had sent. The Joined did no work. Forty Earth-years they lived and toiled, but from First Joining to Final Union there was only joy and music, and they wandered the streets and rang their bells and talked and sang, and other Shkeen gave them food and drink. It was an honor to feed a Joined, and the Shkeen who had given up his meatrolls was radiating pride and pleasure.

"Lya," I whispered, "can you read them now?"

She nodded against my chest and pulled away and stared at the Joined, her eyes going hard and then softening again. She looked back at me. "It's different," she said, curious.

"How?"

She squinted in puzzlement. "I don't know. I mean, they still love us, and all. But now their thoughts are, well, sort of more human. There are levels, you know, and digging isn't easy, and there are hidden things, things they hide even from themselves, it's not all open like it was. They're thinking about the food now and how good it tastes. It's all very vivid. I could taste the rolls myself. But it's not the same."

I had an inspiration. "How many minds are there?"

"Four," she said. "Linked somehow, I think. But not really." She stopped, confused, and shook her head. "I mean, they sort of feel each other's emotions, like you do, I guess. But not thoughts, not the detail. I can read them, but they don't read each other. Each one is distinct. They were closer before, when they were ringing, but they were always individuals."

I was slightly disappointed. "Four minds then, not one?"

"Umpf, yes. Four."

"And the Greeshka?" My other bright idea. If the Greeshka had minds of their own.

"Nothing," Lya said. "Like reading a plant, or a piece of clothing. Not even yes-I-live."

That was disturbing. Even lower animals had some vague consciousness of life — the feeling Talents called yes-I-live — usually only a dim spark that it took a major Talent to see. But Lya was a major Talent.

"Let's talk to them," I said. She nodded, and we walked up to where the Joined were munching their meatrolls. "Hello," I said awkwardly, wondering how to address them. "Can you speak Terran?"

Three of them looked at me without comprehension. But the fourth one, the little one whose Greeshka was a rippling red cape, bobbed his head up and down. "Yesh," he said, in a piping-thin voice.

I suddenly forgot what I was going to ask, but Lyanna came to my rescue. "Do you know of human Joined?" she said.

He grinned. "All Joined are one," he said.

"Oh," I said. "Well, yes, but do you know any who look like us? Tall, you know, with hair and skin that's pink or brown or something?" I came to another awkward halt, wondering just how *much* Terran the old Shkeen knew, and eyeing his Greeshka a little apprehensively.

His head bobbled from side to side. "Joined are all different, but all are one, all are shame. Shome look ash you. Would you Join?"

"No, thanks," I said. "Where can I find a human Joined?"

He bobbled his head some more. "Joined shing and ring and walk the shacred city."

Lya had been reading. "He doesn't know," she told me. "The Joined just wander and play their bells. There's no pattern to it, nobody keeps track. It's all random. Some travel in groups, some alone, and new groups form every time two bunches meet."

"We'll have to search," I said.

"Eat," the Shkeen told us. He reached into the basket on the ground and his hands came out with two steaming meatrolls. He pressed one into my hand, one in Lya's.

I looked at it dubiously. "Thank you," I told him. I pulled at Lya with my free hand and we walked off together. The Joined grinned at us as we left, and started ringing once more before we were halfway down the street.

The meatroll was still in my hand, its crust burning my fingers. "Should I eat this?" I asked Lya.

She took a bite out of hers. "Why not? We had them last night in the restaurant, right? And I'm sure Valcarenghi would've warned us if the native food was poisonous."

That made sense, so I lifted the roll to my mouth and took a bite as I walked. It was hot, and also *hot*, and it wasn't a bit like the meatrolls we'd sampled the previous night. Those had been golden, flaky things, seasoned gently with orangespice from Baldur. The Shkeen version was crunchy, and the meat inside dripped grease and burned my mouth. But it was good, and I was hungry, and the roll didn't last long.

"Get anything else when you read the small guy?" I asked Lya around a mouthful of hot roll.

She swallowed, and nodded. "Yes, I did. He was happy, even more than the rest. He's older. He's near Final Union, and he's very thrilled about it." She spoke with her old easy manner; the after effects of reading the Joined seemed to have faded.

"Why?" I was musing out loud. "He's going to *die*. Why is he so happy about it?"

Lya shrugged. "He wasn't thinking in any great analytical detail, I'm afraid."

I licked my fingers to get rid of the last of the grease. We were at a crossroads, with Shkeen bustling by us in all directions, and now we could hear more bells on the wind. "More Joined," I said. "Want to look them up?"

"What would we find out? That we don't already know? We need a *human* Joined."

"Maybe one of this batch *will* be human."

I got Lya's withering look. "Ha. What are the odds?"

"All right," I conceded. It was now late afternoon. "Maybe we'd better head back. Get an earlier start tomorrow. Besides, Dino is probably expecting us for dinner."

Dinner, this time, was served in Valcarenghi's office, after a little additional furniture had been dragged in. His quarters, it turned out, were on the level below, but he preferred to entertain upstairs where his guests could enjoy the spectacular Tower view.

There were five of us, all told: me and Lya, Valcarenghi and Laurie, plus Gourlay. Laurie did the cooking, supervised by master chef Valcarenghi. We had beefsteaks, bred on Shkea from Old Earth stock, plus a fascinating blend of vegetables that included mushrooms from

Old Earth, groundpips from Baldur, and Shkeen sweethorns. Dino
liked to experiment and the dish was one of his inventions.

Lya and I gave a full report on the day's adventures, interrupted
only by Valcarenghi's sharp, perceptive questioning. After dinner, we
got rid of tables and dishes and sat around drinking Veltaar and talking.
This time Lya and I asked the questions, with Gourlay supplying the
biggest chunk of the answers. Valcarenghi listened from a cushion on
the floor, one arm around Laurie, the other holding his wine glass. We
were not the first Talents to visit Shkea, he told us. Nor the first to claim
the Shkeen were manlike.

"Suppose that means something," he said. "But I don't know.
They're *not* men, you know. No, sir. They're much more social, for one
thing. Great little city builders from way back, always in towns, always
surrounding themselves with others. And they're more communal than
man, too. Cooperate in all sorts of things, and they're big on sharing.
Trade, for instance — they see that as mutual sharing."

Valcarenghi laughed. "You can say that again. I just spent the whole
day trying to work out a trade contract with a group of farmers who
hadn't dealt with us before. It's not easy, believe me. They give us as
much of their stuff as we ask for, if they don't need it themselves and no
one else has asked for it earlier. But then they want to get whatever *they*
ask for in the future. They expect it, in fact. So every time we deal we've
got a choice; hand them a blank check, or go through an incredible
round of talks that ends with them convinced that we're totally selfish."

Lya wasn't satisfied. "What about sex?" she demanded. "From the
stuff you were translating last night, I got the impression they're
monogamous."

"They're confused about sex relationships," Gourlay said. "It's very
strange. Sex is sharing, you see, and it's good to share with everyone.
But the sharing has to be real and meaningful. That creates problems."

Laurie sat up, attentive. "I've studied the point," she said quickly.
"Shkeen morality insists they love *everybody*. But they can't do it, they're
too human, too possessive. They wind up in monogamous relationships, because a really deep sex-sharing with one person is better than a
million shallow physical things, in their culture. The ideal Shkeen
would sex-share with everyone, with each of the unions being just as
deep, but they can't achieve that ideal."

I frowned. "Wasn't somebody guilty last night over betraying his wife?"

Laurie nodded eagerly. "Yes, but the guilt was because his other relationships caused his sharing with his wife to diminish. *That* was the betrayal. If he'd been able to manage it without hurting his older relationship, the sex would have been meaningless. And, if all of the relationships have been real love-sharing, it would have been a plus. His wife would have been proud of him. It's quite an achievement for a Shkeen to be in a multiple union that works."

"And one of the greatest Shkeen crimes is to leave another alone," Gourlay said. "Emotionally alone. Without sharing."

I mulled over that, while Gourlay went on. The Shkeen had little crime, he told us. Especially no violent crime. No murders, no beatings, no prisons, no wars in their long, empty history.

"They're a race without murderers," Valcarenghi said. "Which may explain something. On Old Earth, the same cultures that had the highest suicide rates often had the lowest murder rates, too. And the Shkeen suicide rate is one hundred percent."

"They kill animals," I said.

"Not part of the Union," Gourlay replied. "The Union embraces all that thinks, and its creatures may not be killed. They do not kill Shkeen, or humans, or Greeshka."

Lya looked at me, then at Gourlay. "The Greeshka don't think," she said. "I tried to read them this morning and got nothing but the minds of the Shkeen they rode. Not even a yes-I-live."

"We've known that, but the point's always puzzled me," Valcarenghi said, climbing to his feet. He went to the bar for more wine, brought out a bottle, and filled our glasses. "A truly mindless parasite, but an intelligent race like the Shkeen are enslaved by it. Why?"

The new wine was good and chilled, a cold trail down my throat. I drank it, and nodded, remembering the flood of euphoria that had swept over us earlier that day. "Drugs," I said, speculatively. "The Greeshka must produce an organic pleasure drug. The Shkeen submit to it willingly and die happy. The joy is real, believe me. We felt it."

Lyanna looked doubtful, though, and Gourlay shook his head adamantly. "No, Robb. Not so. We've experimented on the Greeshka, and ..."

He must have noticed my raised eyebrows. He stopped.

"How did the Shkeen feel about that?" I asked.

"Didn't tell them. They wouldn't have liked it, not at all. Greeshka's just an animal, but it's their God. Don't fool around with God, you know. We refrained for a long time, but when Gustaffson went over, old Stuart had to know. His orders. We didn't get anywhere, though. No extracts that might be a drug, no secretions, nothing. In fact, the Shkeen are the *only* native life that submits so easily. We caught a whiner, you see, and strapped it down, and let a Greeshka link up. Then, couple hours later, we yanked the straps. Damn whiner was furious, screeching and yelping, attacking the thing on its head. Nearly clawed its own skull to ribbons before it got it off."

"Maybe only the Shkeen are susceptible?" I said. A feeble rescue attempt.

"Not quite," said Valcarenghi, with a small, thin smile. "There's us."

Lya was strangely silent in the tube, almost withdrawn. I assumed she was thinking about the conversation. But the door to our suite had barely slid shut behind us when she turned toward me and wrapped her arms around me.

I reached up and stroked her soft brown hair, slightly startled by the hug. "Hey," I muttered, "what's wrong?"

She gave me her vampire look, big-eyed and fragile. "Make love to me, Robb," she said with a soft sudden urgency. "Please. Make love to me now."

I smiled, but it was a puzzled smile, not my usual lecherous bedroom grin. Lya generally comes on impish and wicked when she's horny, but now she was all troubled and vulnerable. I didn't quite get it.

But it wasn't a time for questions, and I didn't ask any. I just pulled her to me wordlessly and kissed her hard, and we walked together to the bedroom.

And we made love, *really* made love, more than poor Normals can do. We joined our bodies as one, and I felt Lya stiffen as her mind reached out to mine. And as we moved together I was opening myself to her, drowning myself in the flood of love and need and fear that was pouring from her.

Then, quickly as it had begun, it ended. Her pleasure washed over me in a raw red wave. And I joined her on the crest, and Lya clutched me tightly, her eyes shrunk up small as she drank it all in.

Afterwards, we lay there in the darkness and let the stars of Shkea pour their radiance through the window. Lya huddled against me, her head on my chest, while I stroked her.

"That was good," I said in a drowsy-dreamy voice, smiling in the star-filled darkness.

"Yes," she replied. Her voice was soft and small, so small I barely heard it. "I love you, Robb," she whispered.

"Uh-huh," I said. "And I love you."

She pulled loose of my arm and rolled over, propping her head on a hand to stare at me and smile. "You do," she said. "I read it. I know it. And you know how much I love you, too, don't you?"

I nodded, smiling. "Sure."

"We're lucky, you know. The Normals have only words. Poor little Normals. How can they *tell*, with just words? How can they *know*? They're always apart from each other, trying to reach each other and failing. Even when they make love, even when they come, they're always apart. They must be very lonely."

There was something ... disturbing ... in that. I looked at Lya, into her bright happy eyes, and thought about it. "Maybe," I said, finally. "But it's not that bad for them. They don't know any other way. And they try, they love too. They bridge the gap sometimes."

"Only a look and a voice, then darkness again and a silence," Lya quoted, her voice sad and tender. "We're luckier, aren't we? We have so much more."

"We're luckier," I echoed. And I reached out to read her too. Her mind was a haze of satisfaction, with a gentle scent of wistful, lonely longing. But there was something else, way down, almost gone now, but still faintly detectable.

I sat up slowly. "Hey," I said. "You're worried about something. And before, when we came in, you were scared. What's the matter?"

"I don't know, really," she said. She sounded puzzled and she was puzzled; I read it there. "I *was* scared, but I don't know why. The Joined, I think. I kept thinking about how much they loved me. They didn't even *know* me, but they loved me so much, and they understood — it was almost like what we have. It — I don't know. It bothered me. I mean, I didn't think I could ever be loved that way, except by you. And they were so *close*, so together. I felt kind of lonely, just holding hands and talking. I wanted to be close to *you* that way. After the way they were all sharing and everything, being alone just seemed empty. And frightening. You know?"

"I know," I said, touching her lightly again, with hand and mind. "I understand. We do understand each other. We're together almost as they are, as Normals can't ever be."

Lya nodded, and smiled, and hugged me. We went to sleep in each other's arms.

Dreams again. But again, at dawn, the memory stole away from me. It was all very annoying. The dream had been pleasant, comfortable. I wanted it back, and I couldn't even remember what it was. Our bedroom, washed by harsh daylight, seemed drab compared to the splendors of my lost vision.

Lya woke after me, with another headache. This time she had the pills on hand, by the bedstand. She grimaced and took one.

"It must he the Shkeen wine," I told her. "Something about it takes a dim view of your metabolism."

She pulled on a fresh coverall and scowled at me. "Ha. We were drinking Veltaar last night, remember? My father gave me my first glass of Veltaar when I was nine. It never gave me headaches before."

"A first!" I said, smiling.

"It's not funny," she said. "It hurts."

I quit kidding, and tried to read her. She was right. It *did* hurt. Her whole forehead throbbed with pain. I withdrew quickly before I caught it too.

"All right," I said. "I'm sorry. The pills will take care of it, though. Meanwhile, we've got work to do."

Lya nodded. She'd never let anything interfere with work yet.

The second day was a day of manhunt. We got off to a much earlier start, had a quick breakfast with Gourlay, then picked up our aircar outside the tower. This time we didn't drop down when we hit Shkeentown. We wanted a human Joined, which meant we had to cover a lot of ground. The city was the biggest I'd ever seen, in area at any rate, and the thousand-odd human cultists were lost among millions of Shkeen. And, of those humans, only about half were actually Joined yet.

So we kept the aircar low, and buzzed up and down the dome-dotted hills like a floating rollercoaster, causing quite a stir in the streets below us. The Shkeen had seen aircars before, of course, but it still had some novelty value, particularly to the kids, who tried to run after us whenever we flashed by. We also panicked a whiner, causing him to upset the cart full of fruit he was dragging. I felt guilty about that, so I kept the car higher afterwards.

We spotted Joined all over the city, singing, eating, walking — and ringing those bells, those eternal bronze bells. But for the first three hours, all we found were Shkeen Joined. Lya and I took turns driving and watching. After the excitement of the previous day, the search was tedious and tiring.

Finally, however, we found something: a large group of Joined, ten of them, clustered around a bread cart behind one of the steeper hills. Two were taller than the rest.

We landed on the other side of the hill and walked around to meet them, leaving our aircar surrounded by a crowd of Shkeen children. The Joined were still eating when we arrived. Eight of them were Shkeen of various sizes and hues, Greeshka pulsing atop their skulls. The other two were human.

They wore the same long red gowns as the Shkeen, and they carried the same bells. One of them was a big man, with loose skin that hung in flaps, as if he'd lost a lot of weight recently. His hair was white and curly, his face marked by a broad smile and laugh wrinkles around his eyes. The other was a thin, dark weasel of a man with a big hooked nose.

Both of them had Greeshka sucking at their skulls. The parasite riding the weasel was barely a pimple, but the older man had a lordly specimen that dripped down beyond his shoulders and into the back of the gown.

Somehow, this time, it *did* look hideous.

Lyanna and I walked up to them, trying hard to smile, not reading — at least at first. They smiled at us as we approached. Then they waved.

"Hello," the weasel said cheerily when we got there. "I've never seen you. Are you new on Shkea?"

That took me slightly by surprise. I'd been expecting some sort of garbled mystic greeting, or maybe no greeting at all. I was assuming that somehow the human converts would have abandoned their humanity to become mock-Shkeen. I was wrong.

"More or less," I replied. And I read the weasel. He was genuinely pleased to see us, and just bubbled with contentment and good cheer. "We've been hired to talk to people like you." I'd decided to be honest about it.

The weasel stretched his grin farther than I thought it would go. "I am Joined, and happy," he said. "I'll be glad to talk to you. My name is Lester Kamenz. What do you want to know, brother?"

Lya, next to me, was going tense. I decided I'd let her read in depth while I asked questions. "When did you convert to the Cult?"

"Cult?" Kamenz said.

"The Union."

He nodded, and I was struck by the grotesque similarity of his bobbing head and that of the elderly Shkeen we'd seen yesterday. "I have always been in the Union. You are in the Union. All that thinks is in the Union."

"Some of us weren't told," I said. "How about you? When did you realize you were in the Union?"

"A year ago, Old Earth time. I was admitted to the ranks of the Joined only a few weeks ago. The First Joining is a joyful time. I am joyful. Now I will walk the streets and ring my bells until the Final Union."

"What did you do before?"

"Before?" A short vague look. "I ran machines once, I ran computers, in the Tower. But my life was empty, brother. I did not know I was in the Union, and I was alone. I had only machines, cold machines. Now I am Joined. Now I am" — again he searched — "not alone."

I reached into him, and found the happiness still there, with love. But now there was an ache too, a vague recollection of past pain, the stink of unwelcome memories. Did these fade? Maybe the gift the Greeshka gave its victims was oblivion, sweet mindless rest and end of struggle. Maybe.

I decided to try something. "That thing on your head," I said, sharply. "It's a parasite. It's drinking your blood right now, feeding on it. As it grows, it will take more and more of the things *you* need to live. Finally it will start to eat your tissue. Understand? It will *eat* you. I don't know how painful it will be, but however it feels, at the end you'll be *dead*. Unless you come back to the Tower now, and have the surgeons remove it. Or maybe you could remove it yourself. Why don't you try? Just reach up and pull it off. Go ahead."

I'd expected — what? Rage? Horror? Disgust? I got none of these. Kamenz just stuffed bread in his mouth and smiled at me, and all I read was his love and joy and a little pity.

"The Greeshka does not kill," he said finally. "The Greeshka gives joy and happy Union. Only those who have no Greeshka die. They are ... alone. Oh, forever alone." Something in his mind trembled with sudden fear, but it faded quickly.

I glanced at Lya. She was stiff and hard-eyed, still reading. I looked back and began to phrase another question. But suddenly the Joined began to ring. One of the Shkeen started it off, swinging his bell up and down to produce a single sharp clang. Then his other hand swung, then the first again, then the second, then another Joined began to ring, then still another, and then they were all swinging and clanging and the noise of their bells was smashing against my ears as the joy and the love and the feel of the bells assaulted my mind once again.

I lingered to savor it. The love there was breathtaking, awesome, almost frightening in its heat and intensity, and there was so much sharing to frolic in and wonder at, such a soothing-calming-exhila-rating tapestry of good feelings. Something happened to the Joined when they rang, something touched them and lifted them and gave them a glow, something strange and glorious that mere Normals could not hear in their harsh clanging music. I was no Normal, though. I could hear it.

I withdrew reluctantly, slowly. Kamenz and the other human were both ringing vigorously now, with broad smiles and glowing twinkling eyes that transfigured their faces. Lyanna was still tense, still reading. Her mouth was slightly open, and she trembled where she stood.

I put an arm around her and waited, listening to the music, patient. Lya continued to read. Finally, after minutes, I shook her gently. She turned and studied me with hard, distant eyes. Then blinked. And her eyes widened and she came back, shaking her head and frowning.

Puzzled, I looked into her head. Strange and stranger. It was a swirling fog of emotion, a dense moving blend of more feelings than I'd care to put a name to. No sooner had I entered than I was lost, lost and uneasy. Somewhere in the fog there was a bottomless abyss lurking to engulf me. At least it felt that way.

"Lya," I said. "What's wrong?"

She shook her head again, and looked at the Joined with a look that was equal parts fear and longing. I repeated my question.

"I — I don't know," she said. "Robb, let's not talk now. Let's go. I want time to think."

"OK," I said. What was going on here? I took her hand and we walked slowly around the hill to the slope where we'd left the car. Shkeen kids were climbing all over it, I chased them, laughing. Lya just stood there, her eyes gone all faraway on me. I wanted to read her again, but somehow I felt it would be an invasion of privacy.

Airborne, we streaked back toward the Tower, riding higher and faster this time. I drove, while Lya sat beside me and stared out into the distance.

"Did you get anything useful?" I asked her, trying to get her mind back on the assignment.

"Yes. No, Maybe." Her voice sounded distracted, as if only part of her was talking to me. "I read their lives, both of them. Kamenz was a computer programmer, as he said. But he wasn't very good. An ugly little man with an ugly little personality, no friends, no sex, no nothing. Lived by himself, avoided the Shkeen, didn't like them at all. Didn't even like people, really. But Gustaffson got through to him, somehow. He ignored Kamenz' coldness, his bitter little cuts, his cruel jokes. He didn't retaliate, you know? After a while, Kamenz came to like Gustaffson, to admire him. They were never really friends in any normal sense, but still Gustaffson was the nearest thing to a friend that Kamenz had."

She stopped suddenly. "So he went over with Gustaffson?" I prompted, glancing at her quickly. Her eyes still wandered.

"No, not at first. He was still afraid, still scared of the Shkeen and terrified of the Greeshka. But later, with Gustaffson gone, he began to realize how empty his life was. He worked all day with people who despised him and machines that didn't care, then sat alone at night reading and watching holoshows. Not life, really. He hardly touched the people around him. Finally he went to find Gustaffson, and wound up converted. Now ..."

"Now ... ?"

She hesitated. "He's happy, Robb," she said. "He really is. For the first time in his life, he's happy. He'd never known love before. Now it fills him."

"You got a lot," I said.

"Yes." Still the distracted voice, the lost eyes. "He was open, sort of. There were levels, but digging wasn't as hard as it usually is — as if his barriers were weakening, coming down almost ... "

"How about the other guy?"

She stroked the instrument panel, staring only at her hand. "Him? That was Gustaffson ... "

And that, suddenly, seemed to wake her, to restore her to the Lya I knew and loved. She shook her head and looked at me, and the aimless voice became an animated torrent of words. "Robb, listen, that was *Gustaffson*, he's been Joined over a year now, and he's going on to Final Union within a week. The Greeshka has accepted him, and he wants it, you know? He really does, and — and — oh Robb, he's *dying!*"

"Within a week, according to what you just said."

"No. I mean yes, but that's not what I mean. Final Union isn't death, to him. He believes it, all of it, the whole religion. The Greeshka is his god, and he's going to join it. But before, and now, he was dying. He's got the Slow Plague, Robb. A terminal case. It's been eating at him from inside for fifteen years now. He got it back on Nightmare, in the swamps, when his family died. That's no world for people, but he was there, the administrator over a research base, a short-term thing. They lived on Thor; it was only a visit, but the ship crashed. Gustaffson got all wild and tried to reach them before the end, but he grabbed a faulty pair of skinthins, and the spores got through. And they were all dead when he got there. He had an awful lot of pain, Robb. From the Slow Plague, but more from the loss. He really loved them, and it was never the same after. They gave him Shkea as a reward, kind of, to take his mind off the crash, but he still thought of it all the time. I could see the picture, Robb. It was vivid. He couldn't forget it. The kids were inside the ship, safe behind the walls, but the life system failed and choked them to death. But his wife — oh, Robb — she took some skinthins and tried to go for help, and outside those *things*, those big wrigglers they have on Nightmare — ?"

I swallowed hard, feeling a little sick. "The eater-worms," I said, dully. I'd read about them, and seen holos. I could imagine the picture that Lya'd seen in Gustaffson's memory, and it wasn't at all pretty. I was glad I didn't have her Talent.

"They were still — still — when Gustaffson got there. You know. He killed them all with a screech gun."

I shook my head. "I didn't think things like that really went on."

"No," Lya said. "Neither did Gustaffson. They'd been so — so *happy* before that, before the thing on Nightmare. He loved her, and they were really close, and his career had been almost charmed. He didn't have to go to Nightmare, you know. He took it because it was a challenge, because nobody else could handle it. That gnaws at him, too. And he remembers all the time. No — they — " Her voice faltered. "They thought they were *lucky*," she said, before falling into silence.

There was nothing to say to that. I just kept quiet and drove, thinking, feeling a blurred, watered-down version of what Gustaffson's pain must have been like. After a while, Lya began to speak again.

"It was all there, Robb," she said, her voice softer and slower and more thoughtful once again. "But he was at peace. He still remembered it all, and the way it had hurt, but it didn't bother him as it had. Only now he was sorry they weren't with him. He was sorry that they died without Final Union. Almost like the Shkeen woman, remember? The one at the Gathering? With her brother?"

"I remember," I said.

"Like that. And his mind was open, too. More than Kamenz, much more. When he rang, the levels all vanished, and everything was right at the surface, all the love and pain and everything. His whole life, Robb. I shared his whole life with him, in an instant. And all his thoughts, too ... he's seen the caves of Union ... he went down once, before he converted. I ..."

More silence, settling over us and darkening the car. We were close to the end of Shkeentown. The Tower slashed the sky ahead of us, shining in the sun. And the lower domes and archways of the glittering human city were coming into view.

"Robb," Lya said. "Land here. I have to think a while, you know? Go back without me. I want to walk among the Shkeen a little."

I glanced at her, frowning. "Walk? It's a long way back to the Tower, Lya."

"I'll be all right. Please. Just let me think a bit."

I read her. The thought fog had returned, denser than ever, laced through with the colors of fear. "Are you sure?" I said. "You're scared, Lyanna. Why? What's wrong? The eater-worms are a long way off."

She just looked at me, troubled. "Please, Robb," she repeated.

I didn't know what else to do, so I landed.

And I, too, thought, as I guided the aircar home. Of what Lyanna had said, and read — of Kamenz and Gustaffson. I kept my mind on the problem we'd been assigned to crack. I tried to keep it off Lya, and whatever was bothering her. That would solve itself, I thought.

Back at the Tower, I wasted no time. I went straight up to Valcarenghi's office. He was there, alone, dictating into a machine. He shut it off when I entered.

"Hi, Robb," he began. "Where's Lya?"

"Out walking. She wanted to think, I've been thinking, too. And I believe I've got your answer."

He raised his eyebrows, waiting.

I sat down. "We found Gustaffson this afternoon, and Lya read him. I think it's clear why he went over. He was a broken man, inside, however much he smiled. The Greeshka gave him an end to his pain. And there was another convert with him, a Lester Kamenz. He'd been miserable, too, a pathetic lonely man with nothing to live for. Why *shouldn't* he convert? Check out the other converts, and I bet you'll find a pattern. The most lost and vulnerable, the failures, the isolated — those will be the ones that turned to Union."

Valcarenghi nodded. "OK, I'll buy that," he said. "But our psychs guessed that long ago, Robb. Only it's no answer, not really. Sure, the converts on the whole have been a messed-up crew, I won't dispute that. But why turn to the Cult of the Union? The psychs can't answer that. Take Gustaffson now. He was a strong man, believe me. I never knew him personally, but I knew his career. He took some rough assignments, generally for the hell of it, and beat them. He could have had the cushy jobs, but he wasn't interested. I've heard about the incident on Nightmare. It's famous, in a warped sort of way. But Phil Gustaffson wasn't the sort of man to be beaten, even by something like that. He snapped out of it very quickly, from what Nelse tells me. He came to Shkea and really set the place in order, cleaning up the mess that Rockwood had left. He pushed through the first real trade contract we ever got, *and* he made the Shkeen understand what it meant, which isn't easy.

"So here he is, this competent, talented man, who's made a career of beating tough jobs and handling men. He's gone through a personal nightmare, but it hasn't destroyed him. He's as tough as ever. And suddenly he turns to the Cult of the Union, signs up for a grotesque suicide. Why? For an end to his pain, you say? An interesting theory, but there are other ways to end pain. Gustaffson had years between Nightmare and the Greeshka. He never ran away from pain then. He didn't turn to drink, or drugs, or any of the usual outs. He didn't head back to Old Earth to have a psi-psych clean up his memories — and believe me, he could've gotten it paid for, if he'd wanted it. The colonial office would have done anything for him, after Nightmare. He went on, swallowed his pain, rebuilt. Until suddenly he converts.

"His pain made him more vulnerable, yes, no doubt of it. But something else brought him over — something that Union offered, something he couldn't get from wine or memory wipe. The same's true of Kamenz, and the others. They had other outs, other ways to vote no on life. They passed them up. But they chose Union. You see what I'm getting at?"

I did, of course. My answer was no answer at all, and I realized it. But Valcarenghi was wrong too, in parts.

"Yes," I said. "I guess we've still got some reading to do." I smiled wanly. "One thing, though. Gustaffson hadn't really beaten his pain, not ever. Lya was very clear on that. It was inside him all the time, tormenting him. He just never let it come out."

"That's victory, isn't it?" Valcarenghi said. "If you bury your hurts so deep that no one can tell you have them?"

"I don't know. I don't think so. But ... anyway, there was more. Gustaffson has the Slow Plague. He's dying. He's been dying for years."

Valcarenghi's expression flickered briefly. "That I didn't know, but it just bolsters my point. I've read that some eighty percent of Slow Plague victims opt for euthanasia, if they happen to be on a planet where it's legal. Gustaffson was a planetary administrator. He could have *made* it legal. If he passed up suicide for all those years, why choose it now?"

I didn't have an answer for that. Lyanna hadn't given me one, if she had one. I didn't know where we could find one, either unless ...

"The caves," I said suddenly. "The caves of Union. We've got to witness a Final Union. There must be something about it, something that accounts for the conversions. Give us a chance to find out what it is."

Valcarenghi smiled. "All right," he said. "I can arrange it. I expected it would come to that. It's not pleasant, though, I'll warn you. I've gone down myself, so I know what I'm talking about."

"That's OK," I told him. "If you think reading Gustaffson was any fun, you should have seen Lya when she was through. She's out now trying to walk it off." That, I'd decided, must have been what was bothering her. "Final Union won't be any worse than those memories of Nightmare, I'm sure."

"Fine, then. I'll set it up for tomorrow. I'm going with you, of course. I don't want to take any chances on anything happening to you."

I nodded. Valcarenghi rose. "Good enough," he said, "Meanwhile, let's think about more interesting things. You have any plans for dinner?"

We wound up eating at a mock-Shkeen restaurant run by humans, in the company of Gourlay and Laurie Blackburn. The talk was mostly social noises — sports, politics, art, old jokes, that sort of thing. I don't think there was a mention of the Shkeen or the Greeshka all evening.

Afterwards, when I got back to our suite, I found Lyanna waiting for me. She was in bed, reading one of the handsome volumes from our library, a book of Old Earth poetry. She looked up when I entered.

"Hi," I said. "How was your walk?"

"Long." A smile creased her pale, small face, then faded. "But I had time to think. About this afternoon, and yesterday, and about the Joined. And us."

"Us?"

"Robb, do you love me?" The question was delivered almost matter-of-factly, in a voice full of question. As if she didn't know. As if she really didn't know.

I sat down on the bed and took her hand and tried to smile. "Sure," I said. 'You know that, Lya."

"I did. I do. You love me, Robb, really you do. As much as a human can love. But ... " She stopped. She shook her head and closed her book and sighed, "But we're still apart, Robb. We're still apart."

"What *are* you talking about?"

"This afternoon. I was so confused afterwards, and scared. I wasn't sure why, but I've thought about it. When I was reading, Robb — I was in there, with the Joined, sharing them and their love. I really was. And I didn't want to come out. I didn't want to leave them, Robb. When I did, I felt so isolated, so cut off."

"That's your fault," I said. "I tried to talk to you. You were too busy thinking."

"Talking? What good is talking? It's communication, I guess, but is it *really?* I used to think so, before they trained my Talent. After that, reading seemed to be the real communication, the real way to reach somebody else, somebody like you. But now I don't know. The Joined — when they ring — they're so *together,* Robb. All linked. Like us when we make love, almost. And they love each other, too. And they love us, so intensely. I felt — I don't know. But Gustaffson loves me as much as you do. No. He loves me more."

Her face was white as she said that, her eyes wide, lost, lonely. And me, I felt a sudden chill, like a cold wind blowing through my soul. I didn't say anything. I only looked at her, and wet my lips. And bled.

She saw the hurt in my eyes, I guess. Or read it. Her hand pulled at mine, caressed it. "Oh, Robb. Please. I don't mean to hurt you. It's not you. It's all of us. What do we have, compared to *them?*"

"I don't know what you're talking about, Lya," Half of me suddenly wanted to cry. The other half wanted to shout. I stifled both halves, and kept my voice steady. But inside I wasn't steady, I wasn't steady at all.

"Do you love me, Robb?" Again. Wondering.

"Yes!" Fiercely. A challenge.

"What does that mean?" she said.

"You know what it means," I said. "Dammit, Lya, *think!* Remember all we've had, all we've shared together. *That's* love, Lya. It is. We're the lucky ones, remember? You said that yourself. The Normals have only a touch and a voice, then back to their darkness. They can barely find each other. They're alone. Always. Groping. Trying, over and over, to climb out of their isolation booths, and failing, over and over. But not us, we found the way, we know each other as much as any human beings ever can. There's nothing I wouldn't tell you, or share with you. I've said that before, and you know it's true, you can read it in me. *That's* love, dammit. *Isn't it?*"

"I don't know," she said, in a voice so sadly baffled. Soundlessly, without even a sob, she began to cry. And while the tears ran in lonely paths down her cheeks, she talked. "Maybe that's love. I always thought it was. But now I don't know. If what we have is love, what was it I felt this afternoon, what was it I touched and shared in? Oh, Robb, I love you too. You know that. I try to share with you. I want to share what I read, what it was like. But I can't. We're cut off. I can't make you understand. I'm here and you're there and we can touch and make love and talk, but we're still apart. You see? You see? I'm alone. And this afternoon, I *wasn't*."

"You're not alone, dammit," I said suddenly. "I'm here." I clutched her hand tightly. "Feel? Hear? You're not alone!"

She shook her head, and the tears flowed on. "You don't understand, see? And there's no way I can make you. You said we know each other as much as any human beings ever can. You're right. But how much can human beings know each other? Aren't all of them cut off, really? Each alone in a big, dark, empty universe? We only trick ourselves when we think that someone else is there. In the end, in the cold lonely end, it's only us, by ourselves in the blackness. Are you there, Robb? How do I know? Will you die with me, Robb? Will we be together then? Are we together *now*? You say we're luckier than the Normals. I've said it too. They have only a touch and voice, right? How many times have I quoted that? But what do we have? A touch and two voices, maybe. It's not enough anymore. I'm scared. Suddenly I'm scared."

She began to sob. Instinctively I reached out to her, wrapped her in my arms, stroked her. We lay back together, and she wept against my chest. I read her, briefly, and I read her pain, her sudden loneliness, her hunger, all aswirl in a darkening mindstorm of fear. And, though I touched her and caressed her and whispered — over and over — that it would be all right, that I was here, that she wasn't alone, I knew that it would not be enough. Suddenly there was a gulf between us, a great dark yawning thing that grew and grew, and I didn't know how to bridge it. And Lya, my Lya, was crying, and she needed me. And I needed her, but I couldn't get to her.

Then I realized that I was crying too.

We held each other, in silent tears, for what must have been an hour. But finally the tears ran out. Lya clutched her body to me so tightly I could hardly breathe, and I held her just as tightly.

"Robb," she whispered. "You said — you said we really know each other. All those times you've said it. And you say, sometimes, that I'm *right* for you, that I'm perfect."

I nodded, wanting to believe. "Yes. You are."

"No," she said, choking out the word, forcing it into the air, fighting herself to say it. "It's not *so*. I read you, yes. I can hear the words rattling around in your head as you fit a sentence together before saying it. And I listen to you scold yourself when you've done something stupid. And I see memories, some memories, and live through them with you. But it's all on the surface, Robb, all on the top. Below it, there's more, more of *you*. Drifting half-thoughts I don't quite catch. Feelings I can't put a name to. Passions you suppress, and memories even you don't know you have. Sometimes I can get to that level. Sometimes. If I really fight, if I drain myself to exhaustion. But when I get there, I know — I *know* — that there's another level below *that*. And more and more, on and on, down and down. I can't reach them, Robb, though they're part of you. I don't know you. I can t know you. You don't even know yourself, see? And me, do you know me? No. Even less. You know what I tell you, and I tell you the truth, but maybe not all. And you read my feelings, my surface feelings — the pain of a stubbed toe, a quick flash of annoyance, the pleasure I get when you're in me. Does that mean you know me? What of *my* levels, and levels? What about the things I don't even know myself? Do you know them? How, Robb, how?"

She shook her head again, with that funny little gesture she had whenever she was confused. "And you say I'm perfect, and that you love me. I'm so right for you. *But am I?* Robb, *I read your thoughts.* I know when you want me to be sexy, so I'm sexy. I see what turns you on, so I do it. I know when you want me to be serious, and when you want me to joke. I know what kind of jokes to tell, too. Never the cutting kind, you don't like that, to hurt or see people hurt. You laugh with people not at them, and I laugh with you, and love you for your tastes. I know when you want me to talk, and when to keep quiet. I know when you want me to be your proud tigress, you tawny telepath, and when you want a little girl to shelter in your arms. And I *am* those things, Robb, because you want me to be, because I love you, because I can feel the joy in your mind at every *right* thing that I do. I never set out to do it that way, but it happened. I didn't mind; I don't mind. Most of the time it wasn't even conscious. You do the same thing, too. I read it in you. You can't read as I do, so sometimes you guess wrong — you come on witty when I want silent understanding, or you act the strong man when I need a boy to mother. But you get it right sometimes, too. And you *try,* you always try.

"But is it really *you?* Is it really *me?* What if I wasn't perfect, you see, if I was just myself, with all my faults and the things you don't like out in the open? Would you love me *then?* I don't know. But Gustaffson would, and Kamenz. I know that, Robb. I saw it. I know *them.* Their levels ... vanished. I *KNOW* them, and if I went back I could share with them, more than with you. And they know me, the real me, all of me, I think. And they love me. You see? You *see?*"

Did I see? I don't know. I was confused. Would I love Lya if she was "herself"? But what was "herself"? How was it different from the Lya I knew? I thought I loved Lya and would always love Lya — but what if the real Lya wasn't like my Lya? *What* did I love? The strange abstract concept of a human being, or the flesh and voice and personality that I thought of as Lya? I didn't know. I didn't know who Lya was, or who I was, or what the hell it all meant. And I was scared. Maybe I couldn't feel what she had felt that afternoon. But I knew what she was feeling then. I was alone, and I needed someone.

"Lya," I called. "Lya, let's try. We don't have to give up. We can reach each other. There's a way, our way. We've done it before. Come, Lya, come with me, come to me."

As I spoke, I undressed her, and she responded and her hands joined mine. When we were nude, I began to stroke her, slowly, and she me. Our minds reached out to each other. Reached and probed as never before. I could feel her, inside my head, digging. Deeper and deeper. Down. And I opened myself to her, I surrendered, all the petty little secrets I had kept even from her, or tried to, now I yielded up to her everything I could remember, my triumphs and shames, the good moments and the pain, the times I'd hurt someone, the times I'd been hurt, the long crying sessions by myself, the fears I wouldn't admit, the prejudices I fought, the vanities I battled when the time struck, the silly boyish sins. All. Everything. I buried nothing. I hid nothing. I gave myself to her, to Lya, to *my* Lya. She had to know me.

And so, too, she yielded. Her mind was a forest through which I roamed, hunting down wisps of emotion, the fear and the need and the love at the top, the fainter things beneath, the half-formed whims and passions still deeper into the woods. I don't have Lya's Talent, I read only feelings, never thoughts. But I read thoughts then, for the first and only time, thoughts she threw at me because I'd never seen them before. I couldn't read much, but some I got.

And as her mind opened to mine, so did her body. I entered her, and we moved together, bodies one, minds entwined, as close as human beings can join. I felt pleasure washing over me in great glorious waves, my pleasure, her pleasure, both together building on each other, and I rode the crest for an eternity as it approached a far distant shore. And finally as it smashed into that beach, we came together, and for a second — for a tiny, fleeting second — I could not tell which orgasm was mine, and which was hers.

But then it passed. We lay, bodies locked together, on the bed. In the starlight. But it was not a bed. It was the beach, the flat black beach, and there were no stars above. A thought touched me, a vagrant thought that was not mine. Lya's thought. We were on a plain, she was thinking, and I saw that she was right. The waters that had carried us here were gone, receded. There was only a vast flat blackness stretching away in all directions, with dim ominous shapes moving on either horizon. *We are here as on a darkling plain,* Lya thought. And suddenly I knew what those shapes were, and what poem she had been reading.

We slept.

I woke, alone.

The room was dark. Lya lay on the other side of the bed, curled up, still asleep. It was late, near dawn I thought. But I wasn't sure. I was restless.

I got up and dressed in silence. I needed to walk somewhere, to think, to work things out. Where, though?

There was a key in my pocket. I touched it when I pulled on my tunic, and remembered. Valcarenghi's office. It would be locked and deserted at this time of night. And the view might help me think.

I left, found the tubes, and shot up, up, up to the apex of the Tower, the top of man's steel challenge to the Shkeen. The office was unlit, the furniture dark shapes in the shadows. There was only the starlight. Shkea is closer to the galactic center than Old Earth, or Baldur. The stars are a fiery canopy across the night sky. Some of them are very close, and they burn like red and blue-white fires in the awesome blackness above. In Valcarenghi's office, all the walls are glass. I went to one, and looked out. I wasn't thinking. Just feeling. And I felt cold and lost and little.

Then there was a soft voice behind me saying hello. I barely heard it.

I turned away from the window, but other stars leaped at me from the far walls. Laurie Blackburn sat in one of the low chairs, concealed by the darkness.

"Hello," I said. "I didn't mean to intrude. I thought no one would be here."

She smiled. A radiant smile in a radiant face, but there was no humor in it. Her hair fell in sweeping auburn waves past her shoulders, and she was dressed in something long and gauzy. I could see her gentle curves through its folds, and she made no effort to hide herself.

"I come up here a lot," she said. "At night, usually. When Dino's asleep. It's a good place to think."

"Yes," I said, smiling. "My thoughts, too."

"The stars are pretty, aren't they?"

"Yes."

"I think so. I — " Hesitation. Then she rose and came to me. "Do you love Lya?" she said.

A hammer of a question. Timed terribly. But I handled it well, I think. My mind was still on my talk with Lya. "Yes," I said. "Very much. Why?"

She was standing close to me, looking at my face, and past me, out to the stars. "I don't know. I wonder about love, sometimes. I love Dino, you know. He came here two months ago, so we haven't known each other long. But I love him already. I've never known anybody like him. He's kind, and considerate, and he does everything well. I've never seen him fail at anything he tried. Yet he doesn't seem driven, like some men. He wins so easily. He believes in himself a lot, and that's attractive. He's given me anything I could ask for, everything."

I read her, caught her love and worry, and guessed. "Except himself," I said.

She looked at me, startled. Then she smiled. "I forgot. You're a Talent. Of course you know. You're right. I don't know what I worry about, but I do worry. Dino is so perfect, you know. I've told him — well, everything. All about me and my life. And he listens and understands. He's always receptive, he's there when I need him. But — "

"It's all one way," I said. It was a statement. I knew.

She nodded. "It's not that he keeps secrets. He doesn't. He'll answer any question I ask. But the answers mean nothing. I ask him what he fears, and he says nothing, and makes me believe it. He's very rational, very calm. He never gets angry, he never has. I asked him. He doesn't hate people, he thinks hate is bad. He's never felt pain, either, or he says he hasn't. Emotional pain, I mean. Yet he understands me when I talk about my life. Once he said his biggest fault was laziness. But he's not lazy at all, I know that. Is he really that perfect? He tells me he's always sure of himself, because he knows he's good, but he smiles when he says it, so I can't even accuse him of being vain. He says he believes in God, but he never talks about it. If you try to talk seriously, he'll listen patiently, or joke with you, or lead the conversation away. He says he loves me, but — "

I nodded. I knew what was coming.

It came. She looked up at me, eyes begging. "You're a Talent," she said. "You've read him, haven't you? You know him? Tell me. Please tell me."

I was reading her. I could see how much she needed to know, how much she worried and feared, how much she loved. I couldn't lie to her. Yet it was hard to give her the answer I had to.

"I've read him," I said. Slowly. Carefully. Measuring out my words like precious fluids. "And you, you too. I saw your love, on that first night, when we ate together."

"And Dino?"

My words caught in my throat. "He's — funny, Lya said once. I can read his surface emotions easily enough. Below that, nothing. He's very self-contained, walled off. Almost as if his only emotions are the ones he — *allows* himself to feel. I've felt his confidence, his pleasure. I've felt worry too, but never real fear. He's very affectionate toward you, very protective. He enjoys feeling protective."

"Is that all?" So hopeful. It hurt.

"I'm afraid it is. He's walled off, Laurie. He needs himself, only himself. If there's love in him, it's behind that wall, hidden. I can't read it. He thinks a lot of you, Laurie. But love — well, it's different. It's stronger and more unreasoning and it comes in crashing floods. And Dino's not like that, at least not out where I can read."

"Closed," she said. "He's closed to me. I opened myself to him, totally. But he didn't. I was always afraid — even when he was with me, I felt sometimes that he wasn't there at all — "

She sighed. I read her despair, her welling loneliness. I didn't know what to do. "Cry if you like," I told her, inanely. "Sometimes it helps. I know. I've cried enough in my time."

She didn't cry. She looked up, and laughed lightly. "No," she said. "I can't. Dino taught me never to cry. He said tears never solve anything."

A sad philosophy. Tears don't solve anything, maybe, but they're part of being human. I wanted to tell her so, but instead I just smiled at her.

She smiled back, and cocked her head. "You cry," she said suddenly, in a voice strangely delighted. "That's funny. That's more of an admission than I ever heard from Dino, in a way. Thank you, Robb. Thank you."

And Laurie stood on her toes and looked up, expectant. And I could read what she expected. So I took her and kissed her, and she pressed her body hard against mine. And all the while I thought of Lya, telling myself that she wouldn't mind, that she'd be proud of me, that she'd understand.

Afterwards, I stayed up in the office alone to watch the dawn come up. I was drained, but somehow content. The light that crept over the horizon was chasing the shadows before it, and suddenly all the fears that had seemed so threatening in the night were silly, unreasoning. We'd bridged it, I thought — Lya and I. Whatever it was, we'd handled it, and today we'd handle the Greeshka with the same ease, together.

When I got back to our room, Lya was gone.

"We found the aircar in the middle of Shkeentown," Valcarenghi was saying. He was cool, precise, reassuring. His voice told me, without words, that there was nothing to worry about. "I've got men out looking for her. But Shkeentown's a big place. Do you have any idea where she might have gone?"

"No," I said, dully. "Not really. Maybe to see some more Joined. She seemed — well, almost obsessed by them. I don't know."

"Well, we've got a good police force. We'll find her, I'm certain of that. But it may take a while. Did you two have a fight?"

"Yes. No. Sort of, but it wasn't a real fight. It was strange."

"I see," he said. But he didn't. "Laurie tells me you came up here last night, alone."

"Yes. I needed to think."

"All right," said Valcarenghi. "So let's say Lya woke up, decided she wanted to think too. You came up here. She took a ride. Maybe she just wants a day off to wander around Shkeentown. She did something like that yesterday, didn't she?"

"Yes."

"So she's doing it again. No problem. She'll probably be back well before dinner." He smiled.

"Why did she go without telling me, then? Or leaving a note, or *something?*"

"I don't know. *It's not important.*"

Wasn't it, though? *Wasn't it?* I sat in the chair, head in my hands and a scowl on my face, and I was sweating. Suddenly I was very much afraid, of what I didn't know. I should never have left her alone. I was telling myself. While I was up here with Laurie, Lyanna woke alone in a darkened room, and — and — and *what?* And left.

"Meanwhile, though," Valcarenghi said. "we've got work to do. The trip to the caves is all set."

I looked up, disbelieving. "The caves? I can't go there, not now, not alone."

He gave a sigh of exasperation, exaggerated for effect. "Oh, come now, Robb. It's not the end of the world. Lya will be all right. She seemed to be a perfectly sensible girl, and I'm sure she can take care of herself. Right?"

I nodded.

"Meanwhile, we'll cover the caves, I still want to get to the bottom of this."

"It won't do any good." I protested. "Not without Lya. She's the major Talent. I — I just read emotions. I can't get down deep, as she can. I won't solve anything for you."

He shrugged. "Maybe not. But the trip is on, and we've got nothing to lose. We can always make a second run after Lya comes back. Besides, this should do you good, get your mind off this other business. There's nothing you can do for Lya now. I've got every available man out searching for her, and if they don't find her you certainly won't. So there's no sense dwelling on it. Just get back into action, keep busy." He turned, headed for the tube. "Come. There's an aircar waiting for us. Nelse will go too."

Reluctantly, I stood. I was in no mood to consider the problems of the Shkeen, but Valcarenghi's arguments made a certain amount of sense. Besides which, he'd hired Lyanna and me, and we still had obligations to him. I could try anyway, I thought.

On the ride out, Valcarenghi sat in the front with the driver, a hulking police sergeant with a face chiseled out of granite. He'd selected a police car this time so we could keep posted on the search for Lya. Gourlay and I were in the back seat together. Gourlay had covered our laps with a big map, and he was telling me about the caves of Final Union.

"Theory is the caves are the original home of the Greeshka," he said. "Probably true, makes sense. Greeshka are a lot bigger there. You'll see. The caves are all through the hills, away from our part of Shkeentown, where the country gets wilder. A regular little honeycomb. Greeshka in every one, too. Or so I've heard. Been in a few myself, Greeshka in all of *them*. So I believe what they say about the rest. The city, the sacred city, well, it was probably built *because* of the caves. Shkeen come here from all over the continent, you know, for Final Union. Here, this is the cave region." He took out a pen, and made a big circle in red near the center of the map. It was meaningless to me. The map was getting me down. I hadn't realized that the Shkeen city was so *huge*. How the hell could they find anyone who didn't want to be found?

Valcarenghi looked back from the front seat. "The cave we're going to is a big one, as these places go. I've been there before. There's no formality about Final Union, you understand. The Shkeen just pick a cave, and walk in, and lie down on top of the Greeshka. They'll use whatever entrance is most convenient. Some of them are no bigger than sewer pipes, but if you went in far enough, theory says you'd run into a Greeshka, setting back in the dark and pulsing away. The biggest caves are lighted with torches, like the Great Hall, but that's just a frill. It doesn't play any real part in the Union."

"I take it we're going to one of them?" I said.

Valcarenghi nodded. "Right. I figured you'd want to see what a mature Greeshka is like. It's not pretty, but it's educational. So we need lighting."

Gourlay resumed his narrative then, but I tuned him out. I felt I knew quite enough about the Shkeen and the Greeshka, and I was still worried about Lyanna. After a while he wound down, and the rest of the trip was in silence. We covered more ground than we ever had before. Even the Tower — our shining steel landmark — had been swallowed by the hills behind us.

The terrain got rougher, rockier, and more overgrown, and the hills rose higher and wilder. But the domes went on and on and on, and there were Shkeen everywhere. Lya could be down there, I thought, lost among those teeming millions. Looking for what? Thinking what?

Finally we landed, in a wooded valley between two massive, rock-studded hills. Even here there were Shkeen, the red-brick domes rising from the undergrowth among the stubby trees. I had no trouble spotting the cave. It was halfway up one of the slopes, a dark yawn in the rock face, with a dusty road winding up to it.

We set down in the valley and climbed that road. Gourlay ate up the distance with long, gawky strides, while Valcarenghi moved with an easy, untiring grace, and the policeman plodded on stolidly. I was the straggler. I dragged myself up, and I was half-winded by the time we got to the cave mouth.

If I'd expected cave paintings, or an altar, or some kind of nature temple, I was sadly disappointed. It was an ordinary cave, with damp stone walls and low ceilings and cold, wet air. Cooler than most of Shkea, and less dusty, but that was about it. There was one long, winding passage through the rock, wide enough for the four of us to walk abreast yet low enough so Gourlay had to stoop. Torches were set along the walls at regular intervals, but only every fourth one or so was lit. They burned with an oily smoke that seemed to cling to the top of the cave and drift down into the depths before us. I wondered what was sucking it in.

After about ten minutes of walking, most of it down a barely perceptible incline, the passage led us out into a high, brightly lit room, with a vaulting stone roof that was stained sooty by torch smoke. In the room, the Greeshka.

Its color was a dull brownish red, like old blood, not the bright near-translucent crimson of the small creatures that clung to the skulls of the Joined. There were spots of black, too, like burns or soot stains on the vast body. I could barely see the far side of the cave; the Greeshka was too huge, it towered above us so that there was only a thin crack between it and the roof. But it sloped down abruptly halfway across the chamber, like an immense jellied hill, and ended a good twenty feet from where we stood. Between us and the great bulk of the Greeshka was a forest of hanging, dangling red strands, a living cobweb of Greeshka tissue that came almost to our faces.

And it pulsed. As one organism. Even the strands kept time, widening and then contracting again, moving to a silent beat that was one with the great Greeshka behind them.

My stomach churned, but my companions seemed unmoved. They'd seen this before. "Come," Valcarenghi said, switching on a flashlight he'd brought to augment the torchlight. The light, twisting around the pulsing web, gave the illusion of some weird haunted forest, Valcarenghi stepped into that forest. Lightly. Swinging the light and brushing aside the Greeshka.

Gourlay followed him, but I recoiled. Valcarenghi looked back and smiled, "Don't worry," he said. "The Greeshka takes hours to attach itself, and it's easily removed. It won't grab you if you stumble against it."

I screwed up my courage, reached out, and touched one of the living strands. It was soft and wet, and there was a slimy feel to it. But that was all. It broke easily enough. I walked through it, reaching before me and bending and breaking the web to clear my path. The policeman walked silently behind me.

Then we stood on the far side of the web, at the foot of the great Greeshka. Valcarenghi studied it for a second, then pointed with his flashlight. "Look," he said. "Final Union."

I looked. His beam had thrown a pool of light around one of the dark spots, a blemish on the reddish hulk. I looked closer. There was a head in the blemish. Centered in the dark spot, with just the face showing, and even that covered by a thin reddish film. But the features were unmistakable. An elderly Shkeen, wrinkled and big-eyed, his eyes closed now. But smiling. Smiling.

I moved closer: A little lower and to the right, a few fingertips hung out of the mass. But that was all. Most of the body was already gone, sunken into the Greeshka, dissolved or dissolving. The old Shkeen was dead, and the parasite was digesting his corpse.

"Every one of the dark spots is a recent Union," Valcarenghi was saying, moving his light around like a pointer. "The spots fade in time, of course. The Greeshka is growing steadily. In another hundred years it will fill this chamber, and start up the passageway."

Then there was a rustle of movement behind us. I looked back. Someone else was coming through the web.

She reached us soon, and smiled. A Shkeen woman, old, naked, breasts hanging past her waist. Joined, of course. Her Greeshka covered most of her head and hung lower than her breasts. It was still bright and translucent from its time in the sun. You could see through it, to where it was eating the skin off her back.

"A candidate for Final Union," Gourlay said.

"This is a popular cave," Valcarenghi added in a low, sardonic voice.

The woman did not speak to us, nor we to her. Smiling, she walked past us. And lay down on the Greeshka.

The little Greeshka, the one that rode her back, seemed almost to dissolve on contact, melting away into the great cave creature, so the Shkeen woman and the great Greeshka were joined as one. After that, nothing. She just closed her eyes, and lay peacefully, seemingly asleep.

"What's happening?" I asked.

"Union," said Valcarenghi. "It'll be an hour before you'd notice anything, but the Greeshka is closing over her even now, swallowing her. A response to her body heat, I'm told. In a day she'll be buried in it. In two, like him — " The flash found the half-dissolved face above us.

"Can you read her?" Gourlay suggested. "Maybe that'd tell us something."

"All right," I said, repelled but curious. I opened myself. And the mindstorm hit.

But it's wrong to call it a mindstorm. It was immense and awesome and intense, searing and blinding and choking. But it was peaceful too, and gentle with a gentleness that was more violent than human hate. It shrieked soft shrieks and siren calls and pulled at me seductively, and it washed over me in crimson waves of passion, and drew me to it. It filled me and emptied me all at once. And I heard the bells somewhere, clanging a harsh bronze song, a song of love and surrender and togetherness, of joining and union and never being alone.

Storm, mindstorm, yes, it was that. But it was to an ordinary mindstorm as a supernova is to a hurricane, and its violence was the violence of love. It loved me, that mindstorm, and it wanted me, and its bells called to me, and sang its love, and I reached to it and touched, wanting to be with it, wanting to link, wanting never to be alone again. And suddenly I was on the crest of a great wave once again, a wave of fire that washed across the stars forever, and this time I knew the wave would never end, this time I would not be alone afterwards upon my darkling plain.

But with that phrase I thought of Lya.

And suddenly I was struggling, fighting it, battling back against the sea of sucking love. I ran, ran, *ran, RAN* ... and closed my minddoor and hammered shut the latch and let the storm flail and howl against it while I held it with all my strength, resisting. Yet the door began to buckle and crack.

I screamed. The door smashed open, and the storm whipped in and clutched at me, whirled me out and around and around. I sailed up to the cold stars but they were cold no longer, and I grew bigger and bigger until I *was* the stars and they were me, and I was Union, and for a single solitary glittering instant I was the universe.

Then nothing.

I woke up back in my room, with a headache that was trying to tear my skull apart. Gourlay was sitting on a chair reading one of our books. He looked up when I groaned.

Lya's headache pills were still on the bedstand. I took one hastily, then struggled to sit up in bed.

"You all right?" Gourlay asked.

"Headache," I said, rubbing my forehead. It *throbbed*, as if it was about to burst. Worse than the time I'd peered into Lya's pain. "What happened?"

He stood up. 'You scared the hell out of us. After you began to read, all of a sudden you started trembling. Then you walked right into the goddamn Greeshka. And you screamed. Dino and the sergeant had to drag you out. You were stepping right in the thing, and it was up to your knees. Twitching, too. Weird. Dino hit you, knocked you out."

He shook his head, started for the door. "Where are you going?" I said.

"To sleep," he said, You've been out for eight hours or so. Dino asked me to watch you till you came to. OK, you came to. Now get some rest, and I will too. We'll talk about it tomorrow."

"I want to talk about it now."

"It's late," he said, as he closed the bedroom door. I listened to his footsteps on the way out. And I'm sure I heard the outer door lock. Somebody was clearly afraid of Talents who steal away into the night. I wasn't going anywhere.

I got up and went out for a drink. There was Veltaar chilling. I put away a couple of glasses quick, and ate a light snack. The headache began to fade. Then I went back to the bedroom, turned off the light and cleared the glass, so the stars would all shine through, Then back to sleep.

But I didn't sleep, not right away. Too much had happened. I had to think about it. The headache first, the incredible headache that ripped at my skull. Like Lya's. But Lya hadn't been through what I had. Or had she? Lya was a major Talent, much more sensitive than I was, with a greater range. Could that mindstorm have reached this far, over miles and miles? Late at night, when humans and Shkeen were sleeping and their thoughts dim? Maybe. And maybe my half-remembered dreams were pale reflections of whatever she had felt the same nights. But my dreams had been pleasant. It was waking that bothered me, waking and not remembering.

But again, had I had this headache when I slept? Or when I woke?

What the hell had happened? What was that thing, that reached me there in the cave, and pulled me to it? The Greeshka? It had to be. I hadn't even time to focus on the Shkeen woman, it *had* to be the Greeshka. But Lyanna had said that Greeshka had no minds, not even a yes-I-live.

It all swirled around me, questions on questions on questions, and I had no answers. I began to think of Lya then, to wonder where she was and why she'd left me. Was this what she had been going through? Why hadn't I understood? I missed her then. I needed her beside me, and she wasn't there. I was alone, and very aware of it.

I slept.

Long darkness then, but finally a dream, and finally I remembered. I was back on the plain again, the infinite darkling plain with its starless sky and black shapes in the distance, the plain Lya had spoken of so often. It was from one of her favorite poems. I was alone, forever alone, and I knew it. That was the nature of things. I was the only reality in the universe, and I was cold and hungry and frightened, and the shapes were moving toward me, inhuman and inexorable. And there was no one to call to, no one to turn to, no one to hear my cries. There never had been anyone. There never would be anyone.

Then Lya came to me.

She floated down from the starless sky, pale and thin and fragile, and stood beside me on the plain. She brushed her hair back with her hand, and looked at me with glowing wide eyes, and smiled. And I knew it was no dream. She was with me, somehow. We talked.

Hi, Robb.

Lya? Hi, Lya. Where are you? You left me.

I'm sorry. I had to. You understand, Robb. You have to. I didn't want to be here anymore, ever, in this place, this awful place. I would have been, Robb. Men are always here, but for brief moments.

A touch and a voice?

Yes, Robb. Then darkness again, and a silence. And the darkling plain.

You're mixing two poems, Lya. But it's OK. You know them better than I do. But aren't you leaving out something? The earlier part. "Ah love, let us be true ..."

Oh, Robb.

Where are you?

I'm — everywhere. But mostly in a cave. I was ready, Robb. I was already more open than the rest. I could skip the Gathering, and the Joining. My Talent made me used to sharing. It took me.

Final Union?

Yes.

Oh, Lya.

Robb. Please. Join us, join me. It's happiness, you know? Forever and forever, and belonging and sharing and being together. I'm in love, Robb, I'm in love with a billion billion people, and I know all of them better than

I ever knew you, and they know me, all of me, and they love me. And it will last forever. Me, Us. The Union. I'm still me, but I'm them too, you see? And they're me. The Joined, the reading, opened me, and the Union called to me every night, because it loved me, you see? Oh, Robb, join us, join us. I love you.

The Union. The Greeshka, you mean. I love you, Lya. Please come back. It can't have absorbed you already. Tell me where you are. I'll come to you.

Yes, come to me. Come anywhere, Robb. The Greeshka is all one, the caves all connect under the hills, the little Greeshka are all part of the Union. Come to me and join me. Love me as you said you did. Join me. You're so far away, I can hardly reach you, even with the Union. Come and be one with us.

No. I will not be eaten. Please, Lya, tell me where you are.

Poor Robb. Don't worry, love. The body isn't important. The Greeshka needs it for nourishment, and we need the Greeshka. But, oh Robb, the Union isn't just the Greeshka, you see? The Greeshka isn't important, it doesn't even have a mind, it's just the link, the medium, the Union is the Shkeen. A million billion billion Shkeen, all the Shkeen that have lived and joined in fourteen thousand years, all together and loving and belonging, immortal. It's beautiful, Robb, it's more than we had, much more, and we were the lucky ones, remember? We were! But this is better.

Lya. My Lya. I loved you. This isn't for you, this isn't for humans. Come back to me.

This isn't for humans? Oh, it IS! It's what humans have always been looking for, searching for, crying for on lonely nights. It's love, Robb, real love, and human love is only a pale imitation. You see?

No.

Come, Robb. Join. Or you'll be alone forever, alone on the plain, with only a voice and a touch to keep you going. And in the end when your body dies, you won't even have that. Just an eternity of empty blackness. The plain, Robb, forever and ever. And I won't be able to reach you, not ever. But it doesn't have to be ...

No.

Oh, Robb. I'm fading. Please come.

No. Lya, don't go. I love you, Lya. Don't leave me.

I love you, Robb. I did. I really did ...

And then she was gone. I was alone on the plain again. A wind was blowing from somewhere, and it whipped her fading words away from me, out into the cold vastness of infinity.

In the cheerless morning, the outer door was unlocked. I ascended the tower and found Valcarenghi alone in his office. "Do you believe in God?" I asked him.

He looked up, smiled. "Sure." Said lightly. I was reading him. It was a subject he'd never thought about.

"I don't," I said. "Neither did Lya. Most Talents are atheists, you know. There was an experiment tried back on Old Earth fifty years ago. It was organized by a major Talent named Linnel, who was also devoutly religious. He thought that by using drugs, and linking together the minds of the world's most potent Talents, he could reach something he called the Universal Yes-I-Live. Also known as God. The experiment was a dismal failure, but *something* happened. Linnel went mad, and the others came away with only a vision of a vast, dark, uncaring nothing-ness, a void without reason or form or meaning. Other Talents have felt the same way, and Normals too. Centuries ago there was a poet named Arnold, who wrote of a darkling plain. The poem's in one of the old languages, but it's worth reading. It shows — fear, I think. Something basic in man, some dread of being alone in the cosmos. Maybe it's just fear of death, maybe it's more. I don't know. But it's primal. All men are forever alone, but they don't want to be. They're always searching, trying to make contact, trying to reach others across the void. Some people never succeed, some break through occasionally. Lya and I were lucky. But it's never permanent. In the end you're alone again, back on the darkling plain. You see, Dino? *Do you see?*"

He smiled an amused little smile. Not derisive — that wasn't his style — just surprised and disbelieving. "No," he said.

"Look again, then. Always people are reaching for something, for someone, searching. Talk, Talent, love, sex, it's all part of the same thing, the same search. And gods, too. Man invents gods because he's afraid of being alone, scared of an empty universe, scared of the dark-ling plain. That's why your men are converting, Dino, that's why people are going over. They've found God, or as much of a God as they're ever likely to find. The Union is a mass-mind, an immortal mass-mind, many in one, all love. The Shkeen don't die, dammit. No wonder they don't have the concept of an afterlife. They *know* there's a God. Maybe it didn't create the universe, but it's love, pure love, and they say that God is love, don't they? Or maybe what we call love is a tiny piece of God. I don't care, whatever it is, the Union is it. The end of the search for the Shkeen, and for Man too. We're alike after all, we're so alike it hurts."

Valcarenghi gave his exaggerated sigh. "Robb, you're overwrought. You sound like one of the Joined."

"Maybe that's just what I should be. Lya is. She's part of the Union now."

He blinked. "How do you know that?"

"She came to me last night in a dream."

"Oh. A dream."

"It was *true*, dammit. It's all true."

Valcarenghi stood, and smiled. "I believe you," he said. "That is, I believe that the Greeshka uses a psi-lure, a love lure if you will, to draw in its prey, something so powerful that it convinces men — even you — that it's God. Dangerous, of course. I'll have to think about this before taking action. We could guard the caves to keep humans out, but there are too many caves. And sealing off the Greeshka wouldn't help our relations with the Shkeen. But now it's my problem. You've done your job."

I waited until he was through. "You're wrong, Dino. This is real, no trick, no illusion. I *felt* it, and Lya too. The Greeshka hasn't even a yes-I-live, let alone a psi-lure strong enough to bring in Shkeen and men."

"You expect me to believe that God is an animal who lives in the caves of Shkea?"

"Yes."

"Robb, that's absurd, and you know it. You think the Shkeen have found the answer to the mysteries of creation. But look at them. The oldest civilized race in known space, but they've been stuck in the Bronze Age for fourteen thousand years. We came to *them*. Where are their spaceships? Where are their towers?"

"Where are our bells?" I said. "And our joy? They're happy, Dino. Are we? Maybe they've found what we're still looking for. Why the hell is man so driven, anyway? Why is he out to conquer the galaxy, the universe, whatever? Looking for God, maybe ... ? Maybe. He can't find him anywhere, though, so on he goes, on and on, always looking. But always back to the same darkling plain in the end."

"Compare the accomplishments. I'll take humanity's record."

"Is it worth it?"

"I think so." He went to the window, and looked out. "We've got the only Tower on their world," he said, smiling, as he looked down through the clouds.

"They've got the only God in our universe," I told him. But he only smiled.

"All right, Robb," he said, when he finally turned from the window. "I'll keep all this in mind. And we'll find Lyanna for you."

My voice softened. "Lya is lost," I said. "I know that now. I will be too, if I wait. I'm leaving tonight. I'll book passage on the first ship out to Baldur."

He nodded. "If you like. I'll have your money ready." He grinned. "And we'll send Lya after you, when we find her. I imagine she'll be a little miffed, but that's your worry."

I didn't answer. Instead I shrugged, and headed for the tube. I was almost there when he stopped me.

"Wait," he said. "How about dinner tonight? You've done a good job for us. We're having a farewell party anyway, Laurie and me. She's leaving too."

"I'm sorry," I said.

His turn to shrug. "What for? Laurie's a beautiful person, and I'll miss her. But it's no tragedy. There are other beautiful people. I think she was getting restless with Shkea, anyway."

I'd almost forgotten my Talent, in my heat and the pain of my loss. I remembered it now. I read him. There was no sorrow, no pain, just a vague disappointment. And below that, his wall. Always the wall, keeping him apart, this man who was a first-name friend to everyone and an intimate to none. And on it, it was almost as if there were a sign that read, THIS FAR YOU GO, AND NO FARTHER.

"Come up," be said. "It should be fun." I nodded.

I asked myself, when my ship lifted off, why I was leaving.

Maybe to return home. We have a house on Baldur, away from the cities, on one of the undeveloped continents with only wilderness for a neighbor. It stands on a cliff, above a high waterfall that tumbles endlessly down into a shaded green pool. Lya and I swam there often, in the sunlit days between assignments. And afterwards we'd lie down nude in the shade of the orangespice trees, and make love on a carpet of silver moss. Maybe I'm returning to that. But it won't be the same without Lya, lost Lya.

Lya whom I still could have. Whom I could have now. It would be easy, so easy. A slow stroll into a darkened cave, a short sleep. Then Lya with me for eternity, in me, sharing me, being me, and I her. Loving and knowing more of each other than men can ever do. Union and joy, and no darkness again, ever. God. If I believed that, what I told Valcarenghi, then why did I tell Lya no?

Maybe because I'm not sure. Maybe I still hope, for something still greater and more loving than the Union, for the God they told me of so long ago. Maybe I'm taking a risk, because part of me still believes. But if I'm wrong ... then the darkness, and the plain ...

But maybe it's something else, something I saw in Valcarenghi, something that made me doubt what I had said. For man is more than Shkeen, somehow; there are men like Dino and Gourlay as well as Lya and Gustaffson, men who fear love and Union as much as they crave it. A dichotomy, then. Man has two primal urges, and the Shkeen only one? If so, perhaps there is a human answer, to reach and join and not be alone, and yet to still be men.

I do not envy Valcarenghi. He cries behind his wall, I think, and no one knows, not even he. And no one will ever know, and in the end he'll always be alone in smiling pain. No, I do not envy Dino.

Yet there is something of him in me, Lya, as well as much of you. And that is why I ran, though I loved you.

Laurie Blackburn was on the ship with me. I ate with her after liftoff, and we spent the evening talking over wine. Not a happy conversation, maybe, but a human one. Both of us needed someone, and we reached out.

Afterwards, I took her back to my cabin, and made love to her as fiercely as I could. Then, the darkness softened, we held each other and talked away the night.

Chicago, Illinois
January-February, 1973

215

This book was designed by Lydia Marano for Babbage Press using a Macintosh G3 and Adobe FrameMaker. It was printed by LSI on sixty pound, offset cream-white acid-free stock. The text font is Minion, a Garalde Oldstyle typeface designed by Robert Slimbach in 1990 for Adobe Systems. Minion was inspired by the elegant and highly readable type designs of master printers Claude Garamond and Aldus Manutius in the late Renaissance. Created primarily for type-setting, Minion lends an aesthetic quality to the modern versatility of digital technology.

Printed in the United States
6471